A
Village
Shattered

A
Village
Shattered

Logan & Cafferty
Mystery/Suspense Series

Jean Henry Mead

Printed in the United States of America
ISBN: 978-1-931415-24-8

Cover design by Bill Mead
First edition, 1999
Second edition 2008
Third edition 2011

Dedication

For my dear friend, Marge Hughes,
who can always make me laugh

Reviews:

"This book kept me on the edge of my seat! There's mystery, suspense and, to make things a bit more interesting, some romance thrown in. You don't know who the killer is or why he/she is doing it until the very end. I would recommend this book to anyone who loves a good mystery."

~Rhapsody Magazine

"Readers will love guessing who's killing the residents of the Valley Retirement Village in this delightfully funny and cleverly plotted mystery. A must read for Sherlock fans, but Sherlock himself would be no match for these sassy senior sleuths."

~Sue Owens Wright, mystery writer

Chapter One

Alice's porch light always served as a beacon on Saturday nights, but her house at the end of Mulberry Lane was as dark as a mausoleum. Dana eased her car along the curb and stopped in front of the house. Her dashboard clock said 7:46, so they were only a minute late.

"Something's wrong, Sarah."

Her companion leaned to have a better look. "You're right. Alice would never miss bingo night, unless…"

Dana retrieved a flashlight from beneath the driver's seat. It was then she noticed that all the houses on Alice's street were dark. "How strange," she said, opening the Audi's door. "There hasn't been a brown-out in the village in years."

"Harold must have driven his pickup into one of the power poles."

Envisioning the village's "Mister Magoo," Dana wondered how Harold Samuels had renewed his driver's license. He was much too vain for glasses, and contacts were more than he could manage. Her attention returned to the house. Momentarily scanning the windows for candlelight, she started up the walk, leaves crunching underfoot. The door should be open by now. Alice was always anxious to get there early.

They hesitated on the edge of the jungle Alice called a garden. A giant willow stood dead center in the overgrown tangle of plants, its weeping limbs restless in the evening breeze. The camellias were tall enough to hide a mountain lion, but it was something considerably smaller that streaked past.

Dana turned to track the animal's path. Her flashlight caught two gold eyes peering from behind Sarah's legs. Sighing, Dana knelt to scoop up Alice's cat.

"It's only Mr. Tiger."

"What's he doing out here?" her friend said as she backed away. "Alice never lets him roam at night."

"Something's definitely wrong." Dana prayed it wasn't another heart attack. She tucked the cat beneath her arm and stepped onto the porch. Ringing the bell, they waited long moments for someone to answer. Rummaging through her purse, she found the key Alice had recently given her. When the door creaked open, an overpowering sweet smell greeted them. Sarah held a tissue to her nose and shrieked, "Alliicceee?" in a voice pitched high enough to crack the entry glass.

Dana flipped a switch along the foyer wall. When a lamp failed to light, she flashed her beam around the living room. The coffee table was overturned, knickknacks scattered and broken. The room resembled a miniature battlefield.

Alice was there among the rubble. Face down on her green Berber rug, she clutched a short, knotted cord in her bloated hand. A shattered lamp lay on the floor, its slivers gleaming in her snowy hair. Slowly kneeling beside her, Dana searched for a pulse she sensed wasn't there. "She's gone, Sarah."

"But who would kill sweet Alice?"

Dana felt her throat constrict and made no attempt to reply.

"Everybody loved her."

"Not quite everyone."

A cold, nauseous lump settled in Dana's rib cage. Get a grip, she told herself. You've got to remember the crime scene. Reading glasses were on the floor with the novel Alice had been reading. They knew she watched the afternoon soaps, so she must have died that morning.

Sarah lifted the phone with a soggy tissue. Using a pen, she punched in 911. Moments later she concluded the line was as dead as Alice.

Despite her bulk, their friend had put up quite a struggle. She apparently tried to escape to the kitchen when struck with the lamp from behind. Dana's stomach tied itself in knots. Struggling to her feet, she signaled Sarah to follow. They skirted what they considered evidence and cautiously left through the foyer. After locking and testing the door, they made their way to the car. They then noticed that lights were on and the neighbors were filing into the recreation hall, Alice's favorite hangout. The killer must have known the body would be found on bingo night, unless a stranger had committed the murder.

A light mist settled over the red-tiled roofs of the Valley Retirement Village. As the night deepened, tule fog would form an opaque mist. Dana vowed every fall to leave the San Joaquin Valley, but she couldn't leave her friends. They had saved her from the black hole she'd fallen into when Earl died. Her mystery novels also helped fill the void left by her husband's death.

Dana glanced down at her chubby friend, who seemed to be hyperventilating. Worried, she said, "First, a quick cup of chai tea. Then we'll call the sheriff."

* * *

Sheriff Walter Grayson stood like a military guard. Well over six feet, his once-impressive chest had lost the war with gravity. Most middle-aged men acquired some social polish, but the newly-elected sheriff had all the charms of film patrolman, Robocop. Even his voice was robotic.

"We're not suspects," Dana sputtered. "Sarah and I play bingo with Alice every Saturday night."

Disbelief registered in his heavy, arched brow.

"Not much happens here on weekends when you live a mile from town. Especially when the fog rolls in." Dana wondered why she was making excuses. They had nothing to hide.

The sheriff lifted a notepad from his crisp uniform pocket, his pen ready for answers. "Your full names, ages, and addresses?" he said.

"What does age have to do with the murder?"

"Routine questions, ma'am."

She hesitated long enough to make the sheriff scowl. "Dana Marie Logan. I'm … fifty-nine and I live here in the village." She waited for him to ask for her social security number. Before long they would be tattooed on everyone's wrists.

"You don't look old enough for a retirement village," he said.

"My husband was sixty-seven when he died two years ago."

"I see." He abruptly turned to Sarah. "And you, ma'am?"

"Sarah Anne Cafferty. I'm the same age as Dana. My husband, Terry, was sixty-four when lightning struck him last fall. He was swinging a five iron on the village course."

"How long'd you know Alice Zimmer?"

"Several years." Dana was acutely aware of the sheriff's impatience. "We're all members of the Sew and So Club."

"So and So?"

"Needlework and gossip." Dana pantomimed sewing.

"I want all the members' names. And her friends while you're at it."

"They're one and the same, Sheriff." Dana listed nine women, including herself and Sarah.

"The two of you break in the Zimmer house together?"

"Alice gave us keys. She was afraid of another heart attack."

"Everybody in the club have one?"

"Just Lana, Sarah, and I."

"Three with opportunity." He continued scribbling.

"You can't suspect us." Sarah's voice was shrill. "Alice was our friend."

"Everybody's suspect, Miz Cafferty. Where were you all day?"

"Home," she said indignantly.

"Together?"

"We talked on the phone. I was telling Dana—"

"No alibis," he said, without looking up.

Before they could protest, he asked when they had last talked to the victim.

"Last evening," Dana said, glaring. "Sew and Sos met at her house."

"Any squabbling at the meeting?"

"No, Sheriff, we all get along quite well."

"The Zimmer woman must have had an enemy."

"Alice was well liked in the village. That's what makes her death so baffling."

* * *

Settled among her sofa pillows, Dana watched as Sarah scanned the floor-to-ceiling bookcases.

"You have enough mystery novels to start your own bookstore, Dana. How many do you read a week?"

"Two or three."

"Looks like everything Doyle and Christie ever wrote."

"You'll find contemporary writers as well: Hart, Clark, Grafton, Leonard, Sayers..."

Sarah thoughtfully sipped her tea. "They can help us solve the murder."

"How?"

"We know more about sleuthing than that newbie sheriff ever will."

"That doesn't give us the right to snoop."

"All those mystery novels you've read," Sarah said, "and the tons of reports I typed for Terry..."

Dana envisioned the pink marble urn containing Terry's ashes, which sat on Sarah's mantle. Terry Cafferty had been an anomaly, an unassuming P.I. with one apparent vice, an occasional pipe bowl of Prince Albert.

"...and between us, we can track down Alice's killer."

"This isn't a 'Murder, She Wrote' board game we're playing, Sarah. Suppose the killer discovers us first?"

"We'll be careful."

She obviously wasn't herself so Dana decided to humor her. "Let's discuss the case with Terry. A private investigator's advice is exactly what we need."

"A séance, you mean?"

"Our resident psychic conducts them on a regular basis."

"Tamara?"

"She even owns a crystal ball."

Sarah shook her head, apparently dismissing that idea. "We don't look like detectives, so no one would suspect us of investigating the murder."

Dana surveyed her friend's double chin and glittering light blue eyes. "You do resemble Shelly Winters more than Angela Lansbury."

Sarah mimicked the actress. "And you, Logan? A mature Geena Davis."

Dana deliberately dimpled her cheeks, although she wasn't up to smiling. "All right, where do we start?"

"Suspects."

"I can't think of anyone who'd want to kill Alice."

"I can."

"Who?"

"Harold Samuels."

"You can't be serious."

"Remember that sweet smell in Alice's house?"

Dana nodded.

"She's allergic to perfume."

"That's right, she was."

"Kind of smelled like Harold."

"That horse liniment he wears?"

"Harold's bursitis gave him away."

"Honestly, Sarah, how many seniors use arthritic rubs?" Dana answered the question herself. "Nearly everyone."

"Harold must've killed her."

Dana recalled an argument between them at a recent garage sale. "Harold argues with everyone, including Pastor Williams."

"Alice slapped him a good one when he wrestled that trowel away from her. I've never seen her so mad."

"That's still no reason to kill."

"It might've been enough for the village grump."

Dana shook her head in exasperation. "How do you plan to prove your theory?"

"Return to the crime scene and take another whiff."

"The strangest thing I saw," Dana said, attempting to distract her, "was that cord in Alice's hand. She could have snatched it from the killer, and he panicked and used the lamp."

"Harold could've dropped something."

"The police have sealed the house by now. We'd be suspects if they caught us snooping."

"Set your alarm for three o'clock, and don't forget your sneakers. They make 'em in size thirteen, don't they?"

"Eleven-and-a-half, you mush melon. They're hard to find in my size."

"Then wear that old pair of Earl's you use for gardening." Sarah's impish grin dissolved into a determined line. "If you're not up by 3:15, I'll go alone."

Worried, Dana agreed. Her friend was stubborn enough to investigate on her own, and she thought she knew why. Sarah had understudied her husband for years, just waiting to play detective.

* * *

Both women dressed in dark clothing, each pocketing Terry Cafferty's investigative tools. Heavy flashlights would serve as weapons as well as illuminate the crime scene. The dense fog made Dana claustrophobic, but it didn't deter her friend. Sarah was like an eager child equipped with a magnifying glass.

When they reached Alice's house, yellow crime tape blocked their paths. Carefully ducking beneath the barrier, they stopped for a moment to listen. Satisfied they were alone, Dana fumbled in her pocket, wondering why the sheriff had not impounded their keys. She removed her gloves and crouched to find the keyhole.

"Terry will vacate his urn," she whispered, "when he finds out what we're doing."

The night air was cold and damp, but perspiration trickled from beneath Dana's knit cap, a reminder of the felony they were committing. Her hands trembled as she inserted the key in the lock. At last the tumblers fell and the door swung open, but her friend hesitated on the threshold.

"Where's the cat?" Sarah whispered.

"They must have taken him to the animal shelter." Dana sighed as she nudged Sarah inside. Her fear of felines was a longstanding village joke. Once in the foyer, they switched on flashlights, directing their beams at the floor. Dana cringed when she noticed the chalked outline of Alice's body. The procedure was unnecessary if the body had not been moved, but the inexperienced sheriff must carry his own chalk.

"That sweet smell's gone, Logan."

"It probably aired out when the crime team was here."

"I wonder why they didn't clean up all this fingerprint powder." Sarah swung her light along the baseboards. "Let's search for anything missing."

"Alice's silver tea service is still in place. A burglar would have taken it."

"Somebody might have scared him off."

Dana focused her light on a freestanding bookcase. The contents appeared to have survived an earthquake.

"Her scrapbooks were kept there."

"Why would the killer want them?"

"Sheriff probably took them," Sarah said as she led the way to Alice's bedroom.

Although nothing seemed out of place, the closet door was open. Clothing had been pushed aside and shoes were scattered on the floor.

"Alice's silk blouses are falling off the hangers."

"The bureau drawers have also been searched." Furious, Dana imagined the killer rummaging through Alice's queen-sized underwear. Or had it been the sheriff?

* * *

Dana crouched beneath a window, attempting to peer inside. Dense fog pressed in from all sides, squeezing the air from her lungs. Her peripheral vision picked up a vague figure moving toward her in the fog. An upraised lamp glinted faintly in the haloed street light. Before she could scream, a telephone rang on the sill beside her head. Groping for the receiver, she pulled it to her ear.

Sarah's voice, high-pitched and yawning, jarred her fully awake. "Breakfast, Logan? Crepes are ready for the pan."

"Good grief, Sarah, don't you ever sleep?"

"Bring some blackberry tea, will you?"

Dana berated herself for agreeing to Sarah's crazy scheme. She would convince her—gently, of course—that tampering with the crime scene could earn them time in jail. Rehearsing her lecture, she slipped on pale green sweats. Her ancient sociology degree had not prepared her for sabotage, but Sarah's obsession with solving the murders could get them both killed. She'd have to persuade her to investigate from a distance.

Sarah was smiling when she answered the door wearing a new fuchsia pantsuit and stained butcher's apron. *Dana's mood* lightened in response. Reasoning with her friend would be easier than she anticipated. She followed her into the small, orange and white kitchen. Better to wait until after breakfast, she decided. She would talk to her later about her diet.

Sarah was buttering her third piece of toast when the doorbell rang. Dana waited at the table, finishing her tea. Recognizing the monotone voice, she braced herself for further questioning. She wondered whether the robotic sheriff had been assembled in Silicone Valley. She much preferred Ed McBain's fictional Detective Carella.

Once they were seated in the living room, the sheriff asked how well they knew Betty Wilson.

Sarah said, "She's a Sew and So, Sheriff."

He scrutinized them both. "When's the last time you saw her."

Sarah's hand crumpled the front of her fuchsia blouse. "You don't mean…?"

"Just answer the question."

"When was it, Dana?"

"Yesterday afternoon. Betty was fine."

When Dana pressed, the sheriff admitted that Betty had disappeared. Her husband reported her missing at midnight when she failed to return from bingo.

She sensed Sarah's anxiety and slid an arm around her shoulder.

"I strongly advise you to keep your doors locked until the perpetrator's arrested," he said. "If you have to go out, use the buddy system."

"We're no longer suspects, Sheriff?" Dana noticed he had relaxed his rigid stance.

Ignoring her question, he cautioned them again about security.

Once the door was double-locked behind him, Sarah insisted, "We've got to find Betty."

Chapter Two

Dana braced her feet against the floorboard, her attention riveted to the speedometer. Sarah was taking the minister's "God speed" much too literally. She certainly wasn't worried about a speeding ticket.

When they reached the village, they changed clothes and wore their gardening gloves. By mid-afternoon they had searched the village grounds, cafeteria freezer, and every available dumpster. Tired and frustrated, they rested on a park bench near the nine-hole golf course. Sarah slumped against the wooden slats, convinced that Betty's body was hidden in Harold's trunk.

"He drives a pickup, Sarah."

"Luggage," she said, whipping discarded cardboard to fan her flushed face. "Or he buried her in his yard like that Sacramento landlady who planted her boarders instead of flowers."

"Betty's listed as missing, not deceased."

"Harold killed her. I'm sure of it."

"Why would he?"

"Remember that picnic when he squirted mustard on Betty's brand new blouse?"

Dana agreed she had never seen them both so angry. They behaved more like a married couple than village next-door neighbors. Shading her eyes, she scanned the manicured golf course. Grouped along the perimeter were stark white stucco houses, each topped with a red-tiled roof. Low-walled gardens fronted the homes, some still bright with autumn flowers.

Squinting, Dana located Harold's corner lot. His multi-paned picture window reflected the setting sun.

"Aren't you worried that the killer might be watching us?" Dana said.

"Harold may not wear glasses, but I've seen him at his window with binoculars. He's not only a murderer, he's a peeping Tom."

Dana shivered. "He could be spying on us now." She glanced again at Harold's house but saw no sign of movement. While she continued to scan his yard, Sarah struggled from the bench, her ankles swollen from the walking they'd done that day.

"Let's go back to my place, Logan. I'm working on a plan to trap him."

* * *

Harold Samuels meticulously cleaned his trowel, washing bits of grass and soil down his kitchen sink. He was proud of the job he'd done. Settling his large frame in a favorite chair, he rested mud-caked boots on a distressed coffee table. He started with the comics and worked his way down the page to "Doonesbury." When the telephone rang, he tossed his paper aside to answer before the fourth ring.

"Harold?"

"Whadda ya want?" He knew he sounded gruff.

"It's Sarah. How about having dinner with me tonight?"

Harold smiled in spite of himself. He liked plump blondes. He'd married two of them. "Just you 'n me?"

"Dana will be here."

Disappointed, he said, "You two women scairt of the bogey man?"

"I can't think of anyone we'd rather have protect us."

"A lotta widow women need protectin'. I gotta spread myself around."

"That's awfully nice of you, Harold. We'll expect you about seven o'clock."

"I guess I can make it."

"Good, and don't forget that aftershave you've been wearing lately."

"What kind's that?"

"The stuff that gives us goosebumps."

Harold slathered himself with his dwindling supply of vanilla extract. He had forgotten to ask about the menu, but envisioned roast beef, mashed potatoes, and berry pie. He'd get rid of the amazon after the main course and save the plump little widow for desert.

* * *

Sarah bustled about the kitchen as though a young bride preparing dinner for her in-laws. Tired of getting in the way, Dana removed herself from traffic lanes and seated herself against the wall.

"Don't you think you're overdoing it, Sarah?"

"We'll stuff him so full of mashed potatoes that he won't know he's being interrogated."

"And if he does?"

"We've got plenty of weapons to defend ourselves." Sarah opened a drawer. "Butcher knives." A cupboard door was unlatched. "Rolling pin—"

"Suppose he's not the one?"

"We'll cross him off our suspects' list."

Dana shrugged. "That's great but how many village men are on your possibles list?"

"All of them. At least we're not cowering behind locked doors like the other widows."

"Betty had a husband to protect her."

13

Sarah turned from the range, a mitted hand resting on her ample hip. "You're assuming she's dead. What if she just up and left Pat. Maybe they had a fight."

"Maybe Pat killed her. And maybe he killed Alice to throw the police off the track."

Sarah shook her head in disbelief.

"You're the one who insisted that Harold buried her somewhere."

Sarah banged a metal spoon against the cast iron skillet. Sighing, she said, "I thought with reading all those mysteries, you'd have a clue by now."

"Dame Christie, I'm not. Why is solving this case so important?"

Sarah's chin dropped to her chest, tripling it. In a small voice she said, "I've never done anything special."

"You have great kids. Both successful in their careers."

"Everybody has kids. I guess I always envied Terry's career. It was mostly boring stakeouts but—"

The doorbell's unexpected ring caused Dana's spine to stiffen.

"He's early." Sarah removed her apron and patted her short, blond curls into place. Dana followed her into the foyer where her friend stopped to smooth her dress. Switching on the overhead light, she disengaged the bolt.

"Harold, how nice to see you."

He nearly filled the entry, his stance bordering on arrogance. His mustard-colored jacket sported wide lapels and topped a red, wrinkled western shirt. The ensemble was accessorized by a turquoise bolo tie. His green plaid trousers hung a full inch above his sockless, brown alligator loafers.

"My, you smell as fresh as a batch of vanilla fudge." Sarah was obviously disappointed.

Dana realized immediately that it wasn't the remembered scent.

"I wore it just for you, Sarah. And speakin' of smellin' good..." He sniffed, lifting his bulbous nose.

"Dinner's just about ready. Come keep Dana company while I finish making my special country gravy."

Dana led the way into the kitchen. "I hope you're hungry. Sarah's been cooking all afternoon."

Harold's warm smile surprised her and Dana found his rare display of charm unsettling. When he squeezed and patted her hand, a chill raced to the base of her spine. Withdrawing a few steps, she inquired about his health. While he rattled on about his bursitis, she worried they were making a mistake. Harold could easily overpower them both. He was her own height but outweighed her by at least eighty pounds. Most of that bulged above his low-slung concha belt.

She had warned her friend about her matchmaking. Sarah hadn't delved beyond physical height when she tried to pair them for the picnic at Grover Park. Dana had nothing more in common with Harold than their gardening skills. How would she keep him entertained until dinner?

Sarah chattered while allowing milk to thicken with seasoned, browned flour. The plan was to wait until after dinner to broach the subject of Alice's death.

Dana suddenly realized that he'd stopped talking and was watching her.

"How's your Shishi Gashira doing?" she asked, indicating a chair for him at the table.

"Them big double blooms are comin' in red as can be."

"My Cleopatra's ready to burst into bloom."

"Ya don't say—this early?"

"Grow lights and indoor beds are wonderful, aren't they?"

"Yeah, they keep the water warden from catchin' up with ya. During the big drought I was fined twice for waterin' on even days, and five minutes after the noon hour. One of the neighbors musta turned me in. When I find out who done it, I'll twist her damned neck."

15

Dana was startled by the sound of breaking glass. Turning, she watched Sarah abruptly leave the sink. Before she could ask what had happened, her friend disappeared down the hall. Worried, she glanced back at Harold, who didn't seem to notice Sarah's departure.

"Which types of fertilizer are you using?" she asked, when he stopped to take a breath. Smiling, he ticked off a long list of plant aides. Before long Sarah returned with a tray topped with cocktail glasses.

Dana pretended to listen as she watched her set the tray on the counter, pull a pitcher of fruit juice from the refrigerator, and fill each tall glass.

"I'm a Japonica man," he said, his eyes never straying from Dana's face. "There's hundred-year-old plants hereabouts that grow as high as twenty feet."

"Try this new cocktail," Sarah said as she hurried to the table. "It's light and guaranteed to settle your stomach." She lifted a blue crystal glass from the tray and stood over him while he took a sip.

"Mighty tasty. Ain't you ladies gonna join me?"

Sarah handed Dana a tall, clear glass and took a matching one. "Drink up," she said, as Harold obediently emptied his. "Dinner's ready if you two gardeners can pull up roots long enough to eat."

Harold stared blankly at Sarah, then returned his attention to Dana. "How come I didn't know you was a camellia grower?"

Shrugging, Dana smiled. "I'm partial to Tiffanies." Stealing a glance at her watch she saw that it wasn't yet seven-thirty. It's going to be a long night.

Sarah set the table while Dana listened to Harold's gardening monologue. Moments after they sat to eat, the women shared a wary glance. Their guest had attacked his meal as though ending a hunger strike.

"How's the steak?" Sarah asked.

Harold grunted approval, his attention never straying from his plate. He answered her question about the gravy by spreading it over his mashed potatoes. Neither she nor Sarah had eaten a bite.

Dessert was waiting. Sarah bustled to the refrigerator to withdraw a homemade cherry pie, which she sliced and scooped into serving dishes. Returning to the table, she set one next to his dinner plate.

"Save room for the pie, Harold. I baked it just for you."

He ignored Sarah as he launched into a detailed description of achieving the right acidic soil consistency.

Dana wondered why Harold had failed to mention Alice's death. Was he deliberately avoiding the subject with his nonstop gardening chatter? And how would they change the subject when he was so wrapped up in his camellias?

As she rose to clear the table, he abruptly switched trowels. "I planted Mrs. Charles Cobb under my bedroom window," he said, "alongside Mrs. Nellie Eastman..."

Dana sat down hard in her chair.

"...and I dug up Mrs. D. W. Davis. I replanted her next to Betty Sheffield and Jean May on the north side of the house."

Sarah rushed back to the table with another tall, blue glass. "See if this one's more to your liking, Harold." When the glass was half emptied, she tugged Dana from her chair. "Us girls are gonna freshen up."

His eyelids were edging downward, and Dana wondered if it was past his bedtime. "Wait until we get back to drink that," she said. "We'll have ourselves a toast."

When they reached the living room, Sarah whispered, "We haven't got much time. Now that he's confessed to all those murders, he'll have to kill us too."

"He was planting camellias, not people."

"What?"

"Harold's a camellia expert. He was talking about different varieties of camellias. He owned a flower shop in The City."

"Harold lived in San Francisco?"

Dana nodded.

"Well, anybody that handy with a shovel is still suspect in my book. He probably buried Betty alongside Mrs. Cobb— whoever she is."

"Mrs. Charles Cobb is a beautiful, red peony, semi-double petalled camellia."

"Just 'cause he likes flowers doesn't mean he's innocent." Sarah's fingers curled around a heavy brass candlestick. "Let's go back before he comes looking."

Harold was holding an empty glass. "Thirsty..." he said sleepily. "Don't suppose you got some more?" Yawning, he pulled the napkin from his collar and dabbed at his chin.

"I have a headache," Sarah said as she set the candlestick on the counter. "Mind if we wind this up early?"

"I'm a tad tired, myself." Harold's eyelids appeared heavy as he pushed back his chair.

They followed him to the door where a chilling breeze replaced him as he staggered onto the porch. Quickly closing the door, Sarah shot the bolt again in place.

"He acts like he's drunk, Sarah. What did you put in his glass?"

"Chloral hydrate syrup from Terry's investigative kit."

"You gave him a Mickey Finn?"

"The rolling pin could've killed him."

Dana leaned against the wall, feeling a little faint. "How much did you give him?"

Sarah stared at her patent leather pumps. "A double dose because of his size. The drops are so old, I figured they'd lost their punch."

"Some drugs might get more potent with age."

"You mean lethal?"

"I don't know. We'd better see that Harold gets home, then pray for his recovery."

Harold was nowhere in sight. When they rounded the north side of the recreation hall, they spotted him leaning against the building. Fortunately the fog was light. He could have fallen and not been found until noon the following day.

At the sound of their footsteps, Harold opened an eye. "If you ladies changed your mind about wantin' my company, I'm afraid I—" His speech was slurred and nearly unintelligible.

Dana moved to support him when he slumped to his knees. Sarah hurried to slip under his other arm. Between them they managed to pull him upright, but Harold's feet were not cooperating.

"What'll we do, Dana?"

"We've got to get him home."

"It'll take all night to drag him."

"The gardener's big wheelbarrow is behind the recreation hall. We can lift Harold into it."

"What if somebody comes along?"

"We'll say he had too much to drink."

"But, Dana."

"If Harold dies, you can add murder to our growing list of felonies."

Shamefaced, Sarah disappeared, returning moments later with the wheelbarrow. Planting it nose deep in damp sod, they pulled Harold into a sitting position, then wedged him into the tub. Applying weight to the handles, they lifted him off the ground. Harold's hairy, sockless legs straddled the front wheel. Removing his jacket they folded it to form a pillow under his head and took turns propelling him along the dimly-lighted walkway.

When they reached his house, Sarah searched his pockets for his keys. Giggling, she said, "I haven't done this in years."

"Someone might hear you," Dana warned. She glanced at Alice's house across the courtyard, a cold fist squeezing her intestines.

Tipping the wheelbarrow, they rolled him out, then dragged him as far as his living room couch, where Dana covered him with his jacket.

"Still breathing?"

Dana licked her index finger and held it under his nose. "Barely."

"Check his pulse."

"I'm not a nurse, Sarah. We should call an ambulance."

"We can't do that. How would we explain?"

"What if he dies?"

"He won't. Terry said it just causes a hangover."

"If you're wrong—and I'm quoting you now—'we're in duck pucky up to our earlobes.'"

* * *

A message waited on Sarah's answering machine. The sheriff had arranged a group meeting for the following morning at nine. Only Sew and So members were required to attend.

"We must be prime suspects." Dana sighed, realizing how precarious their situation was. If Harold died they would also be suspects in Alice's murder. Sarah's kitchen clock said nine-fifteen and Dana was exhausted. A hot shower and mystery novel were calling her home.

Her own machine contained the same message. She listened twice and to several disconnects which followed. Wondering who was attempting to get in touch, she decided a legitimate caller would have left a message. Someone was tracking her whereabouts. Grasping the fireplace poker, she searched each room. She decided nothing had been touched, although a stalking killer seldom left evidence.

Dana's heart still thundered as she dialed Sarah's number. Her muffled voice told her she was eating.

"Not the cherry pie."

Sarah laughed. "Couldn't let it go to waste."

Straight to your waist. "Lock the doors and windows. Keep a poker beside your bed and don't answer the door tonight for any reason."

"What's got into you, Dana?"

"You're having a mid-life crisis that could get us both killed."

* * *

Showered and ready for bed, Dana launched into her latest book club arrival. Loren Estleman was a favorite author, but something skulking through her gray matter was ruining her concentration. Worried about Harold, she was convinced his only crimes were social ineptness and lack of body image; both forgivable misdemeanors. Anyone who tenderly cared for flowers couldn't be totally contemptible.

In the middle of chapter six, she climbed from her bed to find her drug guide book. Thumbing through she found chloral hydrate, relieved to learn it was only life threatening in large doses. Bold type discouraged senior citizens from taking the drug, particularly combined with alcohol. Harold was sixty-six and would have a mammoth hangover when he woke. If he woke. When he failed to answer his phone, Dana crawled beneath the blankets, vowing to call him in the morning. She tried again to read, but dozed off before the fictional killer's identity came to light.

She had forgotten to set the alarm and would have missed the meeting, had Sarah not called.

"The sheriff wants us at the rec hall now, Dana."

"I'll be right there."

"Good. I'll get us front row seats."

"Immediately after the meeting, we need to check on Harold."

* * *

Fellow Sew and So members were present when Dana arrived, hastily unbuttoning her jacket. The sheriff shot her a look she hadn't seen since sneaking late into home ec class during the bronze age.

"Up late, Miz Logan?"

She nodded as Sarah waved her into a chair.

"You have an alibi for last night?"

Sarah raised her hand. "She was with me, Sheriff."

"Let Miz Logan alibi herself."

Dana hesitated. "We had dinner with Harold Samuels."

"That's interesting, Samuels seems to be missing."

"Harold must be sleeping in this morning." Dana's voice was louder than she intended. She hoped he was still snoring under that awful mustard-colored jacket.

"He's not answering the door or his phone," the sheriff said, "and his pickup's still garaged."

Dana cringed when Sarah volunteered, "Harold's a very sound sleeper." Rumors they were having an affair would be rampant in the village by noon.

"If Samuels can't be found to verify your alibis, I'll have to take you both in for questioning."

The two women eyed one another, frowning.

Sheriff Grayson cleared his throat. "I have an announcement to make." The hall was suddenly quiet. "Betty Wilson has been found." Removing his dark glasses, he inspected them in the overhead light.

"Where?" Everyone seemed to shout at once.

"Right here in the recreation hall, ladies. She was strangled."

Chapter Three

Sheriff Grayson stood like a palace guard, his massive chest straining his uniform buttons. Scanning the women seated before him, he took careful note of their expressions. He understood their anxiety. His own stomach had tied itself in knots since the Zimmer murder. The longer he stood there watching them, the more Sew and Sos fidgeted. He was counting on at least one of them to let something slip.

Dressed in athletic shoes and pastel sweats, most of the women resembled weight loss clinic refugees. The Logan woman was the exception in her red silky warm-up suit. She reminded him of a long-stemmed rose in a field of dandelions. Why was an attractive widow like her living in a retirement village? Her hostility bothered him more than he cared to admit.

He wondered why anyone would drive to the village to kill two harmless old women. Nothing about this case made sense. The motive in either death didn't appear to be robbery or a crime of passion. Some macho nut case who hated women must have done them in. Probably some old guy in the village who was more than a bubble off.

Grayson's scrutiny settled on a scrawny little woman with red hair and shifty eyes that refused to meet his gaze.

Nervously scratching her bony neck, she said her name was Nola Champlain. "You can't suspect me," she whined. "I liked Alice. Betty, too, but I'm not surprised she's dead."

A group gasp made her shrink even smaller in her chair. He surmised that she'd broken a club rule by publicly criticizing a fellow club member. A deceased one at that.

"Why's that, Miz Champlain?"

Squirming, she whispered. "Betty complained a lot."

"About what?"

"Everything, Sheriff." Green eyes darting at the others, she clapped a hand to her mouth.

He'd get nothing more from her with Sew and So members present. Her cohorts would probably drum her out of the club for what she had to say.

A dumpy woman with gray hair pulled behind her ears tentatively raised her hand. "Lana Nelson," she said. While he scribbled her name, she swallowed half a dozen words before "stranger" escaped.

"Well, that narrow's it down considerably, doesn't it?" He knew his sarcasm was lost on no one. A tiny, troll-like woman informed him they were the Zimmer woman's only friends. Candice Yarborough was her name, but he already had that information.

"Alice didn't have any gentleman callers," she said, "so a burglar must have killed her." Sew and So members grunted their agreement.

"I see. The burglar then sneaked over here to strangle the Wilson woman and steal her ten dollar bingo winnings." He gestured toward the rec hall closet where the body had been found.

A large Portuguese woman rose to her feet, her olive face flushed. "Then a lunatic's loose in the village."

"Your name, ma'am?"

"Michelle Lugundos, but everybody calls me Micki."

24

"Let's not jump to conclusions, Miz Lugundos. Two murders don't constitute a serial killing." *But a darn good start on one.*

Lugundos was still standing when a feisty little blonde sprang from her chair. She seemed so full of energy that she couldn't sit still. "How are you going to protect us?" She was glaring at him. When she ignored his request for her name, someone volunteered, "Carole Lambert."

"No need for armed guards, ma'am. You're gonna use the buddy system. Widows will bunk together so that no one's left alone."

Hands balled on her hips, Miz Lambert was having none of it. He'd have to try another tack. "If the department could spare the men, you'd all be furnished guards," he said in a tone reserved for children. "Just follow the safety rules I've passed out among you."

Carole Lambert flopped back angrily in her chair.

"I'm sure we've seen the last of him," Grayson said. "The perp's probably killing time in Tijuana."

Ignoring the sheriff's attempt at humor, Lambert was back on her feet, mocking him. "You haven't a clue who did it, have you?"

Grayson lowered his voice to a conspiratorial tone. He reminded them, "There's a missing male resident." He should have kept Harold Samuels' disappearance to himself, but the pint-sized blonde was trying her best to humiliate him. He'd drag them all down to headquarters separately, if necessary. Especially the Lambert woman, who had no respect for the law. He wondered whether she was related to Russ Lambert, the former sheriff he had defeated in the last election. He'd have to check that out. She might even be his mother.

As soon as the sheriff left the hall they placed their chairs in a circle. "Harold's the murderer," Sarah confided, once they were all resettled. The others glanced at her, then looked away. Dana knew they were unwilling to suspect anyone in the village. They had already decided that a stranger killed their friends. She blamed their paranoia on the sheriff's lack of diplomacy.

Tamara Merino seemed the most agitated by the sheriff's brashness. "I'll consult my spirit guides to find the killer," she said. "But first let's conduct a group meditation."

Had she said group prayer, the others would have agreed, but they shook their heads self-consciously. Tamara's metaphysical dabblings were an embarrassment to them as a group, although most of them had consulted with her privately.

"Call when you find out who done it," Lana said, getting to her feet. "I'm missing my favorite soap." Carole, her assigned partner, was slow to accompany her.

Anybody can be the killer," Micki said. "I'm barricading my doors till he's caught."

"Have someone with you at all times," Dana warned. "And don't take any chances."

* * *

An hour after her body was found, Betty Wilson's clothing had been boxed for disposal. Her husband Pat kept her gold jewelry and heirloom silverware as remembrances of their forty-year marriage. With Betty gone, he could breakfast on jelly doughnuts and chocolate éclairs. His wife had been a health nut. For the past six years, she had never knowingly allowed sugar to taint her taste buds. Or his. Whenever he wanted a candy bar, he had to sneak one.

Why weren't his neighbors bringing him sweets instead of all this junk food? People seemed to think stuffing one's face with casserole dishes comforted the bereaved. Pat was content with a candy bar for lunch, and pizza and suds for dinner.

"Who needs a woman underfoot," he muttered, rubbing his balding pate. "No chatter boxing all day long and no infernal nagging."

Neighbors had dropped by that morning to express their condolences. It was all he could do to maintain a mournful

26

expression. Tomorrow he'd slip away for a few hours fishing, then spend some time with Sugar. All those sad faces were getting to him. If he didn't leave the village soon, he'd be depressed, and fat if he ate half the food already delivered. Despite the loss of someone to take care of him, his newly found freedom was exhilarating.

An idea abruptly hoisted him from his chair. Eyeing the refrigerator loaded with food, he decided to hold a wake. He'd invite his friends and no one would complain about the noise. The neighbors would simply shake their heads and say, "Poor old Pat's getting rid of his grief."

He was mentally compiling a guest list, a rare cigar clenched between his teeth, when he heard a light tapping at the kitchen door. Sighing, he expected another casserole dish and was annoyed to find Nola Champlain. She was overdressed in black satin, her bright red hair fastened with a rhinestone clasp. Green eyes gleamed mischievously from a pinched face, and she batted false eyelashes at him. She resembled an oversized Chihuahua costumed for a pet parade.

"I couldn't stay away," she said, producing a box of chocolates from behind her back. "I thought we'd share a little sweetness in your hour of need."

Taking the candy, he said, "Since you're here, you can help me plan tonight's wake."

"A wake? You should have told me sooner, dear. I need something new to wear."

"No women tonight, Nola. Just the boys and me."

"But I planned a quiet dinner."

Pat grimaced. "It wouldn't do for the sheriff to find me having dinner with a hungry widow."

"But I'm just consoling you."

"The answer's no."

Eyes narrowed, she muttered, "I wonder what I ever saw in you."

"I owe it to my poor dead wife."

27

"You didn't care about Betty. She said you have a mistress."

"You repeat that and I'll sue you for slander." He plucked at his shirt, now sticking to his chest. "Folks'll think you're a vicious gossip who preys on grieving widowers."

"Grieving, my Aunt Fanny."

"Terrible thing that happened to Betty," he said, pretending to wipe a tear.

"You owe me, Pat Wilson. If there is a mistress…"

Before he could placate her, Nola stormed through the kitchen door, threatening over her shoulder, "Keep an eye on your rump."

* * *

They sat at Sarah's kitchen table, munching muffins and sipping blackberry tea. "Not a word to the sheriff until we've talked to a lawyer."

"But, Dana, I might have killed Harold."

"Don't panic. He's just hiding out to get even for last night."

Dana's call to Riffle, Barrett, and Tomlinson got them nowhere. It was a legal holiday, but not one the sheriff observed. Despite his military bearing, she doubted he was a veteran.

"The only person smiling today is Nola." Sarah's plump hand reached for more nourishment. "I hear she's sweet on Pat, that Archie Bunker clone."

Dana grimaced, wondering how anyone could be attracted to Pat Wilson.

"Did you notice somebody watching us last night?" Sarah swallowed the rest of her blueberry muffin.

"I couldn't tell whether it was a bush blowing in the wind, or someone hiding in Harold's yard."

"Why would—?"

"Wouldn't you be curious if someone Harold's size was stuffed into a wheelbarrow?" Dana frowned, remembering. She refused to believe he was dead. The likelihood was too appalling to dwell on. They needed a lawyer before Sarah talked them both into prison. Tonight they would break into Harold's house. She prayed they wouldn't find him decomposing on his couch.

* * *

Candice Yarborough was a tiny woman, ninety pounds dripping out of her tub, her favorite place to reminisce. She had been alone for seven years since Elmer's death. Occupying her time with the soaps and TV talk shows, she knitted sweaters for family members, although she rarely saw them. Friday afternoons were reserved for Sew and So meetings, the extent of her social life.

She was four months shy of eighty and marking time until her death. Candice wasn't unhappy. She was simply in limbo. So it was no surprise that she rarely locked her doors or asked for identities before she turned the knob.

An uneven number of widows had left Candice without a partner, but she insisted on staying alone. She was in no hurry to dismantle her family shrine to accommodate a live-in companion. Photographs dating back to the Spanish-American War lined her walls, tables, and shelves, as well as the guest room bed. Someone disturbing her pictures was a far greater fear than chancing a killer's visit. Family memories were her only real treasures.

Death, wearing a ski mask and dark clothing, stalked her bathroom that night.

"I wondered when you'd come," she said. "Is this my last bubble bath?"

The intruder said nothing, although obviously surprised by her complacency. Candice watched as a knotted cord was pulled from his pocket.

"You won't need that," she said, leaning her head against the tub. "I won't give you any trouble."

He stood silently, apparently deciding her fate. Gloved hands then plunged into the soapy water to grasp her ankles and jerk her head beneath the surface.

Candice didn't struggle. She had suspected that she was next on the killer's list, and welcomed her demise. She had always been patient, expecting family visits that never came, and she knew that Elmer was waiting.

* * *

They left Dana's house at two the following morning. Palm trees lined a narrow walkway between the two residences, and they crept among the darkest shadows. They might have been seen, but could not have been heard. A party raged at the Wilson house with music and laughter rivaling a country tavern.

Dana stood an anxious watch while Sarah picked the lock. Once inside they switched on flashlights and trained them on the floor. The leather couch was empty, with no sign of Harold. Insisting they check the bedroom, Sarah started down the hall.

Dana's damp palm lost its grip on her flashlight and it hit the floor, trapping her in darkness. Such a klutz, she berated herself. On hands and knees she searched, her fingers finally closing around the plastic tube. Fumbling for the switch, she sighed with relief when an erratic light appeared on the opposite wall. Her heart pounded as she scanned the room, satisfied that Harold had not been sneaking up on her.

The floor plan was identical to her own, and she found her partner searching beneath the bed. Dana insisted they needed more light, but Sarah protested that the house might be under surveillance.

Spraying the unmade bed with light, Dana then aimed at a closet filled with wrinkled clothing. "Looks like he left in a hurry," she said, her breathing easier. "We'd better search the other rooms."

They checked the guest room, kitchen, and bath. Harold was definitely missing.

Once back at Sarah's house, she brewed them each a cup of tea. "No sense trying to sleep till we've sorted things out, Logan."

Eyes closed, Dana's head rested on her palms. "Harold's not the killer."

"Then why'd he disappear?"

"The chloral hydrate may have made him sick and he took a cab to the hospital."

"The sheriff must have checked."

"Grayson seems to be working without a plan, without an advisor."

"What capsizes my cart is the sheriff suspecting us, or any Sew and So for that matter."

"He's new at his job," Dana said. "His only law enforcement experience was training police dogs."

"I heard that the undersheriff quit because Grayson ran the office like a kennel."

"A rumor, but I wouldn't doubt it."

Rinsing cups in the sink, Sarah announced, "We'll continue this investigation in the morning over waffles."

* * *

"Music's pretty loud," John Merino complained. He was sobering up for the second time since the wake began. A reactor ticked in his left hemisphere, ready to trigger a nuclear explosion. He'd never had such a headache.

The place was littered with beer cans and chips. Glad there wasn't a wife present to complain about the mess, he winced, imagining the party at his house. He was surprised that Tamara hadn't arrived to drag him home. He almost wished she had.

Pat had left the wake several hours earlier, without explanation. His neighbor Albert Rodgers kept the party going, although most of the celebrants had passed out or gone home. After playing thirty-seven hands of stud poker, they drummed their way through five Tijuana Brass albums, and swapped World War II stories that grew more improbable with each telling.

Although trim and youthful for his age, John told himself that he was too old for such goings-on. He wished Pat would reappear so he could graciously take his leave. He found it strange celebrating someone's death, but he wasn't Irish.

The others seemed worried about leaving their wives alone, although none of them were Sew and Sos. John knew he should worry too, but Tamara was capable of defending herself. She not only owned a crystal ball, she could bean a burglar with it at twenty paces. His wife had been quite a softball pitcher in her youth.

Pat returned at 3:15, wiping his lips with a handkerchief. John marveled at his recuperative powers. The wake had done him wonders. He resolved to hold a wake of his own when Tamara passed on.

* * *

Tamara discovered Candice's body the following afternoon when she failed to attend a memorial service for the two murdered women. Their tiny neighbor was a compassionate person and her absence was noticed by everyone. Afraid she had suffered a serious fall, Tamara left the chapel to check on her friend. When she found her in the tub, she ran screaming to the church. By four o'clock the Valley Retirement Village resembled an armed camp.

* * *

Sheriff Grayson was unusually brisk when he arrived at Dana's house. Refusing a comfortable chair, he said, "A witness places you both at the scene of all three murders. And you admitted entertaining Samuels the night he disappeared."

"Your witness must be the killer," Dana said. "Nothing else makes sense."

Ignoring her conjecture, he read them their rights. A deputy then escorted them to the patrol car. Seated in the back seat behind the wire screen, Dana whispered, "They're going to separate us when we get to the station. Don't say a word until we've talked to a lawyer."

Anxiety creased Sarah's plump face. "I can't believe what's happened. Three murders and Harold could be number four."

"Corpses don't walk, my friend."

"You think he killed Candice?"

"I think the doomsayers are right," Dana said. "The world's fast approaching an end. Ours, at any rate."

* * *

The room was cold. Seated on a metal chair, Dana faced a detective who might have played for the Lakers. He was so tall that she developed a kink from looking up. A short female deputy leaned against the wall, observing.

"What line of work are you in?"

"I retired from teaching," she said.

"When'd you last see Harold Samuels?"

She insisted on waiting for her lawyer.

Leaning, his face close to hers, he said, "Your friend's already confessed."

"I know better than that." She knew nothing of the sort. Sarah may have told them everything. The door opened, admitting a stout, gray-haired man. Taking a chair beside her, he said, "I'd like some time with my client."

When the others left, Manuel Costera told her that he'd already counseled Sarah. Reaching to pat her hand, he said, "Are you ready to make a statement?"

"I've told them everything, except for Harold Samuels."

"And where might he be?"

"Wherever he is, he's furious. He's probably the anonymous caller who reported us to the sheriff." Harold was either getting even, or suspected them of killing their friends and attempting to poison him. They had to find him to explain.

The deputies returned, the tall one resuming his close-in stance. Rubbing her neck, she lowered her head to stare at the floor. The detective surprised her by asking whether her husband had been a weightlifter. She acknowledged that he had. What did that have to do with the murders? Ignoring her question, he asked about her own physical activities.

"I jog when my friends aren't being killed."

"You have enough money to live on?"

She looked to her lawyer, who nodded. "If I'm frugal and don't live forever. I'm still young enough to work."

"And Mrs. Cafferty?"

"Sarah inherited her—" A hand on her arm stopped her. "My friend doesn't exercise, despite my advice."

The deputy abruptly gathered his papers. "Don't leave the county," he warned, dismissing her.

Sarah was seated in the ante room, her face the color of pasta. Her eyes appeared as though she had attended the Wilson wake.

Dana whispered, "Did you tell them anything?"

"No, but they brought in another body they think might be Harold's. They want us to identify him."

"Why us?" Lightheaded, Dana sank into the nearest chair.

"Harold was a loner. No close friends or family in the valley. I guess all he had were his camellias."

A quiet, middle-aged deputy drove them to the county morgue. Watching them, he slowly pulled the drawer. Turning her head, Sarah pleaded, "You look, Dana. I'll have nightmares."

A deep breath and hand on the edge of the slab kept her from swaying. Guilt overpowered her and Dana nearly confessed. The sheet was pulled below the rib cage, exposing a heavy paunch. Gray skin was lacerated with a dozen stab wounds, as well as a six-inch scrape along his jaw. The bulbous nose was broken and both eyes blackened, making identification difficult. Repelled, Dana hesitated. It was then she noticed small gold studs in both ears.

"Is it him, Dana?" Sarah still had her back to the slab.

"Thank heavens, no. Have a look."

Peering over her shoulder, Sarah's gaze lingered on the large skull tattoo.

"Looks like a senior Hell's Angel," the deputy said. "You sure he's not our man?"

"That's definitely not Harold." Dana said, smiling.

"She's right, officer. Harold fancies himself a ladies' man, but he'd never wear earrings."

* * *

Tamara Merino unwrapped a green silk scarf, revealing Aquarian tarot cards. Carefully arranging them on a white pine board, she selected the queen of swords as her significator. A vague scent of incense further lent an aura of mysticism to the carefully darkened room. Four candles—orange, violet, pink, and green—burned in the table's center. Dana knew they held special meaning, but waited for Tamara to explain.

"I'm laying out a Merino divination," their neighbor said, "instead of the classic Celtic form."

It seemed a bit arrogant, but Dana nodded as though she understood.

Covering the queen with the magician's card, Tamara exclaimed, "Good, my third eye's attuned."

The death card appeared next and was placed across the magician. She explained the card's position as one of opposing force, signifying death as well as possible rebirth. The devil card was then turned up and placed above the magician.

"You didn't stack the cards to scare us, did you?" Sarah reached for the cards and had her hand slapped for disturbing the karma.

"The devil represents a destructive force. Someone selfish with no compassion for others."

"The murderer?"

"Not necessary. The card signifies information you hope to gain." Tamara moaned when the tower card was revealed. "Catastrophe."

"Are you sure?"

"My cards never lie." Placing the fourth card below the queen, she said it symbolized the basis of the matter. She then dealt six additional cards: one on either side of the queen, and four lined up along the edge. She said each card spelled more doom than its predecessor.

When the reversed wheel of fortune card appeared in the number ten spot, Sarah brightened. "A good sign?"

"It means the harder you work, the greater your reward."

Dana sighed. Consulting Tamara had been a waste of time. Their resident psychic was now shuffling cards to find Sarah's significator. Locating the blonde, blue-eyed queen of rods, she placed the cards face up, instructing Sarah to shuffle.

Dana excused herself and left the room. Before she closed the bathroom door, she heard Sarah groan, but when she returned, she found her smiling.

"Look at my cards, Dana."

She shrugged as she glanced at them.

"Beware of the reversed knight of cups," Tamara warned. "A young man with light brown hair and eyes who can't be trusted. He may even be the murderer."

"It's your turn, Dana." Tamara handed her the cards. "Keep shuffling until they feel right. Then, with your left hand, place them on the board in three separate piles."

Dana hesitated but did as she was told. Selecting the middle stack, Tamara dealt ten cards, reading them rapidly.

"Ah, the king of swords reversed. A cruel but brilliant man with evil intentions."

"Describe him, Tamara."

"Dark hair and eyes like mine."

"The killer?"

"Possibly."

Sarah was nonplused. "My cards say he's young with light brown hair."

The doorbell chimed and Tamara predicted that her husband had come to escort her home. "Next time," she said, "we'll use the crystal ball."

When the Merinos left, Dana insisted that she had shuffled her last tarot card. "Tamara will be reading auras next. At least neither description fits Harold."

"But the dark-haired one does fit Tamara's husband."

"John is neither cruel nor brilliant."

"True. He's henpecked as can be. Poor thing's still hung over from the wake."

Dana pulled the deadbolt. "Let's get what you need to spend the night. Then we can settle in with a good novel."

"If you don't mind, I'll study Terry's investigation manuals, instead."

"Fine. Let's get started. Night's coming on."

Chapter Four

Carole Lambert assumed the lotus position. Breathing deeply and deliberately, she succeeded in lowering her heart rate. Lana Nelson's non-stop chatter had driven Carole home to recharge her batteries. No serial killer was going to stop her afternoon yoga.

Unwinding child-like legs, she slid into the cobra position. Lying on her stomach, toes extended, palms beneath her narrow shoulders, she lifted her platinum head toward the ceiling. Exhaling slowly, she congratulated herself on a superb sixty-year-old body. Her violet eyes, rosy complexion, and slender body still turned a few heads in the village, but she had no desire to attract another man. Her goal was to celebrate her hundredth birthday by completing a set of tennis. Good health was all that really mattered.

Carole hated the sheriff's restrictions. She should be out walking the village perimeter or swimming twenty laps in the pool. The buddy system had paired her with Lana Nelson, a confirmed soap opera addict and couch potato. If that weren't enough, Lana daily snacked on chocolate cookies, ate red meat, and drank bituminous coffee by the pot full. No wonder she had so many ailments. She was a candidate for a coronary.

Carole dreaded returning to Lana's house for dinner. In self defense she planned to eat a veggie dish, then honestly claim she wasn't hungry. Tomorrow she would trick her partner into thinking soybean patties were actually hamburgers. Tenting her fingers, she prayed for the killer's capture so her carefully scheduled lifestyle could resume.

She was thawing dinner when staccato knocking jarred her tranquil state. Reaching for her grandson's discarded baseball bat, she stretched to squint through the peephole. Carole was startled by an eye peering back. The knocking resumed, the eye retreating far enough that she recognized Sarah Cafferty. She hurriedly unbolted the door.

"You have a death wish?" Sarah scolded. "The sheriff's liable to lock you up for traipsing around on your own."

Resisting the urge to slam the door, Carole invited her and Dana inside.

Once seated on the couch, Dana explained the reason for their visit. "It didn't occur to me until Sarah was packing an overnight bag to spend the night—"

The microwave's buzzer sounded, and they followed Carole into the kitchen.

"Why didn't you just call?"

"Your phone's out of order."

Carole lifted the wall receiver and listened. She reported the line was dead.

"You might be next on the killer's list," Sarah said. "Alice, Betty and Candice. Next comes Carole and Dana."

Carole crossed her slender arms. "But why?"

"If we knew that, we'd know who's killing our friends."

"Have you discussed this with the sheriff?"

"There wasn't time. You'd better come with us."

The custodian was sweeping the walk when they rushed from the house, Carole carrying her bat. Before they had gone a hundred feet, they heard a shrill whistle.

"Ladies," the custodian called, straightening her willowy frame. "You dropped something." Holding a pair of pink lace panties between her thumb and index finger, she laughed, exposing a space between her teeth.

Carole grabbed the underwear with her free hand. Glaring at the grinning janitor, she said, "If there's nicotine stains on them, you'll buy me another pair."

The custodian laughed. "You still mad about the cigarette burn?"

"You're damned right I am." Carole turned and stalked off, swearing beneath her breath. Still angry when they reached Dana's house, she told them the custodian had caulked her window with a cigarette dangling from her mouth. "She knows I'm allergic."

"Let me guess," Sarah said, fighting an encroaching grin. "She dropped ashes."

"She dropped the cigarette on my white plush carpet. So I chased her out with this." Holding the bat in a menacing manner, she replayed the remembered action.

Dana unlocked her door and urged them both inside. "We need to call the sheriff."

"I already talked to him, Dana. He says carpet burning is a civil matter."

Dana threw the deadbolt and reached for the phone. A minute later her hand covered the mouthpiece. "The sheriff's on patrol." She then said into the receiver, "Tell him our club members were murdered alphabetically. Yes, I know that's strange..." Dana's left hand made a futile gesture. "Yes, Alice Zimmer, Betty Wilson, and Candice Yarborough... No, first names." Her expression was one of pain. "I'm Dana Logan. Yes, D for Dana. But there's someone before me named Carole ... Fine, do that." She slammed the receiver without another word.

"I'm afraid you're losing it, Logan."

"What if your name were next on the killer's list?" Dana's face flushed as she collapsed into the nearest chair.

"It's probably a coincidence." Carole frowned. "If you're wrong, we're acting like fools."

"And if I'm right?"

"I'm the next victim, which means I'll never know."

"It's not going to happen," Sarah said. "There're three of us now. We'll pelt the killer with Dana's books till the sheriff gets here."

"You're not taking this seriously, are you, Sarah?"

"Once my stomach stops growling, I'll think more like a sleuth. At the moment all I can think of is food."

Carole reminded them of her uneaten dinner left in the microwave. "I don't suppose you have any bean sprouts or broccoli?"

"Dana eats them for breakfast."

"I wish the sheriff had paired me with you, Dana. Lana eats like a pregnant whale."

"Ah, like Sarah? Steak a la mode?"

"Exactly."

A shadow flitted across Dana's face. "You left Lana alone, didn't you?"

"Just long enough for yoga and veggies. She doesn't believe in either."

When Dana insisted she call her partner, Carole punched in the numbers and waited. The line was also out of order.

Taking the receiver, Dana warned them not to panic. There could be a line problem or damaged transformer. Carole wanted to believe her, but coincidence was not a word in her vocabulary.

"We'll escort Lana back for an old-fashioned slumber party." Dana reached for the fireplace poker and handed it to Sarah. Arming herself with a three-pound exercise weight, she watched as Carole retrieved her bat. Opening the door little more than a crack, Dana peered into the twilight. It was still the dinner hour, and no one was moving about. Motioning her friends outside, she hurriedly locked the door.

Lana's home bordered the golf course, near a brushy area. They power-walked it in under four minutes, Sarah breathing heavily. When Carole rang the bell, they waited. Twilight had already faded into darkness.

"We were supposed to exchange house keys." Carole stroked her throat to remove the lump that had formed. "Lana must be looking for me."

Bolting before the others could react, Carole ran down the street, turning the corner toward her own house. She knew Sarah could not keep up, and there wasn't time to wait for her. In the darkest area between street lights, she ran into someone the size of a draft horse. He grabbed her before she fell. Growling, he said, "What're you doing out here alone?"

Too frightened to speak, Carole flailed at him with the bat until he wrestled it away from her.

"If I were the killer, you'd be dead by now," he said. "Why aren't you home with your partner?"

"S-sheriff, you nearly stopped my heart."

"I've been looking for you," Grayson said, his voice gruffer than usual. When they moved into the nearest street light, she noticed deep pouches beneath his eyes.

"Where were you? And why'd you leave Miz Nelson?"

"Where is she, Sheriff? Is Lana all right?"

"She called the department at quarter till six, but the dispatcher couldn't understand her. The line went dead and she doesn't seem to be at home. I thought you'd have a key."

Her companions arrived with Sarah out of breath. "The three of you stay together," he ordered, "until I locate Miz Nelson."

* * *

Although Lana's disappearance had dulled their appetites, Carole prepared them a vegetarian dinner. As they sat around her teakwood table, Sarah seesawed in her belief that Harold

43

was the murderer, and fear that he'd been killed. Her friends were noncommittal. When the table had been cleared, they checked that windows and doors were locked, then settled in the living room to talk about motives.

"Nola has her cap set for Pat," Carole said. "You don't suppose that she—?"

"Nola's a schemer but I doubt she's capable of murder." Dana's long, slender legs stretched between a low-backed chair and needlepoint-covered hassock. Lifting shoulder-skimming auburn hair behind her ears, she was obviously struggling to stay awake.

"Pat didn't treat Betty very well," Sarah said. "He's more likely to have killed her than Nola, especially if rumors are true he's a womanizer."

Dana grimaced as though Pat's sex life were repugnant.

Sarah scooted to the edge of her chair. "I think we should consult again with Tamara."

"She does seem to know things, but…" Carole hesitated, uncertain whether to criticize their resident psychic.

"We'll be consulting a Ouija board next." Dana yawned. "All we've gotten from Tamara is silly guesswork."

Sarah seemed disturbed by her friends' skepticism. "Even the police consult with psychics."

"Are we sure Tamara is a psychic?" Dana asked. "She could simply be a mind reader who channels fear."

The phone rang a few minutes before ten. Lana had been found slumped across her bed, an empty fifth of vodka on her pillow. The sheriff surmised that Carole's unscheduled departure had driven her partner to drink. He escorted Carole back to her partner's home, his lecture leaving her seething.

* * *

Pat Wilson awoke with a gargantuan hangover, which he attempted to cure with Bloody Marys. One gulp slid smoothly down his burning throat but, halfway through the second, he bolted for the john. There was no one to prepare

an ice pack or fuss over him. Maybe he should call Nola…
No, that was the worst thing he could do. Her shrill voice
would send him into lunar orbit. Grumbling, he found his
way back to bed. Stumbling over beer cans and trash, he felt
a twinge of regret at Betty's death.

* * *

The doorbell rang next morning while Dana was cleaning
house. Expecting Sheriff Grayson, she ignored the peephole
and immediately pulled the bolts. Her visitor stood between
red nylon suitcases, rendering Dana speechless.

"Surprise." A tall, brown-eyed young woman stepped
forward to embrace her.

"Kerrie. It's good to see you."

"You, too, Mom."

"It's not the best time to visit, dear."

"Why?" The hug ended abruptly.

"The village isn't safe."

"Don't tell me they built it over the San Andreas Fault."

"I wish it were only that."

Kerrie set her luggage inside the door and removed her
leather jacket. "First things first. I lost my job and need a
place to stay."

"Oh, dear."

"I know I'm not the easiest person to live with, but I
promise my best behavior."

"What about Jack?"

"The wedding's off. He doesn't have a clue about fidelity."

"I'm sorry, honey."

"Me, too, Mom." Kerrie's face crumpled and Dana was
afraid she was going to cry.

She led her daughter into the small mauve kitchen where
she poured them each a cup of coffee.

"A friend's occupying the guest room, but we can double
up. Village rules allow visitors to stay sixty days, but there's
something you should know before you unpack…"

Sarah waddled into the kitchen several moments later. Dressed in a green robe, her wet hair was wrapped in a matching towel. Stopping short, she scrutinized their visitor.

"You cloned a beautiful daughter," she said, when Dana introduced them.

Both women smiled.

"Have you told her yet, Dana?"

"Yes, Mom told me, but I'm not worried. Only older women are being killed."

"That's about to change," Dana looped an arm around her daughter's throat, gently pulling her close. "If you're determined to protect this old lady, you'll have to follow the sheriff's safety rules."

"That doesn't mean I have to stay cooped up, does it? My pent-up frustrations demand that I have some fun."

"Not until the sheriff assigns you a partner," Dana said. "There's a psychopath roaming these grounds."

"Safety in numbers, Mom. No psychopath in his right mind would attack two six-foot women."

"I like this girl," Sarah said, laughing.

Dana frowned, shaking her head slightly as Kerrie draped an arm around them both.

Squeezing their shoulders, Kerrie said, "Why don't we start by investigating the local night life?"

"I guess we can manage dinner and a show."

"That's fine for starters. But isn't there somewhere a little more exciting?"

Sarah's eyes danced. "I know just the place, that male stripper club out on the highway."

Dana rolled her eyes.

"I've always wanted to stuff a dollar bill into one of those prancing G-strings."

"You can't be serious."

"Kerrie's right. There's nothing like entertainment to rid your mind of troubles."

46

"Maybe, but a strip joint?"

"I know it's passe, Mom, but I'll bet you've never even seen a stripper."

"You're right, I haven't, and it's never been high on my 'want-to' list."

"Consider it research, Logan. It'll sharpen our observation skills, certainly where the male body is concerned."

Chapter Five

John Merino groaned as he massaged his throbbing head. He blamed stress for his rare bout of heavy drinking. Village residents were jittery as hummingbirds, all of them considered murder suspects. The sheriff couldn't find the killer in a roomful of Buddhist monks. He was surprised Grayson hadn't erected a high wire fence to prevent the seniors from escaping.

He should circulate a recall petition to have the sheriff removed from office. Before Grayson learned his job, there would be mass graves lining the San Andreas Fault. John was fed up with the whole blasted case. He was also fed up to his baseball cap with Tamara's psychic predictions. He admitted that her stock market forecasts had enabled his early retirement, but if Tamara were truly gifted, the murderer's identity would have come to light. The cards had shown her a dark-haired man as well as a light-haired youth. You couldn't have it both ways unless the two of them were working in tandem. Now there was a theory to twist your skivvies in a granny knot.

Since Tamara's crystal ball was too cloudy to divulge the killer, he suggested calling the weather bureau for the next high pressure system. She never appreciated his humor—or him—but whenever he felt neglected, John resisted seeking comfort elsewhere. His wife's crystal ball had him exactly where she wanted him.

* * *

"Where do you want me to put my things?" Kerrie asked, when her mother agreed that a night on the town would hone her detective skills.

Dana, although unconvinced, grudgingly agreed to go along.

Sarah moved her things in with Dana, leaving Kerrie the guest room.

Laying aside black Capri pants and a body-hugging blouse, Kerrie retrieved gold earrings from her small jewelry case. A peace offering from Jack to sooth his conscience? She wasn't sure, but the thought of wearing them suddenly made her ill. She loved the way they dangled, catching the light, but she decided to punish Jack by pawning them, although he'd never know. The distance she had placed between them insured no further contact, but she needed to rid herself of memories. The pain was still too intense.

Her savings would last several months while she found a new direction, but sixty days didn't allow her much time. She had never felt close to her mother, but there was nowhere else to turn. Jobs were scarce, particularly in her field of expertise.

* * *

A "Rockford File" rerun followed the evening news. For the first time that week no mention was made of the murders. They considered the lapse an omen, foreshadowing an end to the killings. Photos of California's most wanted criminals filled the screen instead. Several, the news anchor said, had recently escaped from prison.

"You don't suppose—?" Sarah leaned for a closer look.

"No, I don't think any of them is our serial killer." Dana was adamant. "We're nowhere near a maximum security prison. That's what I like about this part of the valley. No drive-by shootings, no ethnic gangs, unless the Portuguese farmers are organized pheasant poachers."

Sarah laughed. "My word, Logan, you do have a sense of humor."

Ignoring the rib, Dana insisted, "The only serial killings until now have been caused by pesticides, tule fog, and imported bay area smog."

"But, Dana—"

"A stranger is noticed right away. There's nowhere to hide for any length of time, as in The City. I can't imagine an escaped convict drawing attention to himself by committing a series of murders."

"Unless he's a total nut case."

"That's why I'm convinced the killer is someone we know."

"A friend killing off Sew and Sos is worse than menopause."

"Why do you think I'm nervous about Kerrie staying here? She doesn't realize the danger."

"Your daughter's smart. She won't risk her safety. Or ours."

"I wish I had your confidence, Sarah. You know I'm an old worrier—"

"And always have been," Kerrie said from the doorway.

"Don't you look nice." Sarah switched off the TV and struggled to her feet.

Kerrie strode into the room in black Capris and a gold silk blouse, her long, blond-streaked auburn hair freshly washed and shining. Dark, smoky-shadowed eyes were a bit flamboyant for her mother's tastes, but Dana thought it best not to criticize.

"You're as pretty as a Christmas tree," she said, examining Kerrie's attire, "but I wouldn't waste your holiday outfit on us."

Kerrie half-turned, an eyebrow arched in surprise. "How long's it been since you were in a nightclub, Mom?"

"Since Houdini did his underwater act," Sarah said, stroking Kerrie's hair.

"Then it's time we got started, ladies."

Dana decided to bury her misgivings, at least for the moment. She couldn't, however, dismiss the fear that they were tramping through a mine field, every step a life and death venture.

* * *

Nola left her partner's house at 10 p.m., confident that Micki was sleeping. For her entire adult life, Micki had bedded with the chickens and awakened with the cows. A dairyman's wife, Nola thought with distaste. She couldn't imagine retiring at eight and rising at four to cook for a bovine-scented husband. Widowed five years, her partner seemed unable to adjust to leisurely retirement.

From her bedroom window Nola noticed lights in Pat Wilson's house, and decided to pay him another visit. She wouldn't allow him to toss her away like one of his chewed cigars. Pat wasn't the nicest or handsomest man she'd ever known, but Nola was used to second best. Some women used their beauty to get what they wanted. Nola used elbow grease and hated other women for their guile. At sixty-one, when most women were complacent with their lot, she was attempting to bag a second husband. Her meager savings needed a transfusion, but she was too battle-scarred to return to school bus driving.

When she rang his bell, Pat took a long time answering. Grumbling, he blinded her with the porch light.

"Turn it off," she whispered. "We don't want the neighbors knowing I'm here."

"Blast the damn neighbors. Party poops are probably all asleep."

When he didn't invite her in, she nudged the door he was partially holding open. "Aren't you going to invite—?"

"No. An old friend's here to discuss a mutual problem. This ain't a good time for a visit."

Nola ducked beneath his arm, getting far enough into the room to glimpse a pair of black shapely stockings. Pat grabbed Nola and swung her about, depositing her back on the porch.

"We'll do lunch," he said, quickly closing the door.

She heard the lock click as well as several bolts. Enraged, she scooped a handful of rocks from the flower bed. Resisting the urge to hurl them through the draped window, she clamped down hard on her dentures.

"There's more than one way to roast a skunk.

* * *

"We're here."

Sarah drove into the parking lot and searched for an empty space. Large billboard letters spelled "Strippers" diagonally along the building. Dana hung back when they climbed from the car. Deep throbbing sounds reverberated from the building, and she sensed the tavern itself was vibrating. Heavy metal music blasted them as the door opened and a bow-tied, shirtless waiter beckoned them inside. They followed him into the cavernous, dimly-lit interior where small lights swirled about the room in rainbow colors, immediately making her dizzy. The waiter seated them at a tiny round table flanked by three smaller chairs. Cigarette smoke, nearly as dense as tule fog, impaired her vision.

"The girls all look alike," Sarah shouted over the music as she dabbed at her eyes.

Dana nodded, glancing at Kerrie, who was slowly scanning the room. Before they could order a drink, a drum roll gained momentum, ending in a cymbal crash. A baritone voice then announced the floor show.

"Now, ladies, a big round of applause for our first dancer. He comes to us from the centerfold of Playgirl."

Ear-splitting screams surrounded them, reminding Dana of a roller coaster ride. Sarah, she noticed, was clapping fingers against her mouth in a simulated war hoop. Disgusted, Dana covered her ears. Gad, she was feeling old.

* * *

Micki's arthritis woke her before midnight. Slipping quietly out of bed, she made her way to the medicine cabinet. She found a lone aspirin tablet and knowing it wouldn't quell the pain, wondered if Nola had a bottle in her room. Nola's door was open, and she timidly knocked on the frame. Calling softly, she heard no reply. Nola sleeps like a bull, she thought, venturing into the guest room. Patting the coverlet at the end of the bed, she worked her hand higher until she discovered her partner missing. Switching on the bedside lamp, she found the covers undisturbed. Screaming, she rushed back into her room and locked the door. Hands trembling, she grabbed the phone and punched in 911.

* * *

Sarah's head swiveled, her grin like a child's at Disneyland. "Look at all those guys at the bar. I thought no self-respecting man would be caught in a male stripper club."

"What better place to meet women?" Kerrie said.

"I guess they need a few drinks before they shed their clothes."

"If those are the strippers, they'll be laughed off the stage."

The first dancer completed a strenuous set of floor exercises and began his upright maneuvers. Kerrie seemed hypnotized, her eyes narrowed to slits. Swaying with the music, she was obviously enjoying the dancer's sensual moves. Sarah, however, was laughing hysterically, tears trailing down her plump cheeks.

Dana found the dancer's moves disgusting. Squinting through the smoke, she watched young women in twos and threes advance toward the stage. Some danced in synch with the stripper while others stuffed money in his brief. She knew it was useless to suggest leaving while the show was still in progress.

Leaning across the table, Sarah said, "I haven't had this much fun in years."

Dana forced a smile but wanted the show to end. A feeling of uneasiness increased with each dance. Scanning the room, she searched for eyes turned in their direction. Near the end of the bar, a dark-haired man ducked his head when he realized she was staring. Reaching into his pocket, he slapped a bill on the counter, and immediately rose to leave.

Dana got to her feet, nearly upsetting her chair.

"Where're you going, Dana?"

"Restroom," she lied.

By the time she wound her way to the bar, the man had disappeared. The bartender shrugged when she asked where he'd gone. He couldn't remember serving the man and didn't know when he arrived. The bartender seemed more interested in the offstage dancers than he did in tending bar.

They'd call her paranoid if she told them why she left the table. Dana was beginning to doubt her own sanity. What would she have done if the suspect remained on his stool? Ask him if he were the killer? Maybe she should have followed him into the parking lot and written down his license number.

No. That's exactly what he wanted. Rubbing her left brow, she groaned. Sinus headache. Damn cigarette smoke. She had to get away from the bar. The killer could be lurking outside, ready to shoot when they left. No, she reminded herself, he kills with his hands, although he might have changed his MO.

The dance ended to mild applause. She watched another well-built dancer retrieve his costume from the stage. He'd done a competent job of stripping, but the audience wasn't as generous with their applause. They must be as weary as I am, she thought. One more dancer and I'm leaving—killer waiting or not.

Threading her way back to the table, she wondered what she should do. No sense ruining the evening for Kerrie and Sarah, who were obviously enjoying themselves. Neither realized the danger. Any one of those men at the bar could have followed them here. Dana shivered at the thought. If she told them why she was worried, they'd call her an old woman. Her lips set in a grim line. She was a firm believer in reincarnation, but wasn't ready to leave this life to embark on another. Not while a serial killer stalked the retirement village.

* * *

When the door closed behind him, he sank into the nearest chair. That was a close one. He'd have to be more careful. When the Logan woman looked his way, he panicked and left the bar. He should have waited in his car and followed them onto the highway. It would have been easy to run them off the road. Removing the dark toupee and full mustache, he draped them over a Nintendo cassette. No use rushing things. He had other targets. Grinning to himself, he made his way to the bathroom where he removed his dark contacts. After changing his clothes, he donned a baseball cap.

* * *

Carole insisted they watch a horror movie and had turned out all the lights. But Lana was quite capable of finding chocolate cookies in her sleep. Without lighting the kitchen, she renewed her supply of sweets. Both hands and mouth full, she started back when she heard breaking glass. An Oreo lodged in her throat as cookie crumbs sifted through her fingers.

* * *

The third vodka gimlet was lulling Dana to sleep. Laughing, her companions helped her into the car minutes before the bar officially closed. Too weary to remember to check the parking lot for loiterers, she dozed off while Sarah was describing her G-string deposit.

"It wasn't as much fun as I thought," Sarah said, pulling onto the highway. "I might have zigged when he zagged, and we'd both have been embarrassed.

"The only one embarrassed was Mom—"

Floating peacefully, Dana was rudely catapulted from her cloud when the Buick stopped short, nearly colliding with a fire truck. Groping to silence her alarm clock, she wondered why it was so shrill.

"Wake up, Mom. Something's burning."

Dana jerked forward, vigorously rubbing her eyes. A red glow lighted the sky ahead of them.

"Palm tree's on fire," Sarah said as she eased onto the frontage road. "I hope it's not one of ours."

"The whole village could burn if the wind picks up," Kerrie warned

Sarah was adamant. "Stucco houses with tile roofs don't burn."

The landscape was surreal. None of this was making sense. Dana closed her eyes, hoping the nightmare would end. She'd had too much to drink. That's all it was, an alcohol-induced aberration. Rock music mixed with vodka and cigarette smoke had to scramble one's brain. Why had she downed that many drinks? She knew why. It was the only way she could get through the evening. When she opened her eyes, the fire seemed to have gotten worse.

"You all right, Dana?" Sarah glanced sideways, then back at the fire.

"I'm fine, but when does this nightmare end?"

"Not till the sheriff gets some help, I'm afraid."

Kerrie fidgeted in her seat. "I was craving excitement, but I never expected this."

"Excitement?" Sarah turned right on Vineyard Lane. "You should have been here all week."

Thank God Kerrie hadn't arrived earlier, Dana thought, craning her neck to stare at the flames.

Lights were on in all the houses, residents in their night clothes cloistered across the street. A police car with red lights flashing was parked in the middle of the block. When the deputy noticed the Buick, he motioned Sarah to stop. The scene reminded Dana of the Oakland Hills fire in miniature. One house burned so brightly that it seemed to scorch her eyes, the glare intensified by the windshield. She blinked several times and looked away.

Beige-coated firemen with neon stripes were scrambling from the truck, hoses trailing after them. The sound of sirens came from every direction, an ambulance screeching to a halt beside the patrol car. Dana fought to get her bearings, the ghastly scene swirling in her head like a not-so-merry-go-round. Surely the firemen would not attempt a rescue in that inferno.

It wasn't possible that anyone could have survived the fire. Checking the dashboard clock, Dana realized it was two in the morning. Whoever lived there had burned in their beds.

"Oh, my Lord," Sarah shrieked. "Do you know whose house that is?"

Chapter Six

A cold, westerly wind was blowing in from the coast when Kerrie stepped from the car. Excitement made her shiver, despite the fire's intense heat. Sparks spiraling eastward ignited dried fronds of border palms. As far as she could tell, the fire had not yet spread to other houses. A handsome young fireman hesitated when he noticed her. He immediately signaled her to remain where she was.

"Reporter," she shouted over the noise. "Where's the chief?"

He motioned her to follow as he continued toward the pumper truck. Stooping to retrieve a flat-headed axe, he indicated a stout fireman who appeared to be in charge. As Kerrie approached, the stone-faced chief waved her aside. Undaunted, she circled in close on his blind side.

"Kerrie Compton, reporter," she said, when he realized she was there.

"No time for interviews."

"Casualties?"

"None found yet." Frowning, he turned to face her. "Who're you with? I haven't seen you around."

"Correspondent," she said. The fire made her realize how much she missed her job. If another staff writing position failed to materialize, she would freelance as a journalist. The depression she'd experienced since the breakup with Jack had dissipated. She was a free agent and could do whatever she pleased.

Smiling broadly, she said, "One more question and I'm gone."

His pained expression said, *Make it quick.*

"Who lived in the house?"

"Somebody named Nelson."

"First or last name?"

"Last?" Jerking his thumb toward the opposite side of the street, he barked an order at his radio.

"Nelson." She repeated the name as she retreated to the Buick. Sarah was right. Lana Nelson had been incinerated in her bed, along with her partner. Kerrie couldn't remember the other woman's name. Despite the probable casualties, her spirits soared. Ambulance chasing was far from boring, but she had to admit that it kept her in a constant state of flux. Fortunately, she wasn't squeamish, although reporting on others' tragedies did take its toll. As she approached the Buick, Kerrie's heart lurched when she noticed their stricken faces through the windshield.

* * *

"Holy Hannah." Pat Wilson stood at the window in his underwear, the bedroom drapes parted. "Would you look at that." His smaller companion joined him, quietly wrapping herself in an Afghan knitted by his wife. "I hope the fire doesn't spread," she said, hugging herself.

"Not a chance. That's why I bought this place. Burning stucco and tile's like torching concrete. That fire had to start inside."

"Are you sure, Patsy?"

"I wish you wouldn't call me that, Sugar. It makes me sound like a sissy."

Snuggling close, she said, "You're anything but that."

Pat was distracted by movement across the street. Silhouetted by the fire was a small person who turned to stare at their unclothed portrait in the window.

Nola, damn her. What's that crazy broad doing out there by herself? Quickly closing the drapes, he said, "Let's go back to bed, Sugar. The fire can't touch us here."

* * *

Sarah backed around the corner of Peach and Vineyard Lane and slowly headed north. Stopping briefly at home, she allayed her fears that sparks were blowing in their direction. Continuing east to Dana's, she felt drained of emotion, although tears were hovering somewhere near the surface.

"I wonder if the sheriff will evacuate the village."

"I doubt it," Dana said, seemingly sober.

"Maybe we should call the governor and insist on martial law."

Kerrie placed a hand on Sarah's shoulder. "It's not that simple. Apparently the sheriff's in over his head but too stubborn to ask for help."

"What do you suggest, Kerrie?"

"Let's sleep on it."

As they approached Dana's house, headlights spotted movement in the hedge. When Sarah gasped, Dana assured her the shadow was only a dog.

"No, it's bigger than that."

"Then we need a deputy to check it out."

When they pulled to the curb, Kerrie said, "I've earned my karate brown belt." Before they could stop her, she opened the door and rushed around the hedge.

"Cut the lights," Dana ordered, then reached to shut them off herself.

"We should've gone to help her, Dana."

"If she's not back in sixty seconds, we will." Dana stared gloomily at the glowing dashboard clock. The fire's reflected light danced menacingly from the gauges as though a warning from the devil, himself.

"Let's go." Dana reached for the handle and was startled when the door swung outward. Kerrie stood grinning at her.

"Mom, you'll never guess who's hiding in the yard."

* * *

Outside his window, Pat Wilson's snoring rumbled like a defective chain saw. Two-timing sneak. Nola shivered, not only from anger, but the damp cold. She hoped no one was watching when she dribbled gasoline from a five-gallon can along the dried grass. Generously splashing the window frame, she backed to where boards were missing in the fence and set the can aside. Carefully lighting a matchbook, she dropped it into the gasoline trail. As it made a woofing sound and raced toward the house, she ducked through the loose boards. Retrieving the container, she ran.

At Micki's back fence, she pushed in two redwood planks with bottom nails missing. Her breathing was labored when she entered the garage. Replacing the gas can on the floor, she slowly turned the knob. Too late she realized the kitchen was lighted and someone blocked her path.

* * *

Tamara awoke during the night. Frightened, although not sure why, she had gone to the kitchen in search of food. Bananas, she knew, were nocturnal pacifiers. She had eaten one and peeled another when her husband John slouched into the room. The thick, dark hair she'd always loved was shot with gray and disheveled. His deep-set azure eyes were puffy as though he'd had no rest.

"Can't sleep either, I see."

"You're mighty all-fired calm about a fire that could destroy the village," he said.

"Fire?"

"Better wake up your crystal ball and find out who started it."

"You're joking."

"Take a look for yourself." Gripping her arm, he led her into the living room where he roughly parted the drapes.

"Oh, how awful."

"You didn't foresee this happening?"

Tamara lowered her head. "I'm not all-knowing, John. I only know what my spirit guides tell me."

"They must be pretty sadistic to let this happen."

"There's a reason for everything. When the time's right, my guides will tell me who's committing the murders."

* * *

"Why were they hiding in my yard, Kerrie?"

"Shhhh. Don't say a word until we're all safely inside."

"But—"

"Come on. Quiet as you can."

When the door closed behind them, Kerrie rushed to close the drapes. She then switched on a table lamp. Dana shepherded their guests into chairs, asking, "What happened?"

"My house caught fire when we were watching a horror movie."

Lips trembling, Carole added, "Lana choked on a cookie before she could tell me what happened."

Kerrie immediately took charge. "How did the fire start?"

"I heard a window break." Lana's gray eyes widened. "Then an explosion."

"It came from the back of the house." Carole rose from her chair to reenact the scene. "We sneaked out before the fire got to the living room."

Lana wrung her hands. "Then we hid so the killer would think we died."

When Carole suggested that Lana bunk with her, Sarah warned against it. "You can both hide at my house," she said. "The killer won't think to look for you there. Sheriff Grayson will tell the media that you died in the fire."

Carole's eyes blazed. "I don't trust that man."

"He'll know when your bodies aren't found," Dana said. "The sheriff regularly patrols the area. He keeps track of all of us."

"That's all the sheriff's good for, spying."

Dana shook her head. "He's inexperienced, Carole. He's doing his best."

"Not good enough." Carole moved toward the door. "We should all leave the valley before the killer tries again."

"Go where, Carole?"

"He'd never think to look for us in Vegas."

"We can't leave," Sarah said. "In case you've forgotten, we're all murder suspects."

Dana cautioned them not to panic. "We could be followed and disposed of in the Mojave Desert. Let's not do anything stupid."

Disappearing in the middle of a murder investigation, for any reason, would make them all fugitives, Kerrie warned.

"Spending time in jail until they find the real killer wouldn't be fun, either." Sarah sank into the cushions, tired eyes focused on the ceiling.

"It's past my bedtime," Lana said. "We can't all sleep here."

"Not a good idea for anyone to stay," Dana warned. "Both our names are next on the killer's list."

A siren screamed past, accompanied by low-pitched engine noise.

"Another fire." Kerrie rushed to the window. "The truck stopped a few houses down."

"Fire's spreading?" Sarah joined her at the window. "How can that be? We're a good deal north of the blaze."

"The wind must have shifted."

"Now's the time to make the transfer to my house," Sarah said. "Quick. Let's grab you both a disguise."

* * *

A pumper truck arrived first. In less than a minute hoses were at the ready. Before the 500-gallon tank could be emptied of its contents, Pat Wilson sauntered onto the lawn. Dressed in a red terry cloth robe, he yelled. "Fire's already out. Sorry to bring you guys over here on a false alarm."

The truck's captain strode over for details.

"Somebody doused the back of my house with gas and struck a match." A slight smile twitched Pat's lower lip. Now, at least, no one would suspect him of the murders.

"You see who did it?"

"I'm not mentioning any names till I talk to the sheriff." Pat leaned in close to add, "But it's probably not the same one who set the other fire."

"How do you know it was arson?"

"It's obvious, ain't it? Fire started on the inside of the other house, and it burnt up in minutes."

"Nice view you have of the fire," the captain said, his voice suddenly hard. "Make sure you're home the rest of the night. I'll be back to fill out a report."

* * *

They were both too short to disguise as men, so Carole wore one of Dana's shirts with the sleeves rolled up to her wrists. The large silk scarf covering her hair also diminished her. When she looked in the mirror, she remarked that she resembled a gypsy.

Because of her weight, Lana was harder to disguise. She managed to switch clothes with Sarah, her silver hair hidden under Dana's gardening hat.

"Fire truck just left," Kerrie reported from her station at the window. "Must have been a false alarm."

Opening the door a crack, Sarah peered out. Handing Carole her keys, she said, "Don't forget to water the plants, and keep the drapes closed. Hurry."

Both women crept to the car, glancing about as though they expected capture.

Dana groaned. "We forgot to tell them to act naturally."

"All we can do now is pray. I told Carole to call as soon as they lock themselves in."

When the Buick had rounded the corner and disappeared on Vineyard Lane, Dana suggested that her daughter get some sleep. The two older women would retire as soon as they heard from their friends. When the guest room door closed, Dana headed for the kitchen. A kettle of water had been placed on a burner when the telephone rang.

"Dana? We're here."

She heard her own relief amplified in the phone. "Are you sure no one followed you?"

"The only people we saw were firemen rolling up hoses."

"Stay inside and quiet. We'll bring whatever you need."

The kettle was whistling when she replaced the receiver. Dana knew tea at three in the morning wasn't a good idea, but they were both too keyed to sleep. Her friend was obviously in a mood to talk.

"Both my kids called when they heard about the murders," Sarah said, "but I talked them out of coming. I'm glad Kerrie's here, though."

"I'm not, for several reasons."

"What went wrong between you two?"

Dana glanced up from her steaming mug. "Meaning?"

"I don't want to pry, but there's something not quite right between the two of you."

Dana spread her long fingers and seemed to be counting age spots. "Symbiosis," she said at last. "Or lack of it."

"What?"

"Kerrie was a change of life baby."

"I thought she was born during your thirties."

"She was, my only attempt at motherhood, and it certainly changed my life."

"It should have brought you closer, not at arm's length."

"I was widowed the same month Kerrie was born. My first husband had no life insurance, and I worked two jobs to support us."

"I'm sorry." Sarah reached to squeeze her hand.

"Kerrie was raised by a series of babysitters, so we missed that early bonding. Then, when I was hired by the school district and had more time at home, she didn't need me."

"That explains her independence. But she's here now. She must need you."

"I wonder."

"Go easy on Kerrie. She's hurting."

A rare smile brightened Dana's face. "Did you notice tonight, the way she took charge?"

"Proud of her, aren't you?"

"Very."

"Why don't you tell her?"

"When the time's right." Dana rose from the breakfast nook. "I think I can sleep now."

"Me, too, Logan. We'll solve the murders tomorrow."

* * *

Pat Wilson was clearly agitated. "You gotta leave," he said. "If they find you here—"

"I know," she said, pulling on her pale blue cashmere sweater.

"Did I tell you what that fireman said?"

"At least a dozen times. Don't worry. There's nothing they can pin on you."

"I dunno, Sugar. Everything's out a whack. I don't think we should see each other for awhile."

"Whatever you say, Patsy."

"I told you not to call me that."

A long red acrylic nail moved to his lips, silencing him, her almond-shaped eyes questioning. "Are you going to tell them about Nola?"

"Maybe."

"If you don't, they'll suspect you of torching your own house to avert suspicion."

"I didn't think of that."

"And what about your alibi?"

His ruddy skin paled. "I'd have to say I was with you."

"That, my dear Patsy, would make you a prime suspect in your wife's murder." Maintaining eye contact while buttoning her calf-skin coat, she said, "Killing the other women isn't going to fool the sheriff."

Face reddening, he said, "For all I know, you done the old ladies in."

She smiled. "With these little hands?"

"The killer used a lamp and a drapery cord."

"And what was my motive, dearest?"

"You probably thought with Betty out of the way—"

"That you'd marry me?" Her laughter sliced through to his spleen. "Be serious, Patsy. I only stick around till the bank account's empty."

He glared at her, so enraged that he couldn't move, but when she backed toward the door, he lunged. With the grace of a star running back, Sugar managed to twist free of his grasp. The door opened, as he fell to one knee, and slammed in his face.

Palms sweaty, he wrestled with the knob. When he managed to jerk the door open, he faced the fire chief.

"Going somewhere, Mr. Wilson?"

"I— I wondered if the fire was out."

"Mind telling me who just left?"

"An old friend from outa town."

"Her name?"

"Sugar."

"Does Sugar have a last name?"

"My memory's not what it was."

"Try." He stepped across the threshold, fumbling in his pocket for a pen.

"Uh, Brown. That's it. Sugar Brown."

The chief smiled as he wrote Brown, Sugar on his notepad.

"Mind if I have a seat?"

"It's pretty late, Chief."

"This won't take long."

Chapter Seven

"Nola. I thought you were dead."

The stout, olive-skinned woman froze in the act of making coffee. Behind Micki Fugundos, the craggy face of Sheriff Grayson scowled.

"Yes, Miz Champlain," he growled. "Where have you been?"

Nola's knees trembled as she stood inside the kitchen door. Summoning all the control she could muster, she said, "I wanted to see the fire."

The sheriff's eyes narrowed, his thick brows forming an angry frown. "You've been gone for hours. The fire didn't start until after one-thirty."

Before Nola could answer, Micki bellowed, "Don't you care that you worried me?"

Nola stared at the linoleum without a trace of remorse. "If you must know, I left to see my boyfriend."

"His name?" the sheriff demanded.

"Can't tell you."

"Why not?"

"He's married." She glanced through her lashes to gage their reactions.

"Nola, how could you?" Micki wailed.

"This boyfriend help you start the fire?" Grayson moved closer, dwarfing her in his shadow from the overhead light.

"We sparked our own little fire."

"I see." Grasping her wrist, the sheriff leaned to sniff her fingers. A contemptuous smile played across his lips. "Looks like I caught the arsonist as well as the killer, all sealed up in one little package."

She shrank even smaller as Grayson read Nola her rights. When he got to "the right to an attorney," she was sniffling. "I only wanted to scare him."

The sheriff abruptly turned her about, snapping handcuffs on her wrists, which were so thin she could have easily pulled free. For the moment, she was too afraid to try.

"You've got the wrong person," she said, hiccupping. "I saw who set the fire. That's how I got the idea to teach Pat a lesson."

"Lie to your lawyer," Grayson said, gripping her arm. He pulled Nola into the living room where they heard Micki's voice echoing from the kitchen. "You're leaving me here alone? What if she's not the one?"

"If she's not, her boyfriend is," Grayson said, turning back. "If you're afraid to stay alone, call a friend."

"My sisters." She reached for the phone.

* * *

Nola spent a restless night in county jail. She had no lawyer and balked at mortgaging her home to hire one. If only she had held her temper. Pat Wilson wasn't worth losing her house, let alone risking a prison sentence. What was she going to do?

* * *

News of Nola's arrest struck the village with the speed of a ballistic missile. Between a barrage of incoming calls, Dana phoned the fire-bomb refugees.

"Stay put until we know for sure," she warned. "Sheriff Grayson's inexperienced, and I doubt that Nola's guilty."

"We'll hide here as planned," Carole said. "But for heaven sake, keep Lana supplied with sweets. She's driving me crazy looking for chocolate cookies."

Dana promised to raid an Oreo display and learn what evidence the sheriff had on Nola.

* * *

Kerrie awoke in the guest room after nine, unaware of the commotion. Dana marveled at her daughter's sound sleeping habits and worried about her hearing. When told of Nola's arrest, Kerrie asked, "Has she done this sort of thing before?"

"All we know is that she and her husband came from Bakersfield." Sarah blew dark waves in her blackberry tea. "They never said much about their lives, and I've often wondered how those two got together.

"Meaning?"

"Nola's quiet and sneaky. And Joe was so out-going."

"Opposites attract," Dana said.

"Yes, but when Joe died, Nola bought herself a brand new wardrobe. Not your average grieving widow."

The others nodded agreement.

"People react differently to grief." The question of Nola's guilt still sat uneasily on Dana's mind.

Kerrie suggested they research the Champlain's background.

"A trip to Bakersfield?"

"Not necessarily. A friend lives there. She might agree to research their past. I'll give her a call."

"Good idea, Kerrie."

Sarah hesitated before asking, "Did your friend work with you in Los Angeles?"

"Yes, but she married a TV anchor from Bakersfield."

"Did you quit your job because your friend left?"

"I'd rather not talk about it, Sarah." Kerrie turned to leave the room.

71

"Jack worked there," Dana said quietly. The job loss had been as painful as Kerrie's breakup with Jack.

Sarah broke the uneasy silence with: "Cabin fever. That's what I've got. Why don't we shop for something special for dinner?"

"We've plenty of food."

"Bean sprouts and cookies for our fugitives."

"I'm afraid they need more than that." Kerrie stood in the doorway and yawned. "The media will soon be reporting no bodies found in the fire."

"We have no choice," Dana said. "We'll have to tell the sheriff our friends are still alive."

Kerrie offered the others a second cup of tea. She wondered aloud whether it was safe to leave the village, even for a sack of groceries.

"Why?"

"The killer might try a triple murder. What easier way than to tamper with your car, Mom. Like cutting the brake lines, or something under the hood."

"A rental car would be safer. But first things first, hand me the phone."

* * *

Tamara huddled over her crystal ball, warming the sphere with her palms. The fog refused to lift. Frustrated, she returned to her cards. Bewildered by the hermit, the ninth card of the major arcana, she consulted her tarot reference book. Over the past three days the hermit had regularly appeared both in the upright and reversed positions. The hermit card denotes withdrawal, she read, as well as life's contemplation. Reversed it usually meant weakness and dishonor.

But who did the hermit represent? Running over a list of village residents, she settled on Harold Samuels. Of course. Harold fit the description almost perfectly. But where could he hide, kill, and retreat, without being seen?

She had consulted the crystal ball the moment she learned of Nola's arrest. Her spirit guides said Nola could not to be trusted. But a murderess? Why didn't they just whisper the killer's name in her ear? No, the guides expected her to ferret out the truth.

If only the crystal ball would clear.

* * *

While Tamara searched for answers, her husband John was looking for some of his own. Sifting through soggy ashes, he used the cane he bought for occasional gout attacks. What a mess. Lifting charred timbers, he poked around in what had been the master bedroom. There were no bones that he could find. The fire department must have collected them in body bags and dropped them off at the morgue.

Had it actually been forty years since he was sworn in as a Sacramento police officer? John shook his head, remembering. The liquor store shootout that left him near death had ended his law enforcement career, but he later did quite well in real estate. There were times when he regretted his decision to leave police work. Now was one of them.

He found he couldn't move through the debris without soiling his clothes. His golf duds were streaked with charcoal, his large hands sooty and as dark as his brooding eyes. He'd have to shower and change before teeing off at one.

John thought it strange that no mention of the bodies had been made during the morning news, although no one had seen the missing women since the fire. Maybe he'd have a little chat with the sheriff. Butter him up first. Tell him what a great job he'd done capturing Nola Champlain. John laughed at the thought of Nola behind bars. An idiot would know that she was too small to tackle someone Alice Zimmer's size. And strangling feisty Betty Wilson would take more strength than Nola had. He thought of his wife Tamara, who could be a wildcat when cornered. It would take more than a shattered lamp or drapery cord to kill his wife.

* * *

Carole slapped Lana's hand. "No looking out the drapes. You want to give us away?"

"I can't stand being closed in. It's like living in a bat cave."

"Better than buried in one."

"Nola's in jail. How'd you know it wasn't her that killed our friends?"

"Can a mouse kill an elephant?" Carole's tone was biting.

"Anything's possible." Lana retreated from the drapes, sulkily settling herself in Sarah's favorite chair.

"Let me put it another way. Could somebody my size wrestle a woman like you to the floor?"

"Maybe."

"How?"

A grin lifted the corners of Lana's generous mouth, smoothing her facial lines. "You could jump from some high place, like they do in the movies."

"Somebody Nola's age? She's not Clint Eastwood, you know."

"Clint Eastwood's older than Nola, and he's probably got a stand-in."

"Nola has a stand-in? Is that what you're saying—an accomplice?"

"Maybe so."

Carole walked a circle in the beige carpet, a hand ruffling her short, platinum hair. She was amazed that Lana had any reasoning power left after ingesting all that chocolate.

"Who's her accomplice?"

Lana's grin was wicked. "Who do you suppose, Miss Know-it-All?"

Carole stopped short. "Who?"

"Pat Wilson. That's who."

"Lana, I've misjudged you. All those chocolate chips have over-stimulated your brain."

74

Lana continued in earnest. "They killed Alice to bamboozle the law, then killed Betty so they could get hitched."

"But why kill Candice?"

"Maybe they hated their mothers."

Carole shook her head. "Let's get serious, shall we? Setting fire to your house was taking quite a risk. A neighbor might have woke up when the fire bomb broke the glass. Somebody could have seen the killer."

"If you hadn't insisted on turning out the lights to watch that horror movie, Nola wouldn't have dared burn my house."

"Oh, so now it's my fault—"

The sound of tires scraping the curb frightened them both to silence. Lana placed a finger to her lips as she waddled to the window. Carole tiptoed after her, tugging at her arm. She knew Lana would part the drapes to have a look

"It's the sheriff."

In her haste to retreat, she nearly flattened Carole. "Where can we hide?" she whispered hysterically.

"Anywhere but the kitchen. He's sure to look for you there." The telephone's sharp ring startled them both. Carole grabbed the receiver before it made another sound. She listened, covering the mouthpiece with her hand.

"Hello?" she heard. "This is Dana. The sheriff's on his way. We had to tell him—"

"You didn't." Carole said, breaking her silence. "How could you?"

"Sarah's right behind him," Dana said. "They'll explain when they get there."

Carole dropped the phone when she heard a key in the lock. Holding one hand for reassurance, she beckoned her partner into the hall. Some hiding place this is. She didn't know who to trust. Suspicious by nature, Carole had learned from past experience only to trust herself, but she had gotten soft living in the retirement village. Trusting Sew and Sos had been her undoing. One of them was obviously killing the others. It could even be Lana. No, she decided, Lana wasn't smart enough.

Motioning her partner into the nearest room, she pulled the door within an inch of closing. She could hear someone knocking lightly at the door.

"Security bolts are on," Lana whispered from somewhere behind her. "Sheriff'll know we're here."

"Sarah's with him," Carole said.

"Under arrest?"

"No, in cahoots."

"We can't lock her out of her own house."

"Sure we can. She had no right to betray us."

* * *

Sarah looked up anxiously into the sheriff's glowering eyes. "They're afraid to answer the door."

"Didn't Miz Logan call to tell them to expect us?"

"They must be terrified after last night's fire."

Grayson scowled. "If they don't open up, I'll have to break in."

"No, Sheriff," she wailed. "Let's call them from Dana's house." Sarah already regretted revealing their hiding place.

The sheriff grumbled as he turned to leave. Halfway to his patrol car, he stopped. "I almost forgot. You'll be staying with Miz Lugundos."

"Why?"

"Her partner's in jail."

Sarah sighed. Micki was a nice gal, but living in the same house would be an endurance test. Rising regularly at four in the morning would fell a giant redwood.

"Wait a minute." She rushed to intercept the patrol car before it left the curb. Impatient, he rolled down his window.

"Sheriff? If you're convinced Nola's the killer, why are you still pairing Sew and Sos?"

"New evidence," he said, as the window began its climb.

* * *

"Mortgage my house? Are you insane? Why should I pay a lawyer when I can defend myself?"

The deputy shrugged as he left her cell.

Nola sank onto the hard, lumpy mattress. Her eight by ten cell was closing in on her. She felt like a monkey on display. If only Joe were alive. She was still angry with him for dying. He never liked Pat Wilson, and would flop in his casket if he knew what she had done. Her small hands twisted as her legs bounced against the metal bunk.

Her own lawyer? Even Nola realized what folly that was. She didn't know much about the legal system, except what she had watched on TV. She doubted they had a law library in the podunk jail. Next time the deputy swaggered by, she'd ask. She'd also ask if he were married.

* * *

The telephone duel ended in a draw. Although Grayson insisted that he question them in person, Carole and Lana refused.

"We've told you everything," Carole contended. "There's nothing more we can say."

"You're breaking the law by not allowing me in."

"When you can guarantee our safety, we'll be happy to oblige. In the meantime, you're drawing attention to our whereabouts."

The sheriff slammed the receiver, fuming. "Damn stubborn women."

"You can't blame them, Sheriff. They don't trust anyone."

"And that's my fault, Miz Logan?"

"An innocent woman's in jail and a killer's roaming free. That doesn't instill much—"

"That's left to be seen." He rubbed the back of his sun-leathered neck. "Miz Champlain might not have done the actual killings, but her partner's about to be arrested."

"And who might that be?"

77

"That's police business, Miz Logan. You'll be knowing soon enough."

"While you're reeling in another innocent person, the village is collecting a defense fund for Nola."

A short bark came from Grayson's throat. "You're wasting your money." Turning abruptly on his heel, he left.

Kerrie emerged from the guest room with a sympathetic smile. "How can you stand that man? There's got to be some way of circumventing his authority. I've never heard of a murder investigation botched quite so badly."

"Sarah and Micki are coming for dinner and a brainstorming session. Maybe we'll come up with some answers."

"Why don't we meet after dinner at Sarah's house? Include Carole and Lana in the discussion. I'm sure they're bored with each other by now."

Dana appraised her daughter, sans makeup and uncombed hair. She was not only beautiful, she was brilliant. "I'm almost glad you decided to stick around to help in the investigation.

"Almost?"

Dana covered Kerrie's hand with her own. "Mothers always worry about their kids, at least until they reach retirement age."

"You needn't worry about me, Mom. I'm not going to jeopardize my life with heroics."

Dana sighed. "We'll watch each other's backs and, between us, we'll keep an eye on Sarah."

"Where shall we start?

"I was remembering one of Conan Doyle's short stories, where Sherlock Holmes spent hours searching a murder scene at Boscombe Pool. In the end he accurately described the killer, down to his left-handedness, limp, and cane."

Kerrie's dark eyes lighted from within. "The fire."

"Exactly. I thought we might find evidence that hasn't already been trampled."

"Or burned."

Chapter Eight

A cold breeze ruffled their hair, carrying with it the damp, acrid smells of a recently gutted house. Morning sun hid behind thick, gray clouds, rendering the retirement village gloomy. Concerned the curious would be out en masse, they were relieved to be mistaken. Houses along the street had their drapes drawn, as though neighbors were denying the fire had happened.

Dana shivered in the fall wind. Treading carefully along the side yard, she thanked God her friends had survived the fire.

Kerrie had taken the opposite side of the house, and they glimpsed one another through skeletal timbers. A frayed palm frond nearly tripped her up as Dana approached the rear yard. It was strange how many footprints were visible in Lana's muddy flower beds. Wilted chrysanthemums were ground in among the firemen's boot treads. Lana would be heart sick to learn what had happened to her mums. So many hours spent on painful, arthritic knees. Gardening had always been her passion.

Dana lowered herself into a weed-pulling position, pushing half-glasses further up her nose. There didn't seem to be any footprints she could measure for size, or type, for that matter. Maybe clues were more easily found around back where the fire had started. She found Kerrie already there, kneeling in the littered grass, examining something.

"Evidence?"

"I'm not sure," she whispered back. "But look at this." Kerrie flattened her hand, revealing a small ring.

"Hasn't been here long. The gold's not tarnished or dirty. Where did you find it?"

Kerrie pointed to a grassless area several feet from what was left of the exterior wall. "It might be Lana's, or one of her grandchildren's."

"Possibly, and a good question to start the meeting with tonight."

They assigned themselves yard areas and searched until noon. Disappointed they weren't able to find further evidence, they walked home for lunch.

"A tossed salad's fine," Kerrie said, attempting to match the ring with one of her fingers.

Dana stopped shredding lettuce to take a closer look. "Fit your pinkie?"

"Not really. It's a little large. Doesn't fit my ring finger, either."

Taking the ring from Kerrie, she reached for her glasses. "There's a number on the side. A class ring, maybe?"

"Could be, but I've never seen one quite that plain."

"Suppose he lost it when he tossed the bomb in the window?"

"He? Or she?"

Dana sighed. "Nola could be responsible for the murders, but she must have had help."

"Pat Wilson?"

"All signs point to him."

Changing after lunch into Dana's old clothes, they returned to sift through the ashes.

Dana scooped ashes with a small gardening spade while Kerrie dropped burned objects into a canvas sack.

"Someone's been here before us." Dana pointed to a footprint in the former master bedroom. "Not a fireman's," she said, bending to examine it. "You can tell by the lack of tread."

"Looks like a man's print." Kerrie placed her own shoe next to the outline. "Wider and longer than mine. A size thirteen, maybe? A big man."

"What else can we tell from the print?"

"He's probably as dirty as we are." Kerrie brushed the legs of her jeans with a grimy hand. "Don't wet ashes make lye? This stuff will probably eat through our clothes."

"Besides that."

"Beats me, Mom. You're the Sherlock expert."

"See how the imprint is missing along the outer edge of the heel?"

"Yes."

"Must be worn down because of the way he walks."

"Swell. We can play Prince Charming with a plaster cast instead of a glass slipper."

Dana grimaced. "I can't see myself walking up to someone, saying, 'I have a foot fetish. Mind if I check your heels?' I guess we could watch people walk by, from one of the park benches."

"And catch pneumonia long before we spot the killer?"

"You're right, dear." Dana pulled her jacket collar higher. "It does feel like rain. Too bad it wasn't pouring rain last night before the fire. And thank heavens it wasn't foggy.

"Wait a sec." Kerrie stooped to examine a blackened piece of tile. "What are these strange little circles?"

Dana squinted through her reading glasses. "Huh. I noticed one near the footprint. You don't suppose they were made by a cane?"

Something snapped behind them. Straightening, they noticed the coveralled custodian standing in what remained of the hallway.

"Looking for something, ladies?"

"Charcoal briquettes," Kerrie said, grinning.

"Did they send you over to clean this place?" Dana asked.

"Only the yard," Beverly Bryant said sullenly.

"Notice anyone here earlier? A man, maybe?" Dana removed her glasses and gestured with them.

"As a matter of fact." The custodian nodded in the affirmative.

"Who?" they asked in unison.

"I don't know his name, but he's married to the woman who claims she's a psychic." Beverly was apparently a skeptic.

"Tamara?"

Dana turned to her daughter. "John's feet probably would fit the print. And he sometimes uses a cane."

"Excuse me?" Beverly's attractive face seemed puzzled.

Dana said, "We were just thinking of restoring this place."

"But I thought the owner died."

"Oh, yes, she did."

"A burned-out building is such an eyesore," Kerrie said quickly to cover Dana's lapse. Glancing at Beverly's shoes, she asked what size she wore. "I wear an eleven. You can't imagine how hard it is to find cute shoes in my size. Maybe you know of a store—"

"If I could afford to live in a place like this, I'd shop on Rodeo Drive."

"Really? Well, that's quite a ways from here."

"Time to go, dear." Dana took Kerrie's arm and they cut a sooty path around the janitor.

* * *

Sarah tried to talk to Micki, but the dairyman's widow refused. A rare occurrence indeed. Micki hadn't slept well the previous night. That had to be the reason. Sarah suggested she take a nap before they left for Dana's."

"Don't feel like going."

"It's an important meeting tonight, Micki. I can't go without you."

"It doesn't matter. I'll stay here alone, like I did when Nola left."

"But the sheriff—"

At the mention of Sheriff Grayson, the Portuguese woman swore in her native tongue. Sarah was glad she didn't speak the language.

"Nola is a strange person, but she didn't do the murders," Micki said a moment later. "I know she didn't burn Lana's house."

"How do you know?"

"I checked my gas can this morning. It was nearly full."

"Maybe she had one of her own."

"No, she used mine."

"You're sure?"

"Sheriff was here when Nola sneaked in the garage. We both heard her set the gas can down."

"Some people think she had an accomplice."

"Then he knows how to burn houses. Nola doesn't."

"Did you tell the sheriff that?"

Micki's laugh was bitter. "That man doesn't know the difference between tadpoles and frogs."

"Huh?"

"You hear those bullfrogs croaking at night, down at the river?

Sarah nodded.

"The sheriff grabs the first tadpole that swims by. He doesn't wait to gig a frog. You understand?"

"I think so… Our friends should hear what you've got to say. Their lives might depend on it."

* * *

The small living room was crowded with surviving Sew and Sos. Dana opened the meeting by cautioning them to keep their voices down. She didn't want the killer to hear their plans. "We've two bits of evidence to discuss first off," she said. "Kerrie has a ring we want you to examine. She found it in Lana's yard."

At the mention of her former home, Lana wrung her hands. Shown first, she was unable to identify the ring, nor was anyone else. The consensus was a man's pinkie ring, owner unknown. When Micki described Nola's arrest, her friends agreed the sheriff made a mistake, but Nola's defense fund had only netted forty-seven dollars.

"She'll have to stay in the pokie till the real killer's caught." Sarah shook her head sadly. "At least she's safe in jail."

"Serves her right for messing around with somebody else's husband." All eyes focused on Micki.

"Pat Wilson?"

Kerrie glanced questioning at her mother. Her lips formed John Merino's name.

"Yes, it could have been him." Dana then told the others about the footprint.

Lana said, "I wondered why Tamara wasn't here. Has she seen the ring?"

"Not yet. I first wanted to talk it over with all of you."

"That John's a handsome flirt." Lana's eyebrows arched in disbelief. "But what could he possibly see in Nola?"

"It doesn't make sense."

"Unless Nola isn't involved." Kerrie seemed to be thinking aloud.

"And why would John kill us?" Sarah's hands lifted in a helpless gesture.

"That's what we plan to find out. Any suggestions?"

They quietly stared at one another.

"Pat Wilson," Carole insisted. "Nola's after him."

Someone groaned.

"But why trade Betty for Nola?"

More silence. More head shaking.

"Men don't have the sense God gave 'em."

"Let's not turn this into a male bashing session, Carole. We've got to sift clues quickly."

Sarah agreed. "The killer could finish us off tonight by bombing my house. If the sheriff knew his job, we wouldn't be here."

Lana shivered, glancing nervously at the closed drapes. "We shouldn't be meeting like this."

"We won't again," Dana assured her. "But this meeting could bring out facts we might not otherwise consider."

Carole laughed. "Six old ladies brainstorming. Isn't that a joke? I can't remember what I had for lunch."

The others nodded agreement.

Frustrated, Dana glanced at her daughter. "Kerrie's friend will be checking into Nola's past. The rest of you keep a pen and notepad handy to jot down possible clues, before you forget them."

With that the meeting ended.

"Didn't do much good," Kerrie said as soon as they were home.

"Maybe, but now the girls know how to help. Our next job is to pay Tamara a visit."

* * *

John Merino watched his wife assemble a Celtic divination. Peering over the edge of his newspaper, he watched her fling down cards.

"What's wrong, sweetheart?"

"They just won't answer my questions. And this darn hermit refuses to stay in the pack. I must be losing my gift."

Rustling the paper, John grunted in accord. Her last stock market prediction had cost him plenty. "You're tired," he said. "Why not turn in early. I'll be along soon."

Smiling wearily, she gathered the cards and stuffed them in a small pine box. "You're right, I'm exhausted."

Twenty minutes after she'd gone to bed, he quietly retrieved his coat from the hall closet. Tiptoeing down the hall to their bedroom, he was relieved to hear her softly snoring. He wouldn't be gone long. Half an hour should do it.

* * *

Pat Wilson couldn't concentrate on his favorite TV show. His mind kept returning to events of the previous night. Damned fire chief had grilled him like a tough steak. Sugar should have been there to take some of the heat.

He fondly remembered the old days, before women's lib, when the weaker sex obeyed. Variety had, and always would be, the spice a man required. Any attractive woman not nailed down—but mostly the ones that were—presented a welcome challenge. A conquest. If a man's headboard didn't boast a dozen notches, he wasn't really a man.

Pat had to admit that Nola was a mistake. Only once he'd dallied with her and look what had happened. Dumb broad thought he was in love with her. He should have told her right off he was only practicing. Why didn't she understand the rules?

Furious, he slammed a meaty fist into his chair. The worst part was being taken for a fool. Sugar had gone through his bank account like an IRS audit. And he'd bought the cheapest coffin for Betty so Sugar could have her cruise. Then the ungrateful bitch up and left him. Somewhere in the back of his fuzzy brain was a longing for Betty. Betty, who took care of him. Betty, who cleaned up after him...

He had to admit he was a fool of the highest order. How would he get through his wife's funeral tomorrow?

* * *

"Foolish, aren't we, Dana? We should have talked to Lana's neighbors as soon as the fire was out."

"I'm glad you called. I was thinking along the same lines."

"How about tomorrow after Betty's funeral? We'll talk to the people next door and the ones across the street," Sarah said. "Kerrie can do the interviewing. She's our expert."

"I'm glad you reminded me of the funeral. I can't get over the irony of Alice's cremation immediately after the autopsy. And just before the fire."

"The memorial service didn't do her justice." There was a catch in Sarah's voice.

"And then Candice's relatives shipping her body off to Wisconsin, to some pre-paid family plot. We didn't even have a chance to pay our respects."

"The sheriff wouldn't have known she was murdered if the killer hadn't left those camellia petals in her bath water."

"I know you think Harold committed the murders," Dana said, "but anyone could have picked those flowers. Or bought them."

"I'm tired of sitting around doing nothing. I've decided to do a stakeout."

"Of whom?"

"John Merino," Sarah said.

"But I thought—"

"That footprint in Lana's bedroom convinced me someone else could be the killer."

"Walking around in ashes isn't a crime, you know." Dana frowned.

"Why would he be poking around in that mess so early in the morning, unless he was looking for bodies?"

"You could be right."

"Somebody needs to keep an eye on him," Sarah said. "And we can't ask Tamara to do it."

"Is Micki willing to help?"

"If she agrees, we'll use her Chevy. The car sits in the garage most of the time and I doubt John would recognize it. It's perfect for undercover work. Pale green with no fancy trim."

"Don't take any chances. If he notices you, leave the area posthaste. Check in when you get back, no matter what time it is." Dana recognized the excitement in Sarah's voice, and couldn't stop her own heart from pounding.

Chapter Nine

When Micki agreed to the stakeout, Sarah suspected that her life had been dull. What could possibly happen on a dairy farm to quicken one's pulse? A burning haystack? A calving heifer? The subject would be rife for discussion while they waited in the car.

Dressed like her cohort in dark clothing, Micki unearthed two of her late husband's hats. Sarah discretely checked hers for manure stains. Finding none, she covered her short blond curls with the small black straw.

"Antonio's Sunday hat," Micki explained, satisfied that it fit. Pulling it from Sarah's head, she dusted it.

"A few specks of lint won't show in the dark, Micki."

Inspecting the hat in the overhead light, she said, "If he kills us in the car, the neighbors will say we were dirty."

"You're afraid of being murdered, yet you're willing to go along?"

"Nothing better to do."

"Don't worry, we'll be careful."

They packed a late night snack and filled a coffee thermos. Micki's brownies were known village-wide for their immorally good taste. Sarah knew she would gain five pounds on tonight's stakeout.

Micki meticulously dusted the Chevy before she allowed Sarah to back it from the garage. Checking her watch by the dome light, she carefully noted the time: 10:49 p.m. PST in a small black notebook. Switching off the garage light, Micki climbed in beside her, making a production of punching the garage door opener. Sarah then started the engine.

"Still purrs like a Siamese," Micki said with obvious pride.

Sarah disliked the analogy nearly as much as she feared cats. Her hair stood on end whenever a feline rubbed her leg. Recurring nightmares plagued her from a childhood incident with a newly adopted tabby. She remembered waking during the night with those glowing eyes inches from her own, the cat inhaling her breath, or so it seemed. Her screams awakened the rest of the family and half the neighborhood.

They crept half a block on Apricot Street, looking for the darkest place to park, although few houses still had their lights on. Three palm trees grew in graceful columns across from Tamara's house, but there wasn't enough undergrowth to hide them. Sarah drove past searching for an unlighted spot.

"There." Micki pointed to a monstrous oleander threatening to conquer a neighbor's yard.

The Chevy's lights switched off as it rolled into the driveway and backed in the opposite direction. Pulling slowly along the curb, Sarah proclaimed the location perfect. They could see both front and side entrances of the Merino house, a quarter block away, yet were shielded from view by the mammoth shrub. Sarah silently thanked the owners for neglecting to trim their poisonous plant.

Sliding low in the seat, they resigned themselves to a long, arduous wait. If John Merino left the house, Sarah was committed to follow. Or Tamara, for that matter. Even one of the neighbors would warrant a tail, if they left at this late hour.

"What's it like on a dairy farm?" Sarah asked when her lids began to droop.

"Very busy."

"Doing what?"

"Can you think of something better to talk about?"

"All right, you ask me."

"How is it married to a detective?"

"Private investigator," Sarah clarified.

"Whatever."

Sarah abruptly leaned across the steering wheel to track the progress of a large, shaggy cat. Sneaky destructive creature. Once, when she'd left her shiny new Buick in the driveway overnight, a cat had scratched the hood. Look at that one. Stalking something, probably a brand new car. A dangerous animal running loose without a license, free to wake people in the middle of the night with all that loud screeching.

"Sarah, look."

Headlights approached from the rear, perhaps a block away. Ducking from sight, they cautiously peered over the edge of the windshield when the sports car had driven past. Brake lights glowed as the car rolled smoothly into the Merino driveway.

"It's him," Micki whispered.

"He left Tamara alone."

"What'll we do now?"

Sarah didn't know.

"He's getting something out of the car. What is it?"

"If I had ex-ray vision, I could see through the sack."

"What if it's a rope to strangle his wife?"

Sarah turned the key and the Chevy purred to life. Before she could pull from the curb, a sharp crack on the driver's window nearly triggered a stroke. A sudden shaft of light blinded her.

"Roll the window down," a faceless voice demanded.

"No." Micki warned. "It might be the killer."

"I said roll your window, Miz Cafferty."

"Sheriff Grayson," Sarah muttered, obediently cranking the glass.

"You're not doing what I think you're doing?" Voice gruff, his breath was heavy with garlic.

"Guess we are," she said.

"Do you know how dangerous—?"

"Somebody's got to do it."

"I'll pretend I didn't hear that. As of 0800 hours Monday, there'll be special deputies to guard each and every one of you."

Sarah was dumbfounded.

"Now, tell me, Miz Cafferty, who're you watching?"

* * *

They passed the sheriff's car as it pulled into the driveway. Sarah had to admit that Grayson looked haggard. Maybe he wasn't a greenhorn after all.

"You think he'll arrest Tamara's husband?"

"I don't know, Micki. I'm too stuffed with your wonderful brownies to wonder about the sheriff's procedural techniques. What do you say we hit the haystack?"

"I would say we found the needle everybody is looking for. I hope the sheriff arrests that man before he kills again."

"Amen."

"Can we go home now?"

"Before we turn in, I've got to call Dana."

As they approached Micki's driveway, she punched the electronic opener. When the garage door opened, the Chevy's headlights illuminated an enormous black cat. Sitting patiently in the middle of the garage, it seemed to be waiting for them.

Sarah hit the brakes.

"What's wrong?"

"Your cat, Micki?"

"Never saw it before."

It had to be an omen. Sarah hesitated. Should she back the car from the driveway or shoo the cat away? They sat long moments eyeing the feline, who refused to move.

"You think somebody's trying to scare us?"

"I think they already did," Sarah said. Backing into the street, she headed for Dana's house.

* * *

Sheriff Grayson used his nightstick instead of ringing the bell.

When Merino opened the door, he was clearly agitated. "This official, Sheriff?"

"Let's call it unofficial for the moment." He assumed his relaxed military stance. "Where've you been the past hour?"

"Here, of course."

"I watched you pull in not five minutes ago."

Merino shook his head as if to clear it. "I just ran to the store for a minute."

"Left your wife alone?"

"She was sleeping and I didn't want to disturb her."

"You left her defenseless and not even aware you'd gone?"

"I locked everything up tight before I left," he said, staring at the floor. "I wasn't gone long."

"Have you looked in on Miz Merino?

"Uh— not yet. I was just putting things away."

"I think we'd better check on her, don't you?"

Merino threw his hands in a "why not" gesture and turned to lead him down the hall. Pausing at the bedroom door, he said, "She'll be mad if I let you see her in bed."

"Just open the door, Merino. But don't turn on the light."

Grayson switched on his long-handled flashlight and waited for the door to open. When Merino stepped back, the sheriff swung his light along the bed, stopping just short of the sleeping woman's face. Something about the position of her head bothered him, as well as the disheveled blankets.

Easing into the room, he crouched against the wall while he checked for other occupants.

"Get the light," he barked.

"What's wrong?"

The softly lit bedside lamp confirmed what Grayson feared. The Merino woman lay on her back; face blue, tongue protruding from her lips. A red welt was visible above her pajama collar.

"Call an ambulance. Do it now." Dropping his light, he gripped her wrist. Was it his imagination or was there a faint pulse? In the background he could hear her frantic husband calling 911. His hysteria seemed real, but maybe he feared arrest.

Pulling the pillow from beneath her head, he started CPR. Come on, Miz Merino, his mind pleaded. You've got to pull through. Between puffs he glanced at her husband, who seemed on the verge of collapse. Guilt or grief, he wasn't sure. Didn't he realize what he was doing when he left his wife alone? What could he need at the store that couldn't wait till morning?

Checking his watch, he figured he'd been working on the woman for nearly five minutes. Placing fingers on her throat, he held his breath. Still alive but barely. He resumed helping her breathe. In less than ten minutes an ambulance arrived, its siren cut short like a dying calf. She was still holding on but he didn't think she'd make it to County General. He'd heard about her psychic dabblings and hoped her so-called spirit guides would pull her through.

When paramedics lifted her onto the stretcher and rushed her from of the room, the sheriff turned to her husband. The lanky man seemed to have shrunk to fit his chair, his head held trembling at knee level.

"Now, what's so important that you had to rush to town?"

Merino lifted his head, his tanned face as white as the wall behind him. "I wanted to surprise Tamara with a brand new deck of tarot cards."

The sheriff swore beneath his breath. "You expect me to believe that?"

Merino wrung his hands. "The hermit kept turning up whenever she laid out the cards. I thought if I got her a new deck, one that wasn't tainted—"

"Tainted cards? Where'd you expect to find a new deck at this hour?"

"The supermarket stays open all night. I thought I'd find them in the card section."

"Let's see them."

"I couldn't find any, sheriff. They had pinochle and regular old playing cards."

"I ought to cuff you and salt you away forever," Grayson muttered.

"Beg your pardon?"

"I'll drive you to the hospital as soon as the crime lab gets here. Hopefully, you'll arrive in time to kiss your wife goodbye."

Merino's expression made him wish he'd swallowed his words. The guy could actually be that dumb. Grayson hadn't been sheriff long, but he'd known guys with a few beans missing. He figured Merino for early Alzheimer's.

As soon as he checked in at the hospital, he'd pay the supermarket a visit. He was sure the clerks would remember a nut who came in asking for tarot cards.

Sliding wearily into his patrol car, Grayson knew he was in trouble. Reporters were hounding his dispatchers for interviews, but he had nothing new to report. It wouldn't be long before state and county officials would be asking why he hadn't put a wrap on the case. If he didn't collar the perp soon, Sew and Sos would string him up in effigy, but that was the least of his worries.

Sarah rang the bell a third time. Dana had apparently gone to bed. It was nearly midnight, but she had to talk to Logan.

She tried the doorbell again.

"Maybe we should come back tomorrow," Micki said, yawning. It was hours past her bedtime.

"Not with that black cat waiting in your garage. It's got to be a warning."

"Like a rattlesnake shaking his tail, you mean?"

The porch light switched on and Dana invited them in. Before the door closed, Sarah began filling her in on all that had happened.

"Are you sure it was John?" Dana rubbed her eyes.

"As sure as I'm a natural blonde."

"The sheriff's talking to him now?"

"Yes, and Monday morning at eight we'll each have our own bodyguard."

Dana sat down in the nearest chair. "Why wasn't that done sooner?

"Kind of like building a garage after the car's stolen. But if it prevents another murder, it's worth having a shadow."

"I wonder if the guards will be staying in, or outside our homes."

"I'd rather have them inside, wouldn't you?" Sarah looked to Micki, who nodded, yawning.

A siren's wail from the highway prompted Dana to part the drapes.

"I hope no one's had a heart attack," she said.

"Or another fire?" Sarah's heart pounded unevenly, her breathing becoming shallow. No, it had nothing to do with John Merino. It was simply a coincidence. But as the siren grew louder, she realized that the sheriff's visit to the Merino house might have gone wrong. Grabbing her purse, she rushed to the door.

Chapter Ten

The morning sun blinded them when they left the funeral home. Dana and Kerrie flanked Sarah as they descended the steps and crossed a wilted lawn. Sarah's Buick was parked half a block away, and Dana insisted on driving.

"There weren't many mourners." Sarah dabbed at her eyes with a soggy tissue.

"It's not because Betty wasn't liked."

"Maybe her husband's presence kept them away," Kerrie said from the back seat.

Dana sighed. "Friends will probably visit the cemetery later with flowers."

They watched as the coffin was loaded into an aging, dark gray hearse. Pat Wilson and a male companion then climbed into a waiting limo. When both vehicles left the curb, the Buick joined a short line of mourners leaving the service.

"The man with Pat looks enough like him to be his twin," Kerrie said.

"Two Pat Wilsons?" Sarah said, shuddering.

Dana agreed they must be brothers.

"I can't believe how awful Betty's casket looks," Sarah said between sobs. "Pat could afford better."

"Well, at least he looks grief-stricken." Men's emotional displays always left Dana uncomfortable, but she was relieved that Pat was mourning.

"Crocodile tears. That's all they are."

Kerrie leaned to stroke her mother's shoulder. "Are we stopping by the hospital to see how Tamara's doing?"

"Yes, but she's probably still unconscious."

"John must have strangled her," Sarah said, "but why was he sitting beside the sheriff, instead of behind the wire screen?"

"When?" Kerrie asked.

"After the ambulance left with Tamara. I got there just as they were leaving."

Dana turned to glare at Sarah. "That was foolish of you to rush out of the house alone last night."

Sarah shrugged. "John wasn't here for Betty's funeral, so Sheriff Grayson must have locked him up."

"Tamara starts with a T," Kerrie said. "The killer's now working out of alphabetical sequence."

"Oh, dear." Sarah clutched the front of her blouse. "That means I could be next."

Dana worried during the short drive to the cemetery how Tamara's impending death would affect surviving club members. Carole was ready to bolt, and the others were so scared they would probably be hospitalized with nervous disorders. She was especially worried about Lana, who had been deeply depressed since the fire. Her doctor prescribed tranquilizers.

* * *

Pat absently chewed a cigar as the limo followed the hearse through Westside Cemetery. He refused to acknowledge the hearse, as he'd done earlier with the casket. He couldn't bring himself to view his wife's body, although a brief side glance convinced him that Betty would come back to haunt him.

A deep voice beside him asked, "How come none of Betty's people showed up for the funeral?"

"Didn't I tell ya, Bub? Betty was the last of the Cragan's. An only child."

"No cousins or other kin?"

Pat's eyelids squeezed together as he whined. "They live back East. Guess I forgot to notify 'em."

"They didn't hear about the murders on network TV?"

"Mennonites don't have television sets." Pat surveyed the ill-kept graves along the narrow lane.

"You married a Mennonite?"

"No. Betty's old man got himself shunned by the elders. So he ran away and came west where he married a Sacramento school teacher."

"I'll be."

"Yeah, well…"

"What'll you do now, Bro?"

Pat turned from the window to glance at his brother, a slightly younger version of himself. "Ain't a whole helluva lot I can do. Not till this murder thing's cleared up."

Bub Wilson sucked his thick lower lip. "They don't suspect you, do they?"

"Now why would I kill my sweet little wife?" Pat tried, but was unsuccessful at raising his own temper.

"Folks talk. You know they do."

"Who's saying what?"

Bub twisted his short, thick fingers, then turned to stare through the tinted glass.

Pat repeated his question but got no response. Savagely gripping his brother's arm, he gritted his teeth. "You tell me what they're saying, or I'll break you in two—like I did when we were kids."

The younger man stiffened, his gray eyes narrowing. "All right, I'll tell. I heard folks at the funeral home saying you killed Betty 'cause you got another woman."

Pat tightened his grip. "Who's they?"

"People—just people."

The limousine stopped and the driver stepped out to open Pat's door.

Releasing his grip on his brother, Pat hissed, "We'll discuss this later."

* * *

The graveside ceremony was brief and cold in the chilling November wind. They stood facing the backs of metal chairs where Pat and his brother were seated, heads down as though they were praying. A bank of floral wreaths swayed on wooden easels as the plain gray metal casket was lowered into the ground. Each mourner in turn dropped a rosebud on the coffin and said a brief goodbye. Everyone but Dana left the service crying.

The most bereaved was Micki, if grief were measured in decibels. Her visiting sisters from Fresno accompanied her to the funeral. Their wails were nearly as loud as Micki's, although they had never met Betty Wilson.

Dana's own tears had been spent on two departed husbands and the cancer deaths of both her parents. Her ducts had since been drained by Kerrie's adolescence. She was glad a protective wall had formed around her heart. Dana would mourn later. She sat motionless behind the wheel, watching Pat Wilson. Was that a smile as he shook the minister's hand? Men were such strange creatures. The older ones were conditioned to hide their emotions, but the young ones—what was the expression they used? Let it all hang out.

Was Pat actually grieving his wife's death, or was Sarah right about him playing to an audience? She didn't think he had actually killed Betty or the others, but he certainly was obnoxious. Why had Betty stayed with him all those years? They had no children to bind them together. Their relationship was just another piece in an increasingly complicated puzzle.

"Want me to drive?" Sarah asked, then loudly blew her nose.

"No, I'm fine. I was just considering the Wilson's marital relationship."

"Honestly, Dana. This is a strange place to be thinking about sex."

* * *

The county hospital was perched at the east end of Industrial Road, a colorless block building that seemed to lack warmth. Dana found a parking space across the street and hurriedly left the car. She knew Sarah was just as worried about Tamara's condition. Another death might be more than any of them could bear.

"Why'd they bring her here?"

"It's closest to the village. It may have saved her life."

"For how long, Dana?"

Dana shrugged. She had already steeled herself for another death. A full recovery was more than she could hope for. Numbness was preferable to disappointment and further pain.

Tamara's tiny room was on the second floor. As expected, an armed deputy sat outside her door. His chair was tipped against the wall, his attention riveted to a techno-thriller. Although his head was down, Dana surmised that he was young, long-legged, dark-haired, and handsome.

When he glanced up, Dana was surprised by his instant grin. He seemed too nice for an effective guard. The legs of his chair hit the floor and the deputy was on his feet. "Ladies?" he said, reaching to touch the brim of an absent uniform cap.

Kerrie stepped forward "We're here to see Tamara Merino." His eyes lighted in response.

"Family members?" he asked.

"No, close friends."

"Only family's allowed." His tone was apologetic.

"Was her husband here to see her today?" Dana asked, inching toward the partially opened door, hoping for a glimpse of Tamara.

"Not on my shift."

Their brows lifted in unison.

"Can we peek in at her from the doorway," Kerrie pleaded, moving closer to the deputy.

Redness spread from his collarbone to his hairline, and Dana couldn't help but smile at the young man's discomfort.

Exaggerating his movements as he peered down the hall, the deputy said, "I guess it wouldn't hurt, just for a second or two."

They wasted no time looking in, fearing he'd change his mind. The bed was parked against the far wall, its occupant pale-faced and limp beneath the hospital blanket. Tamara's dark hair was disheveled, her eyes deep in their sockets. The tube inserted in her nose and IVs connected to her wrists reminded Dana of an ancient black-and-white horror movie.

"Oh, my dear Lord," Sarah said softly.

Dana was surprised at her own sudden anger. How dare someone do this to their friend? "Don't allow anyone in this room," she told the deputy. "The killer might try to finish her off."

"Mother." Kerrie wailed.

"T-The sheriff already gave me those orders. I hope you won't tell him I let you break the rules?"

"Of course not. You'll have to forgive my mother. She's very upset about her friend."

"I think we'd better find Tamara's doctor and check on her prognosis." Dana started down the hall with Sarah in pursuit. When they reached the nurse's station, she noticed Kerrie was missing.

"She's still talking to the deputy," Sarah said, when Dana craned her neck. "He's a nice looking young man. About her age."

"You're an incurable matchmaker, Sarah."

"A harmless hobby."

"Harmless, my sciatica. You tried to match me with Harold Samuels."

"Too bad he disappeared." Sarah raised an inquisitive eyebrow. "You two were hitting it off."

"Oh, so you've changed your mind about Harold being the killer?"

"No, but just in case…"

A stout, hard-faced nurse returned to her station, glaring as though she resented their intrusion. Rustling through papers on her desk, she told them that Tamara's doctor was unavailable for consultation until later that afternoon. But since they weren't related to the patient, he probably wouldn't see them.

"Tell us Tamara's going to live," Sarah begged.

"Her condition is listed as grave."

Dana gripped her friend's arm and steered her away from the desk. "Our best bet is the deputy," she whispered, as she led Sarah down the hall.

* * *

"Brother or no brother, I won't hear any more talk about hiring a lawyer."

Bub hung his head. His scalp shone like a bowling ball with large knuckles inserted.

"If it was me, I'd get some legal advice."

"Are you saying I'm guilty?"

"No. I'm saying the sheriff might haul you in, if he can't find the killer."

"I'll worry about that when the time gets here."

Bub moved to the kitchen window to stare at golfers on the course. Absently tapping the sill with an index finger, he said, "Word's out about your lady friends. That's reason enough."

"Hell, everybody's got friends. Even you, Bub."

"Yeah, but I'm divorced."

Pat grumbled to himself. "I never thought I'd admit this to anybody…" He clamped down hard on his unlit cigar. "…but I haven't got one woman on the string."

Bub turned from the window, laughing. "Lost your touch, big brother?"

"The sheriff's on my tail. How would it look?"

"Left you flat, didn't she?"

"Get the hell out of here." Pat Wilson glared menacingly, but didn't make a move.

"I'm gone. And when I get back to Beaumont, I'll send a Key Lime pie with a bolt cutter in it."

"Don't do me any favors."

"By the looks of Betty's coffin, you can't afford a lawyer, anyhow. Maybe you oughta head for parts unknown. I hear they're hiring roughnecks in Siberia."

"I know how you Texans operate. If I didn't know better, I'd say you set the fire and "baked the old ladies."

Chapter Eleven

Kerrie and the deputy were quietly talking when they returned to Tamara's room.

"Jim invited me to dinner," Kerrie announced brightly when she noticed them.

"Jim?"

"Dalton, ma'am." The deputy grinned.

"One of the Dalton boys?" Sarah was clearly amused.

"As a matter of fact, I am related to the old outlaw gang."

"I hope you're half the marksman they were," Dana said, scrutinizing him.

"Practice every day, ma'am."

Dana sighed. "Too bad there isn't one of you on every shift."

"The sheriff put his best men on this detail." He flushed, lowering his head. "I hope you don't think I'm braggin' on myself."

"Not at all. May I call you Jim?"

When he nodded, she asked, "Has Mrs. Merino regained consciousness?"

"Not to my knowledge."

"Has anyone been here to visit?"

He shook his head no.

Sarah moved between them. "Is Tamara going to live?"

"I hope so, ma'am."

"Maybe you could take a peek at her chart."

"If I did, I wouldn't know what I was reading." Jim shifted his weight uneasily. Kerrie came to his rescue, insisting they leave the hospital to interview Lana's neighbors. Halfway down the hall, she turned back to wave.

Dana was struck by the deputy's lovesick expression, reminding her of an old family adage. "He's a gone gosling," she said beneath her breath.

The drive to the retirement village was completed in silence, each of them immersed in her own thoughts. As they climbed from the car, Kerrie said, "Well, what do you think?"

Sarah suppressed a giggle. "A freshly brewed cup of tea should chase the chills away."

"And muffins to fortify us for the interviews," Dana added solemnly.

"You know I'm referring to Jim."

"We'll wait until he brings you home from dinner to form an opinion," her mother said. "And don't forget the curfew."

"I'm not a teenager, Mother."

"We're living in a war zone, dear. You'd better get used to it."

* * *

Micki was pleased when her sisters arrived from Fresno. When Josie and Francesca phoned to confirm their arrival, she warned them the serial killer might be hiding in the village. Nothing short of blinding fog could deter sister Josie when she made up her mind. She had always been the dominant one of eight Costa sisters, and unofficially accepted as the son Papa never had.

Their mother had died in childbirth when the youngest daughter Phillipa was born. Papa never took an interest in another woman—not that his daughters would have accepted a surrogate mother. Micki, the eldest, had immediately assumed that role, and when she married Antonio at twenty, Francesca had taken her place.

Poor Papa. He died shortly after Phillipa was married.

A small tear hesitated on Micki's check. No man would ever be as saintly as Vasquez D. Costa. Not even her late husband Antonio.

Her sisters moved into the bedroom vacated by Sarah, and Nola Champlain before her. When Micki wondered aloud whether they should visit Nola in jail, Josie had vetoed that notion.

"What if Nola's guilty?" she asked. "What will the neighbors think?"

"Forget the neighbors, Francesca concluded. "What will the family say?"

"That's why we're here," Josie said, standing over her seated elder sister. "To protect you and our family name."

Micki laughed. "The only time our family name was dragged through the manure was when you stayed out all night."

Josie stamped her tiny foot, reminding Micki of the spoiled child she had spanked on more than one occasion. "We're here to protect you," Josie insisted.

"The deputies will soon be on guard."

"A lot can happen before then."

She knew Josie was aggressive, but Micki had married before her younger sister's tyrannical traits had surfaced. Her happiness at their arrival quickly turned to dread. How would she persuade them to leave before they made her crazy?

* * *

The interviews did not go well. Florence Baxter, whose house faced Lana's, was hostile to their questions. She reacted as though she were suspect. Even Kerrie was unable to sooth her feelings. The Millers, who lived to the west of Lana's burned-out home, were already building a redwood fence along their property line to hide the eyesore—despite home-owner covenants. By late afternoon the three women were aware of rampant paranoia. Their last stop was the Carter house, located on Concord Lane, directly behind Lana's former residence.

Harry Carter met them at the door, his usual friendliness fading when he learned why they were there. "We told the sheriff everything," he said, his brown eyes nearly hidden by thick, white scowling brows. Deciding on another tactic, Kerrie gave him her best smile.

"I'm writing a feature story about the courageous village residents." Before he could argue, she said, "People like you, who aren't afraid to stay while a killer roams these grounds."

"Well, I don't know about that." Carter returned her smile and hesitantly unlatched the door. "The sheriff said no one's allowed to leave."

When they entered the living room, his wife Molly appeared from the kitchen. As small as her husband was large, she, at least, seemed pleased to have company. The spicy aroma of Irish stew filtered into the room as she welcomed them.

Motioning them to be seated, she said, "Won't you stay for supper? I've made enough stew for an entire brigade."

Kerrie thanked her, mentioned her dinner date, then smoothly launched the interview.

"We told the sheriff about the man who set the fire," Molly said. "Maybe you should talk to him."

"I'm afraid that Sheriff Grayson's too busy solving murders to submit to an interview."

"But we saw him twice on TV."

"I'm a print journalist. The sheriff seems to prefer anchor women."

"Well— Harry actually saw what happened," Molly said, turning to her husband.

With a little coaxing, Carter said their poodle had been sick, and they had taken turns putting her out. His eyes glazed in recall. "I'm the night nurse because Molly shouldn't be opening the door, unprotected."

They nodded their approval.

"I was letting Fifi in when I heard a noise and saw this flash of light. Then a man jumped our fence. The yard light was on and I got a look at him."

"Are you sure it was a man?"

"Yeah, he moved like someone in combat. I was a marine during World War II, and believe me, there's no mistaking a man on maneuvers."

"Anything distinctive about him?"

"He was hunched over so I couldn't tell how tall he was. Looked like he was wearing a baseball cap."

"What about clothing?"

"Dark, probably black."

"Did you see his face?"

"Not really."

"What about his feet."

"Black sneakers like running shoes."

"Do you think he saw you?"

"I'm not sure. I had snapped off the kitchen light when I heard breaking glass."

Kerrie glanced at her mother, whose frown mirrored her own. The Carters should also have an armed guard. When she decided the couple had told her everything, she thanked them, and the women took their leave.

Checking her watch, Kerrie realized she had forty minutes to prepare for her date. At the thought of Jim Dalton, she experienced a warm glow. There had been an instant attraction between them, and a dozen adjectives came to mind. Foremost was nice. He was better looking than Jack, and seemed to have none of his undesirable traits. She wondered how Jim looked out of uniform.

* * *

Jim Dalton arrived promptly at six, dressed in a new denim suit. His crisp blue shirt was precisely the color of his eyes, and he was wearing a spicy cologne. Dana was impressed. She had heard of mothers choosing a son-in-law and if she had a say in the matter, Jim would certainly top her list. Sarah caught her eye and winked. Her smile said she also approved of Kerrie's date.

"Where are you kids going for dinner?" Dana asked.

Kerrie raised a brow at the word "kids."

Jim, smiled broadly and seemed oblivious to the exchange "I thought Kerrie might like a chuck wagon steak grilled at the Hitchin' Post."

Kerrie glanced down at her jade silk shift and laughed. "Why don't you fill the ladies in on your day while I make a quick change." She disappeared down the hall before he could protest.

"Sit down, Jim," Dana said. "I have some questions for you."

Jim eased himself into the nearest chair and smoothed his new denim jacket.

"Did Mrs. Merino have visitors after we left the hospital?"

Silent for a moment, he seemed undecided whether to tell her. Biting his lip, he finally said, "There was this woman who said she was her sister, but she wouldn't show her I.D. When I didn't let her in the room, she got real mad and walked."

"Who was she?"

"Don't know. I couldn't follow her 'cause I was on guard duty. But I used my radio to call for backup." His right hand moved to his belt where the appliance usually rode.

"Did they find her?"

"Afraid not. Nobody saw her leave."

Dana was about to ask for the woman's description when Jim volunteered. "She looked like she was wearing a wig 'cause I've never seen that color red. And her black straw hat had a rose on one side."

"Do you remember the color of her eyes?"

"Big sunglasses covered half her face."

"What about her age?"

Jim scratched his ear. "Danged if I know. Her dress didn't have much shape so I couldn't tell what her figure looked like."

Sarah laughed. "Is that how you tell a woman's age?"

"That and other things."

"Her hands, maybe?" Dana asked.

"She was wearing gloves."

"The chin and throat are dead giveaways," Sarah said.

"That may be, but she had a scarf wrapped around her neck. And I was too busy keeping her away from Miz Merino to notice much about her."

Kerrie returned in designer jeans and a colorful print blouse. Jim left his chair as though seated on a spring. His appreciation was apparent.

"Don't forget to wear a warm jacket," Dana said. And to Jim, "I'd feel much better if I knew you were carrying."

He smiled, patting his left shoulder. "I wouldn't leave without it. Not while I'm protecting someone as beautiful as your daughter."

Kerrie smiled shyly, and Dana could have sworn she blushed. She realized how little she knew about her grownup daughter. When the door closed behind them, Sarah said, "You're not worried, are you?"

"I'd trust Jim with my life, but we don't know what the killer's up to. He may have a gun of his own."

Sarah suggested they call the hospital to check on Tamara's condition. "That nasty nurse should be off duty by now."

"Good idea."

The switchboard operator took her time answering. Dana waited for what seemed an eternity for a second floor nurse to pick up the phone. An Hispanic voice asked her to wait. Minutes later the same voice apologized for keeping her on the line.

"I'm Tamara Merino's Aunt Celia," Dana said, carefully crossing her fingers. "How is she?"

Dana listened for a moment before asking, "Which room? Oh, two-twenty-one." She motioned for Sarah to write down the number.

She heard papers rustling. The voice then said, "I'm sorry, she's no longer here."

Was she moved to another room?"

"No. She's no longer in the hospital."

"That's impossible. She was unconscious."

"I just came on duty. You'll have to call tomorrow."

"Wait. What time did she leave?" Dana listened as more papers were shuffled.

"Says five o'clock."

"But how did she leave?"

"Call back in the morning," the voice said.

Before Dana could ask for her supervisor, the line was disconnected. Stunned, she dropped the receiver.

"What's wrong, Dana?

"Tamara has disappeared. She was taken from the hospital the same time Jim got off duty. Grab a coat. We're going to the Hitching Post."

They parked down the block and walked back to the restaurant. Their hands were buried in their coat pockets to protect them from a light, chilling fog. The Hitching Post was filled with Saturday night diners, the waiting list nearly an hour long.

Sarah insisted that Dana stand guard just inside the door while she investigated. Pushing her way to the desk, she spoke to an attractive young receptionist dressed in western attire. When she entered the dining room, Dana studied cattle brands on the wall, wondering whether Sarah had joined the couple for dinner when she finally reappeared.

Red-faced, Sarah whispered, "They're not here. I asked every waitress and busboy in the place if they'd seen them. Kerrie's so tall and pretty, I'm sure they would have noticed her."

"They didn't?"

"No. We'd better call the other steak houses. Maybe the kids got tired of waiting."

"I still trust Jim. Let's check the hospital first to see what's happened to Tamara." Biting her lip, Dana hoped the time factor was only a coincidence. She was rarely wrong about people, and Jim Dalton seemed like such a nice young man.

They entered County General by the emergency room entrance, ignoring the bespeckled young clerk at her desk. When they reached the second floor, they slipped past the nurse's station. A dark-haired woman with her back to them was bent over a stack of files. Peering down the hall, they saw no deputy on duty. When they reached room 221, it was empty.

"That nurse knows what happened to Tamara," Dana insisted.

"You're right. If we have to, we'll shake the information out of her."

Chapter Twelve

"I apologize for being so owly at the funeral today, Bub. Losing a wife does that to a man."

Pat's brother eyed him over the edge of his beer.

"I hope you'll reconsider leaving tomorrow. I could sure use some company."

"By the looks of this place, you could use a housekeeper."

"You volunteering?"

"No, but I'll help you find somebody."

"You mean you'll stay?"

"We'll see how it goes."

The two men sat before the TV set in Pat Wilson's living room. Fast food wrappers littered the coffee table, empty beer cans stacked in a pyramid against the wall. Dust on the TV screen made the football field appear as though it were socked in with fog.

"By the way, Bub. I've still got those old costumes you left at the folk's house before they died. Remember when you used to dress up like women for the hometown parades?"

"Why would I want that old stuff?"

"Might come in handy someday."

"Guess I could give them to the grandkids."

Pat appraised his brother, whose face was beginning to blur. It was like looking into a carnival mirror.

"You're lucky you never had any rug rats," Bub said. "Or child support to pay."

"Oh, I don't know. It woulda been nice in my old age for a son to chauffeur me around, or to watch a football game with."

They heard a tapping noise but decided it was wind blowing a limb against the outer wall. The doorbell rang a moment later. Pat rose, grumbling, to answer. When the porch light switched on an unwelcome apparition greeted him. He would have preferred his wife's ghost to Nola, but there she stood, small, pinch-faced, and shivering. Clutching his chest he gasped something unintelligible.

"I'm back, honey babe." Slipping past him, she said she had just been released from jail. "I came to spend the night. Heat's off at my place. It's colder than Antarctica."

Backing into the living room, she kept her eyes on Pat. The fire's warmth had to feel good, yet she resisted the urge to warm herself. Steeled for his reaction, she winced when a deep voice startled her.

"Who do we have here, Pat? One of your lost strings?"

She turned and saw a Pat Wilson clone. Shock registered on her face as she crumpled into the nearest chair.

"T-twins?" she stammered.

"Not quite," Bub said. "Thirteen months apart. We gave Ma fits."

"You can't stay here." Pat shouted.

"And why not?" his brother said. "A little female company is exactly what we need."

"Focusing his attention on Nola, Bub Wilson asked, "You do housework?"

"All the time."

"You're hired."

Pat stomped over to his brother. "This is still my house."

Bub slid an arm around his shoulder, rocking his brother affectionately. "We were just discussin' a housekeeper, right? And this cute little gal needs a place to stay."

Pat eyed Nola. "You think she's cute?"

"Sure do."

"She's yours."

Scowling menacingly at Nola, Pat said, "Before I agree to anything, I want to know why you tried to burn my house."

"Revenge," she said coolly. "I wanted to hurt you as much as you hurt me."

"By cremating me?"

"No, that person…"

"Sugar? Why, she's nothing but a bed warmer."

Nola jumped from the chair fighting mad. If Bub hadn't stepped between them, she would have seriously clawed Pat's face.

"You can be my sugar," Bub said, swinging her off her feet. When she struggled, he said, "I always wanted a little wildcat."

* * *

A nurse looked up from her files when they approached the second floor station. She informed them visiting hours were over.

"Where's Tamara Merino?" Dana struggled to keep her voice from rising.

"I'm sorry, Mrs. Merino died."

Sarah gasped. "When?"

"Sometime this afternoon."

"Where was the body taken?" Dana gripped the edge of the counter so hard that she chipped one of her nails.

"Probably Farlen's."

"Probably? Don't you know?" Dana thought she detected fear in the young nurse's eyes.

"That's where most County General patients are taken."

"Charity cases?"

The nurse nodded.

"But Tamara wasn't—"

"Sheriff Grayson made the arrangements."

So the sheriff had spirited Tamara away—to protect her? Or had she actually died? How could they learn the truth before Monday when government offices were open? Dana suggested they check other hospitals and the funeral homes. She looked to Sarah who had tears in her eyes.

"What about Kerrie?"

* * *

The band was playing "Cotton-Eyed Joe," the dancers stepping to a country line dance.

"I don't know when I've had more fun," Kerrie said, catching her breath.

"Are you sorry we didn't stay for dinner at the Hitchin' Post?"

"I love cheeseburgers and fries, especially in the company of a good-looking cowboy."

Jim ducked his head. His ears flushed as red as his western bolo tie. His lack of sophistication was his most endearing trait. Kerrie feared she was falling in love with him.

Checking his watch, he said, "It's almost midnight. I better get you home."

"I'm not Cinderella."

"But the curfew, Kerrie."

"I'm quite safe with an officer of the law. Arrest me, if you must. I'll go along willingly."

His Adam's apple bobbed nervously. "You mean you'd go to my apartment?"

"Maybe just a peek. You can tell a lot about a man—"

"But I promised your mother."

"She's been asleep for hours. You don't think she still waits up for me?" Four beers had made Kerrie bold. Someone had to take the lead. Jim was as slow as a snail in hibernation. He hadn't even tried to kiss her.

* * *

Damned bureaucratic red tape was going to ruin him, politically as well as emotionally. It had nearly taken an act of Congress to fund special deputies to guard the old ladies at the retirement village. Three had already been killed, the fourth on a downhill slide. If only the Merino woman would regain consciousness long enough to identify her assailant. With his luck, she never saw a thing.

John Merino was in protective custody, but he'd have to charge him soon or let him go. Releasing the Champlain woman was a stroke of genius, he thought, mentally patting himself on the back. She'd run straight to Wilson. The problem was proving Wilson killed the other women to cover his own wife's murder. The downside was the neighbor's description of the arsonist, who moved like a much younger man. Wilson could have hired a hit-man, but that was risky business that could lead to blackmail. He'd probably have another corpse on his hands before the night was over.

When the special deputies were in place, he'd have inside information filtering back around the clock. Someone would eventually let something slip. He was counting on leaks to crack the case. A framed photograph of his canines caught his eye. Retrieving the group shot from his cluttered desk, he touched each image fondly. What had possessed him to run for sheriff? Dogs were so predictable and far more trustworthy than humans.

Checking his calendar, he decided to call the hospital to check on Jane Smith. If she didn't come around soon, he'd have a bigger problem. That husband of hers was sure to make trouble. If only he could pin the murders on John Merino.

The clock on his office wall said a quarter past midnight. No use going home to an empty house. He'd sleep on the couch in the day room. Hopefully his uniform wouldn't wrinkle. Tomorrow was Sunday so he needn't worry about reporters. The hundred plus hours he'd put in that week were indelibly recorded on his face. He avoided all mirrors, not because of exhaustion, but the growing defeat in his eyes. If Sandra hadn't left him five months earlier, she certainly would now. And if he didn't solve the murders soon, there would be a recall election. Then what would his grown kids think of their old man?

Opening his desk drawer, he retrieved a special number that bypassed the switchboard. The phone at the other end rang five times. He was about to hang up when a woman answered.

"Sheriff Grayson here. Any change in Miz Smith's condition?"

"None, sir. We have instructions to call if and when there is."

The telephone's shrill ring startled him when it sounded the instant he replaced the receiver. Few had his private number and he was hesitant to answer.

"Sheriff?"

"Yes, ma'am." Her voice was familiar, but his brain was already on standby.

"This is Dana Logan. Not only is my daughter out past curfew with one of your deputies, Tamara Merino is missing from the hospital."

His large hand reflexively shot to his forehead. "Now calm down. Is Miz Cafferty with you?"

"Yes, of course she is."

"Let's start with your daughter. Which of my deputies has she eloped with?"

"This is no time for jokes."

"I was merely complimenting you on your beautiful daughter, ma'am. I'm sure all my single deputies would like a date with her. "

"Indeed."

"Who's the lucky fellow?"

"Jim Dalton."

"No need to worry, then. Dalton's one of my best, but when it comes to women, he's—"

"Shy?"

"You might say that." He heard her sigh of relief.

"But they've broken curfew."

Grayson groaned. Didn't he tell those young yahoos to strictly adhere to the rules? They hadn't been told not to date the village residents, considering their ages. But he'd forgotten about Kerrie Compton.

"Don't worry, Miz Logan. I'll send a man around to Dalton's hangouts. I'm sure we'll find your daughter soon."

"Good. Now about Tamara Merino—"

"Hospital tell you she died?"

"Yes, but where have they taken her?"

"Uh, state lab for an autopsy."

"Sacramento?"

"Yes."

"And her husband John? Where is he?"

"Protective custody."

"Does he know about Tamara?"

Why can't she leave well enough alone? "Miz Logan, due to the nature of this case, I'm not at liberty to answer more of your questions."

"When the news media learns of Tamara's death, they'll be hounding you for answers. I think that we, the potential victims in this case, deserve preferential treatment. You must know by now that Sew and So members are not responsible for the murders."

"No one's been ruled out, Miz Logan." He thought her heard her teeth grinding.

"If you don't tell us the truth about Tamara Merino, we're going to notify the *San Francisco Examiner, Sacramento* and *Fresno Bee, Modesto Review-Journal,* and every radio and television station."

"Now hold on. There's no need for that. Why don't I stop by your place tomorrow?"

"Tonight, Sheriff. We have to know tonight."

"Why's that?"

"Someone broke into my home."

"I'll be there in fifteen minutes." If I don't fall asleep at the wheel. He rummaged in his desk drawer for his box of caffeine tablets. With no one around to make him coffee, he'd been eating them like candy. No wonder his hands were shaking.

Chapter Thirteen

He arrived twenty minutes later, weaving along the walk as though he had been drinking. Miz Logan opened the door before he had a chance to knock.

"They're still missing, Sheriff, and it's going on one o'clock."

"We'll be hearing something soon," he said wearily. "Tell me about the break-in."

"Whoever it was left this." She showed him a short length of drapery cord wrapped in clear plastic.

"You didn't touch—?"

"No, I used a pair of tongs."

"Smart lady," he said. "Any sign of forced entry?"

"None that we can find."

"Door or window left unlocked."

"No. We routinely check them."

"I'm glad to hear that."

"But that odor was in here."

"What odor?"

"Same sweet smell as Alice's house the night she was murdered."

"Gone now?" he said, sniffing the air.

"Unfortunately. The killer probably left when he heard us coming." Dana Logan hugged herself, as though she were cold. He wondered how she would feel in his arms.

"What'd it smell like?"

"We're not sure, but it's very distinctive."

Too tired to remain standing, he asked permission to be seated. It was the first time he had allowed himself to relax around suspects, although these two had already been downgraded to witnesses.

Noticing his fatigue, both women insisted on pouring him a cup of coffee. He declined, claiming caffeine overload. While they were recounting their evening, the telephone rang. Handing him the receiver, they listened intently to his side of the conversation.

"Your daughter and my deputy have been found," he said, handing back the phone. Both women looked at him expectantly.

"Where, Sheriff?"

"Dalton's apartment." He lowered his gaze to the carpet.

"I trusted that young man," Dana said angrily.

"Don't be too harsh on Dalton, ma'am. I'll suspend him for a few days if—"

"I'll talk to my daughter first," she said, visibly struggling to regain control. "Now, about the break-in."

"I'll post a deputy outside till guards are on duty Monday … tomorrow," he said, glancing at his watch.

"You're aware that Carole Lambert and I are next on the killer's list."

"I'm well aware of that. I hope the perp still thinks Miz Lambert's dead. I ought to place both her and her partner in protective custody."

"You'll have a fight on your hands, if you try."

* * *

Lana's restlessness interrupted Carole's sleep, but she preferred a bedmate to sleeping alone in the guest room. If the killer broke in during the night, they would challenge him together. An arsenal of weapons lined both sides of the bed, Lana's pillow hiding a World War Two bayonet. No wonder she squirmed as though she were on maneuvers.

Carole's only defense was napping during the day while Lana watched her soap operas, listening to all that melodrama through headphones. They had discussed strategy in the event of a break-in, and had worked out a system of guard duty. It wasn't a bad arrangement. They were leading separate lives under the same roof. If only they had twin beds.

* * *

Never pursued by a man in her entire life, Nola found the situation unsettling. She insisted that she sleep on the couch, although Bub was leering at her. He was the stalker, not the stalkee. This was going to take some getting used to.

She had never liked housework, but here were two needy bachelors wading in their own litter. How could she turn them down? Smiling to herself, she swept assorted trash from the low-backed sofa, fitting a sheet as best she could to the contours of the cushions. Nola hadn't packed an overnight bag, expecting eviction, but she didn't mind sleeping in her clothes. Reaching for the fireplace poker, she wiped the metal clean with a fast food napkin. She then made a deliberate show of placing the poker at her side.

"No funny business," she warned, "or I'll quit the house-keeping job."

"Ain't she somethin'?" Bub said, slurring his words.

* * *

Sarah was exhausted but wired with worry that Dana would make a scene. As much as she admired her friend, she shrank from her rigidity. Dana was still living in the fifties when it came to sexual mores. No wonder her gentleman callers never lasted longer than a month.

When the sheriff left, Dana sat muttering to herself. Sarah tried to reason with her, but was told not to interfere. She sensed

125

that her two friends were going to need an arbitrator, *whether they w*anted one or not. Rising heavily from her chair, she made her way to the kitchen to brew a pot of tea. She anticipated a long night.

When the second cup had been drained, the front door opened and the two young people stepped inside. Dana was instantly on her feet.

"Sit down." she demanded.

Flinching, Jim Dalton did as he was told.

"There's no reason to be cranky, Mom."

"Really."

"Yes." Kerrie smiled as she snuggled close to Jim. Winding her arm through his, she quickly launched her rocket.

"We're engaged."

Jim Dalton's adam's apple jerked upward, nearly choking him.

"Is this true, Jim?"

Recovering quickly, he turned to smile at Kerrie. "Yes, ma'am."

"But you've known each another only a few hours. How can you be in love?"

"We just are, Miz Logan."

Dana was a developing tornado. Sarah sensed it was time to intercede.

"Take things a bit slower, kids. Get to know each other better."

"Good idea, Sarah. We'll talk about it later." Kerrie rose and tugged Jim to his feet. Pecking him on the lips, she led the way to the door.

"Call me during your lunch break," she said, giggling.

Dana stopped him before he could leave. "What do you know about Tamara Merino?"

Jim ducked his head. "Sheriff'll have my job."

Dana lowered her voice to a whisper. "Don't say a word. Just nod your head if she's still alive."

He quickly nodded.

"Good. Did he take her to another hospital?"

He nodded again. "But I can't tell you where."

"Don't worry, the sheriff will never know."

When Jim left, Kerrie started for her room.

"This engagement thing is far from settled," Dana warned.

"Tomorrow," Kerrie drawled, lifting a limp wrist to her forehead. "I'm so tired my knees have turned to jelly."

"Later this morning, Miss Scarlet O'Hara, we'll plant those knees in concrete. And it won't be in Hollywood."

***

"Don't be so hard on the kids," Sarah said over breakfast rolls. Kerrie was sleeping in.

"They're not children. How could they be so irresponsible?"

"Remember young love?"

"I never went to a man's apartment. And certainly not on a first date."

"Times have changed."

"I'm not an interfering parent, Sarah."

"Good. The less said the better. Personally, I think they're putting us on. Nobody gets engaged that quick."

"You're probably right. We won't say another word, except to enforce the curfew."

"The sheriff will take care of that."

* * *

Late Sunday morning, red-eyed and stubbled, the sheriff squared off with his deputy. Jim Dalton wore a worried frown, although the hint of a grin kept creeping onto his lips. The sheriff fumed and fused, making circles with his arms. Jim kept his lip buttoned while Grayson spoke his piece, the sheriff resting his massive arms on the desk.

Leaning forward Grayson said harshly, "Do I make myself clear?"

"Yessir, Sheriff, I won't break the curfew again for any reason."

127

"And you'll stay away from Miz Compton till the case's wrapped up?"

"No sir, I can't do that."

"Why not?"

"'Cause we're engaged."

"I ought to put you on garbage detail—"

"It's the truth, Sheriff. We told her mother last night."

"Lust at first sight?"

"No, it's love. I'll be shopping for a ring on my lunch hour."

Complications, always complications. Grayson had planned to place Dalton with the Logan woman as guard. Now that was impossible. He'd have to rearrange his schedule. Dismissing Dalton, he booted up his computer. Selecting a newly compiled "Special Deputies List" from the main menu, he scrolled through the names.

It was a blasted chess game, matching personalities with potential victims. The Logan woman was right when she called them that. What was her name? Dana, that's it. A very attractive woman. Young for a retirement village. And she was smart. He admired a woman's intelligence. He'd had his fill of bimbos since taking on this job.

Forcing his concentration on the screen, he decided to switch Art Menlo with Dalton, placing his best deputy with Miz Lugundos. He'd then round up Nola Champlain and take her back to her partner. The Lugundos woman would pitch a fit when her sisters had to leave. He needed a decent night's sleep before he tackled that job. He wrote "Evict visitors" on his Monday calendar for eight o'clock and "Drag Champlain back to Lugundos house at eight-thirty." He'd stop by the Logan place at nine to check on Dana. He might even accept a cup of coffee.

* * *

Kerrie slept until noon and was awakened by Jim's call. Her head ached and mouth felt as though it were filled with cotton.

When she answered the phone in her mother's room, she sank into the king-size bed, propping herself with pillows.

"It's me, sweet thing. The sheriff said I couldn't see you for awhile, but I told him we're engaged."

"You what?" Despite her pounding head, Kerrie scrambled to her feet. "That was to placate my mother."

There was silence on the other end.

"Jim? I'm sorry. I thought you knew."

"But you said you love me."

"Don't be silly. People don't fall in love that fast." Or do they? She felt her throat constrict.

"I guess I made a fool of myself."

"Please don't feel that way. I'm sorry I used you. I'm really very fond—" She heard a click and the dial tone. Moaning, she replaced the receiver and slouched back to her own room. What had she done?

A timid knock sounded an hour later as she was dozing. She didn't want to talk to anyone, especially her mother. But when the door opened quietly, she prepared herself for the inevitable.

"I'm not feeling all that great," she said, when Dana asked.

"We need to talk."

Sighing heavily, she said, "I'm sorry. I made a mess of things."

"You didn't sleep with—?"

"No, Mom. Jim's the perfect gentleman. Too perfect. If I hadn't been drinking, I would never have pushed him so far."

Dana blanched, recalling her own recent overindulgence. "I'm afraid we both have little tolerance for alcohol."

"You're right. Now what am I going to do about Jim?"

"Tell him the truth and ask for his forgiveness."

"I already did, but he'll never forgive me."

* * *

Nola awoke with a start. A nubby face was grinning down at her as she reflexively gripped the poker.

"Aw, now, little darlin', don't go gettin' hostile."

Events of the previous evening came flooding back. The homely face could have been Pat's, except for the Texas drawl. She made a mental note to ask why one had a southern accent, the other a nasal twang.

Pushing herself from the couch, she carried the poker to the kitchen. The mess she found was more than she could bear. Food-caked dishes filled every inch of the sink and counter, as well the breakfast nook.

"How about breakfast at McDonald's," his voice drawled behind her.

"Great idea, Bub. By the way, what's your real name and are you married?"

"Elsibub. And no, I'm divorced."

Nola laughed. "Elsibub? Why'd they name you that?"

"My great-granddaddy was a captain in the Civil War. Elsibub Wilson. Ain't that a hoot?"

Nola smiled as she set the poker aside. She decided this southerner was harmless. The longer he talked, the more she liked him. Shaking her head, she wondered aloud why Bub's brother was so different.

"Good question, little darlin'. Ol' Patrick left home right after high school. Headed west and never did come back. I still don't know why he stays in California. Too crowded and polluted for me. Then there's earthquakes, fires, fog, and floods. . ."

"If that's how you feel, why're you still here?"

Chuckling, Bub rubbed his prickly jaw. "Thought I'd better stick around till Pat recuperates. But he's gettin' on my nerves."

"Pat gets on everyone's nerves."

Bub reached to gently draw her close. "How about you 'n me puttin' on the feed bag?"

"Let's leave now before the grump wakes up."

* * *

It was a quarter past eleven when his feet touched the floor. Checking his bedside clock, Pat rubbed his growling stomach. He liked the idea of a housekeeper, but why couldn't he smell breakfast cooking? Lazy wench was probably still asleep, unless Bub was distracting her.

Rushing into his clothes, he started for the living room. It was time to get rid of his brother.

Chapter Fourteen

The sheriff hesitated at the door, chilled to his kidneys in the early morning fog. Confronting a household of screaming woman was not the way he wanted to start his week. He should have called ahead to warn them of the eviction. Miz Lugundos would pitch a fit when he demanded that her sisters leave. With arms the envy of any weight lifter, she could toss him out as well. He figured she'd helped her husband buck hundred-pound bales of hay.

Shivering, he rang the bell.

Still clad in their nightclothes, three stout women surrounded him, chattering in Portuguese-peppered English. He knew Latin women loved to flirt, but this was ludicrous. Breakfast scents filtered in from the kitchen like nerve gas, momentarily incapacitating him. Clearing his throat, Grayson managed to signal immediate silence.

"The village is too dangerous for visitors," he said, the words getting caught his throat. "So I must insist that you pack your bags and leave."

Josie, the smallest, challenged him, her determined chin inches from his chest. Dark eyes sparking, she nicked his instep with her spiked-heeled slipper. "What about Dana Logan's daughter? You're making her leave too?"

He'd forgotten about Kerrie. This feisty little Portuguese woman might file a discrimination suit. He said, "Miz Compton is a newspaper correspondent writing about the murders."

"And I'm a true crime writer." She backed away, planting two small fists firmly on her hips.

"No, you're not," Micki said, grinning.

Josie's face resembled a cranky cherub's. "Uncle Luis from the Azore Islands will put a curse on you."

Her sister Francesca agreed.

"Ay, Sazush." Micki shook a finger at her younger sisters, more amused than angry. She surprised him by winking.

He watched them retreat to the guest room, knowing full well he couldn't force them to leave. His only hope was that they had some respect for the law. Exiting with as much dignity as he could muster, he shook his head, still incredulous at Miz Lugundos's behavior. He'd thought she despised him, but he was admittedly no judge of women.

* * *

Nola spent another night on the Wilson couch, abandoning the poker. She had rebuffed Bub's offer to share his bed, but intended to keep the carrot dangling. She wouldn't have him thinking she was loose.

"How about breakfast at Burger King this mornin'?" he said as she yawned and stretched herself awake.

"You're spoiling me, Bub."

"We'll shovel out the house when we get back. Then old Pat won't throw another hissie." He leaned to plant a wet kiss squarely on her lips. Freshly shaven, he smelled of Brute and Scope. Nola nearly floated in ecstasy from the couch.

The doorbell rang as she was combing her hair. A moment later Bub's deep voice told her through the bathroom door that the sheriff had arrived. "He knows you're here, darlin'."

Breath caught in her throat. "He's taking me back to jail?"

Bub laughed. "The sheriff says you'll be stayin' with somebody named Lugundos."

Nola could not believe her luck. Now Bub could court her properly, without his brother grumbling in the background. And she wouldn't have to clean his filthy house. The sheriff stood glowering near the door. Biting back a sarcastic remark, she went along willingly, which visibly surprised Walter Grayson. Promising Bub she'd meet him for brunch, she climbed into the patrol car. The sheriff watched her curiously, which caused Nola to grin. He expects me to beg to stay with Pat, she thought, as the cruiser pulled from the curb.

"Sheriff?"

"Yeah?"

"This is the best day of my life."

"How's that?"

"I finally found him."

"That right?"

"Mrs. Elsibub Wilson," she said dreamily. "Has a nice ring to it, doesn't it?"

* * *

Aunt Mattie was right. She'd warned him about city women. Deputy Dalton rolled over to check his luminous clock. Four-fifteen, less than three hours until the alarm went off. How would he manage his new assignment without any sleep? He couldn't call in sick. It was his first day to guard the Lugundos woman. Good thing the sheriff had taken him off the Logan detail. He'd rather shovel manure than face Kerrie again, although her image kept crowding out the horses he was counting. No matter how he tried, he couldn't imagine horns sprouting from her hair. She was a devil all the same.

He arrived promptly at eight, after little more than an hour's sleep. He crossed himself, amazed he'd found his way through the fog. Miz Lugundos greeted him warmly. He further thanked his luck she was nice. He didn't think

135

he could handle a belligerent woman. Agreeing to coffee, he gratefully settled into a red recliner chair positioned near the door. In less than a minute he was asleep, dreaming of jumping the pasture fence on old Whizzer. Before horse and rider reached the road, the deputy was rudely shaken awake. His own pistol was inches from his nose, a vaguely familiar voice scolding him. It couldn't be Aunt Mattie 'cause she was back at the ranch.

When his vision cleared, he realized the woman he was guarding held his gun.

"Some bodyguard you are."

"Didn't get much sleep..."

"Out partying, I'll bet."

"No ma'am. Woman problems."

Her expression softened as she returned his gun. "Sheriff's coming up the walk with Nola Champlain. You better wake up quick."

Jim stumbled from the chair and headed where she pointed. Finding the bathroom sink, he splashed his face with water while she ushered in her guests. He'd not only lose his job, if the sheriff caught him napping, his hide would be tacked to the squad room wall.

"How're you two getting on?" the sheriff asked when Jim appeared.

"Just fine," the lady chirped. "He reminds me of my son."

Jim struggled to maintain a professional stance. "Miz Lugundos makes fine coffee," was all he could think to say.

Nola Champlain stood nearby, giving Jim the once over. "I'll take some coffee," she said. "And a croissant, if you've got one."

"You'll have to settle for linguisa and eggs," Micki said, frowning. "And from now on I'm locking you in at night."

"No problem," the Champlain woman said. "I'll do whatever you say."

Eyebrows raised as the new arrival hauled her suitcases into the guest room. Miz Lugundos's prodigal partner had returned.

* * *

When he climbed the steps to the porch, the Logan house was quiet. No music or television sounds, or early morning voices. He wondered whether the dense fog had caused them all to oversleep. The sheriff also wondered if he should ask Dana Logan out to dinner. No, that would have to wait until after he collared the killer. It wouldn't stop him from dropping in, now and then, to check on the ladies. As he knocked, an old maxim came to mind. Dana wasn't getting preferential treatment because she complained the loudest, but he had to admit it factored into the equation.

Dana was yawning when she opened the door. Signaling the sheriff to follow her, she made her way to the kitchen. He seated himself at the table while she poured them each a cup of coffee. Hot with a hint of spice, it was the best he'd ever tasted. Sitting across from her, Walt Grayson momentarily forgot his mission. He could see where her daughter got her looks. Even more important, Dana could carry on an intelligent conversation. He was amazed at her knowledge of police procedures.

"No time for books since I took this job," he said, when she asked about his reading habits. "I used to read Wambaugh and McBain, as well as several others. Now I'm living and breathing all that stuff."

"Crime novels make police work seem glamorous, Walter. Did your reading influence your decision to run for sheriff?"

No one had called him Walter since the seventh grade, but Dana could call him anything she pleased. He lowered his gaze, unsure he should admit she was right.

"It might have indirectly influenced me—"

"I'll wager you wish you were still training police dogs."

"Not true," he said. "I'm on the verge of wrapping up this case."

"That's wonderful, Walter."

Her lack of enthusiasm irked him. He felt she could read him like one of her mystery novels. Abruptly rising, he left, claiming official business. He had relaxed his guard and overstepped his own rules of protocol. He needed a friend and Dana was the best that he could find, but she had to be kept at arm's length until he collared the killer.

His next stop was to check on the survivors.

* * *

Deputy Dan Avila was amazed at their inventiveness. Not since watching the movie, "Home Alone," with his young son Pete, had he seen so many jerry-rigged traps. Carole Lambert and Lana Nelson had missed their callings. They should have worked for the CIA.

"Do you mind if I write down some of your weaponry?" he asked, taking out his notebook. Miz Lambert thought that one over before she agreed. Maybe a patent or copyright was in order. A book on self-defensive living wasn't a bad idea.

"Draw a copyright symbol next to your notes," she said. "I'm planning a 'how-to' book for senior citizens."

The deputy snapped his notebook closed. "Then I won't infringe on your rights."

When the doorbell rang, Avila bolted from his chair to peer through the curtains. Frowning, he opened the door.

The Lambert woman laughed at the procedure. "As if the killer would ring the bell," he heard her say. Her mood changed to contempt when the sheriff entered the room. "Solved any murders yet, Grayson?"

"We're working on it," he said, ignoring her sarcasm.

The deputy nervously cleared his throat. "Everything's fine here, Sheriff. The ladies have set themselves up a fine defense system. I feel sorry for the fool who tries to crash this place."

Grayson shook his head thoughtfully. "Seems we're not needed here. Maybe I ought to pull you off the case."

Lana Nelson immediately objected. "Carole's tired and cantankerous. Don't listen to her, Sheriff."

"No offense taken. I know you ladies are under considerable stress."

"How nice of you to notice." Lambert was relentless. "Call 911 and ask for assistance. That's the only way you'll crack this case."

Grayson surprised his deputy by reining in his temper. "The perp's about to be collared, ma'am. Don't trouble yourself worrying how." Heat rose in the sheriff's face. Turning to his deputy, he said, "Don't allow yourself to be distracted. Make your rounds and stay alert. I'll check with you later."

"Don't bother, Sheriff. We're taking care of ourselves."

The Lambert woman's scorn was oppressive. For an instant the sheriff hesitated. Avila knew he was deciding whether to place them both in protective custody. Carole Lambert's shrill voice probably changed his mind. She'd drive the jailer bonkers.

* * *

The dispatcher called him just after he slid into his patrol car. "Highway pileup, Sheriff, and we're short on deputies."

"Notify the highway patrol," he barked, and immediately regretted his tone. He was mad at Lambert, not Liz, his blonde dispatcher.

"CHP's tied up, sir. Fog's causing wrecks all over the valley."

He had never worked a fender-bender, let alone a multi-car crash. When he didn't respond, the dispatcher said, "Randall's working this one on his own, sir."

"The rookie?"

"Yes, sir. Six vehicles involved. Three miles north of town. Southbound lanes. Two killed, seven injured.

"Emergency facilities called in?"

"Fire trucks, wreckers, and ambulances already there, Sheriff."

"Ten-four. I'm on my way."

Scattered patches of fog still remained when Grayson reached the scene. It would only get worse as the season progressed. If not for the flares, he would have rear-ended a dark sports utility vehicle parked in the right lane.

Two wreckers were working the accident, one hooked-up and ready to roll. Randall came running over as soon as he spotted Grayson. His boyish face was streaked with grease, his hatless hair disheveled.

"Terrible accident, sir. Two people killed and—"

"I know," Grayson said, leaving his patrol car. "Have you interviewed the witnesses?"

"Just those who already left in the ambulances. Not the ones still standing around."

The sheriff hesitated. "I'll take care of it. Get back to whatever you were doing."

Before he approached the witnesses, he'd have a look at the vehicles involved. As he watched, the fire truck finished hosing down a pickup truck struck by a tractor-trailer. Firemen pried open both doors. Sprawled out behind the moving van, like a small derailed train, were three compact cars and the SUV. Sprung hoods and trunks stood at attention, as though soldiers saluting an officer.

The cars in the middle were totaled and would probably wind up as scrap. He marveled that there had not been more fatalities. Fortunately, the car following the eighteen-wheeler stopped just short of hitting the ICC bumper. The second compact must have plowed into the first, resulting in the domino effect.

The medical examiner was standing by, fitting himself with a mask and latex gloves. Grayson wasn't aware until then that passengers were still in the pickup, burned beyond recognition. Breakfast stirred in his stomach, threatening to return for lunch. The stench of hot oil and burned flesh was intolerable, and he backed to where a slight breeze allowed him to breath. Fog floated between him and the coroner as the older man pulled a passenger from the wreckage. Grayson cringed when he noticed how small the corpse was. Probably a child.

When the driver had been laid out in near fetal position, the ME searched through what was left of the clothing. He held up a charred object in his gloved hands.

When asked what it was, the ME said, "Wallet, Sheriff. They're so compressed in a pocket that they rarely burn clear through." Gingerly opening the black lump, he retrieved a warped driver's license.

"Looks like it's from Texas. Name was … Elsibub Wilson. You don't hear that moniker anymore, except in history books. They must have been on vacation. Four suitcases were burned in the truck bed."

"What about the other victim?" Grayson was feeling queasy.

"Looks to be a woman, but we haven't found a purse."

The sheriff managed two steps backward before he heaved.

* * *

The eighteen wheeler was in the right lane, lightly damaged where its bumper struck the pickup. Traffic was crawling by on the left, shepherded by Randall's line of flares.

Where the hell was the highway patrol? Stuck in a fog bank, or still clearing accidents along Highway 99? First fog days of the year were notorious for their havoc.

The big rig driver was leaning against his tractor, leisurely smoking a cigarette. His pregnant shape was appropriately draped in biker's black and low slung charcoal jeans. He was stout but short, seemingly too small to drive a rig of that size. Grayson wondered if he needed extensions on the pedals.

"I happened to be looking in my mirror when this pickup came alongside," the driver said. "He swerved right in front of me. If the fog hadn't made the road slick, the jake brake woulda been on to help shut me down. As it was, I hit 'em almost broadside before the pickup exploded."

"Exploded?"

"Yeah, an older model truck. Musta had one of them outside fuel tanks."

"How could you see what happened in the fog?"

"It was patchy, like now. We just came out of this pea soup cloud when it happened. Tooley fog causes pileups every year. But I've never seen anything like this." His cigarette gestured toward the pickup.

Grayson blanched as he glanced down at his trousers and once-shiny boots. He hoped he wouldn't embarrass himself again.

"How fast were you going?"

"Below the speed limit, Sheriff. Most of them four-wheelers passed me like it was a sunny day. They don't pay attention to them lit-up, slow-down signs. Always in a hurry. They seem to think truckers can stop on a dime. It's a wonder more of 'em don't get killed."

Grayson managed to take the driver's statement, leaving mid-tirade about dishonest trucking brokers, substandard trailers, and outrageous fuel prices. He then looked around for other witnesses.

Attendants were lifting a young woman with a bandaged head into a waiting ambulance. She had driven the dark blue SUV, the last vehicle involved in the crash. She hadn't seen a thing. The second ambulance driver said a young couple with three children had already been taken to the hospital. One of the kids was in critical condition although her sisters were nearly unscathed.

"Hard to figure, Sheriff. They were all wearing seat belts, or buckled in an infant seat."

"Yeah, it's a real crap shoot when you get this kind of wreck. You never know who's going to get hurt. Or killed."

"Too bad about that pickup. They never had a chance."

Until now Grayson had suspected that Nola Champlain was involved in the murders. Maybe she had known too much. If the woman's body was hers, she and Wilson were running away, as evidenced by the smoldering suitcases. If that were the case, Pat Wilson was his prime suspect. He would keep a close, twenty-four hour tail on him. And it wouldn't be a bad idea to watch his first reaction to the accident. He'd have a final word with Deputy Randall, then pay his suspect a visit.

Randall appeared as though he'd slept in a furnace, his face streaked and sweating, his uniform ruined.

"You run that license plate to double check the driver?"

"Yes, sir. Belonged to Elsibub Wilson."

If Wilson was driving, the woman must be Nola Champlain—unless Elsibub shared his brother's appetite for women. He pulled in front of Wilson's house a quarter of an hour later. The fog had nearly burned off, and he switched his Polaroids for Ray Bans. The accident had not only been his first, he'd never had to notify relatives. He hoped he wouldn't botch the job.

When Pat Wilson answered the door, his eyes were crimson, his shave overdue. Grayson remembered with discomfort that the suspect had recently lost his wife. It was too late to call in an experienced deputy. He'd have to handle this one on his own.

"I'm afraid I have bad news," he said as he stepped across the threshold.

"That right?"

"Your brother and his friend were killed on the highway in the fog."

"Huh."

The sheriff closely scrutinized him. "You been drinking, Wilson?"

"No law against a man having a beer in his own home."

"True, but—"

"You told me, now get out."

"Don't you want to know how it happened?"

"I'll read about it in the paper, or watch it on the tube."

"Suit yourself, but don't drive in your condition."

"No problem, Sheriff."

"You need help with arrangements?"

"Somebody else can do it. I don't hold with cremation."

"How'd you know about that?"

"Police band radio," he said, as he turned and weaved from the room.

Baffled, Grayson hesitated, deciding he couldn't arrest him. He had no proof. But he would double the guards to prevent Wilson from running, even if he had to pay for the extra deputy himself.

The sheriff sighed as he returned to his patrol car. He needed to notify the Lugundos woman of her partner's death, following a positive I.D. He'd then shuffle Miz Cafferty back over there.

His batting score was lousy. The Portuguese woman was no doubt furious with him for running off her sisters. Or was she? Had he only imagined the wink as he left her house that morning?

Chapter Fifteen

"Nola killed? But how?"

"Six-car pile-up, ma'am. It could have been much worse."

"She's dead. How could it be worse?"

"More bodies, Miz Lugundos."

"Are you sure it was Nola?"

"A dentist identified her dentures."

Micki gasped as she clapped a hand to her mouth.

"Did Miz Champlain leave here with Bub Wilson?"

"Not long after you did, Sheriff."

"Why'd she leave?"

"She got a phone call from a man. Then she ran out without saying goodbye."

They couldn't wait to escape, he thought, slapping his hat against his thigh. He was still not convinced that Nola Champlain was innocent.

"Poor Nola," she said, wiping shimmering eyes. "She finally found her a man."

Grayson shifted his weight uncomfortably. "They both died instantly, if that's any comfort."

"Then their souls will always be together." Her doleful gaze rested on the ceiling.

The sheriff nodded in agreement, but wondered in which direction the couple actually departed. He couldn't quite picture them wearing halos.

Her large bosoms heaved in a heavy sigh. "I'm all alone again. I feel like I'm running a boarding house."

When he promised another companion, she gazed at him wistfully. "Why not stay for supper, Sheriff? I'm a very good cook."

Surprised, he shuffled backward. "I'm sure you are, ma'am, but I-uh-have a dinner date. Besides, you've got a deputy to cook for." He noticed Dalton grinning at him from the red leather recliner.

"If you haven't tasted Portuguese food, you're missing a real feast," she said, pursuing him. "Tomorrow night then?"

Tensing, he felt as though he were under attack. What's got into her? Two days ago she hated me.

"Who's your date?" She sounded like his mother

"My wife," he lied, tripping over the braided rug as he backed against the door.

"The newspaper said she divorced you."

"Women change their minds." Grayson wrenched the door open and escaped to his patrol car.

* * *

The sheriff expected tears from Miz Cafferty but was surprised that Dana's eyes were also misty. He was losing his subjectivity. How could he anticipate the killer's next move if he couldn't predict the women's reactions? Dog training had taken on an uncommon glow.

"Poor Nola," Dana said. "She tried so hard to find a husband. And look what happened?"

"What did happen, Sheriff?" her daughter wanted to know.

He admitted lab tests were incomplete, but conceded that someone had tampered with Bub Wilson's truck. He didn't tell them the steering mechanism had been loosened, causing the driver to lose control. He figured Wilson had been headed back to Texas. The accident could have happened anywhere along Highway 99.

Kerrie asked, "Did anyone know they were leaving?"

"Pat Wilson must have known," the Cafferty woman said. "He could have sneaked into the garage while his brother was sleeping."

"He parked his pickup out front, ma'am."

Kerrie shook her index finger thoughtfully. "It was so unbelievably foggy this morning. You couldn't see past your eyelashes."

"True," her mother said. "Someone could have crawled under the truck."

Grayson glanced at Dana, wondering how she knew where the damage had been done. She had probably taken one those women's mechanics courses, but he couldn't quite imagine her in greasy overalls.

Kerrie rose to refill their cups. "So it happened after the fog rolled in. But why?"

"Nola was a Sew and So," Sarah Cafferty reminded her.

"Pat's brother wasn't, and he's the only non-member killed."

"Harold wasn't a club member either, and we're assuming he's dead."

"Which leads us back to Wilson," the sheriff said. "He might've been jealous of his brother and Miz Champlain."

They shook their heads in concert. Nola had admitted Pat was through with her, Dana said. "Some egos can't stand competition. It's like waving a discarded bone under a dog's nose. If another dog wants it, the previous owner will usually challenge him."

"Brilliant deduction," Miz Cafferty said. "But would Pat kill his own brother?"

"I doubt it. Those two looked enough alike to be identical twins."

"Sibling rivalry, maybe?"

"Speaking of siblings." Dana's attention focused on the sheriff.

"Wasn't a young girl critically injured in the accident?"

"Yes, that's true."

"What kind of animal would subject innocent children to a death trap?"

"A nut case," Grayson said vehemently.

"A lot of children could have been killed this morning," Miz Cafferty said. "Remember that ninety-seven car pileup some years back, north of Bakersfield?"

"Killer fog," Dana replied. "I've sworn every fall to leave the San Joaquin Valley. Now, a maniac's using fog as camouflage."

"What worries me most, Dana, is that he's trying to outdo himself. He bashed Allie with a lamp, strangled Betty with a cord, and drowned Candice in her tub. Then he tries cremating Carole and Lana. When that didn't work, he sabotaged Bub and Nola."

"You didn't mention Tamara. I wonder if the killer knows she's still alive. Or Carole and Lana, for that matter."

The sheriff pounded the table with his fist. "You know about Miz Merino?"

When they nodded, he asked, "How?"

"We called all the funeral homes, Walter." He noticed Dana crossing fingers in her lap. "We don't know where you transferred her. If we did, we'd form a prayer circle to bring her out of her coma."

Her unvoiced request made him squirm. "I'm afraid I can't allow you to do that."

"Then Tamara's life is in your hands."

Kerrie said, "I think we all agree no woman's capable of the murders. Or strong enough, for that matter."

The Lugundos woman's muscular arms came to mind, but he dismissed the idea as inane.

"What's the killer planning next? And why?" Kerrie wondered.

"Seems he's trying to cop a prize. Get himself into the serial killer's hall of fame. Remember those trading cards with Ted Bundy and other wacko's pictures? Kids collected them like baseball cards." Grayson rose from the table when the deputy beckoned to him.

"Fog's starting to roll back in, Sheriff. I thought you'd want to know."

Checking his watch, Grayson realized he'd overstayed his visit. Envisioning a banner headline: SHERIFF PARTIES WHILE VICTIMS DIE, he stood and said his goodbyes.

Miz Cafferty packed an overnight bag, saying she felt like a much-used ball in a spirited game of tennis. She preferred to stay with Dana, but Miz Lugundos needed a friend.

"Micki's old-fashioned," she said. "She won't be comfortable staying alone with young Dalton."

At the mention of Dalton, Kerrie said, "Make him understand I didn't mean to hurt him, Sarah."

"That's me. Poor man's 'Ann Landers.' I'll see what I can do, Hon."

"I'm really very fond of him…"

"I'm sure he feels the same, but you've got to let him make the first move."

"How'd you get so wise?" Kerrie hugged her.

"Experience, my dear. I was quite a belle in my day."

"I'll bet you were." Kerrie smiled. "Did you know her then, Mom?"

* * *

Next morning Dana and her daughter picked up Sarah at nine. Snares and weapons installed in Sarah's home required their inspection.

"When this is over," Sarah said, her blue eyes apprehensive, "I might get killed in my own house with a forgotten land mine."

"We'll do a thorough search before you move back in," Dana promised, as they pulled into Sarah's driveway.

149

Deputy Avila greeted them at the door, his handsome face solemn. Carole appeared a moment later dressed in a pink floor-length robe. She resembled a surly child who had missed her nap.

"Where's Lana?" Sarah asked, when she had apologized for the intrusion.

"She's in the bedroom having a breakdown."

"I thought she'd feel safe with Deputy Avila here."

"That's not what's bothering her," Carole said, plopping her small frame on the edge of a wingback chair. "She's been watching that shopping channel before her soaps. I guess she gets bored while I'm napping."

Sarah was sympathetic. "It's a good way to replace what she lost in the fire."

"Twelve padded yellow envelopes arrived this morning, and five packing boxes. She's yet to receive the insurance check for her house, and Lana's worried about her credit card bills."

Sarah groaned, recalling her own TV shopping experiences. "You can certainly lose track of what you're spending."

"That's not the worst of it," Carole said, frowning." Lana's afraid to open them because the killer might have planted a letter bomb."

"A copy cat Unabomber?" Dana shook her head, thinking it highly improbable. She glanced at the deputies, who were pretending not to listen. Nodding toward Avila, she whispered, "I'm surprised Lana didn't ask him to call in the bomb squad."

"Lana took care of that herself. She scalded the packages in the bathtub."

They laughed as Kerrie left for the bathroom. She returned a moment later. "You've got to see this," she said, beckoning them to follow.

"Be careful," Carole warned. "Lana nearly flooded the place."

Glaring, Sarah rushed to her kitchen. When the pantry door opened, an iron fell from the cupboard, narrowly missing her head. Her shriek brought both deputies to her rescue.

"I forgot about the iron trap," Carole said sheepishly.

"It's a wonder you haven't killed each another. You've probably forgotten where half the traps are planted."

Sarah's rare display of temper surprised them. She was somewhat placated when Carole said she'd drawn a map.

Filing out of the kitchen, they discovered Lana leaning against Sarah's bedroom door.

"Ciji's dead," Lana said sobbing, "and that nasty Chip killed her."

Sarah abandoned the mop to embrace her. "Who's Ceegee?" she asked, worried.

"She's been watching that soap opera rerun. Lana gets so wrapped up in them, she thinks she's eavesdropping on the neighbors."

Getting Lana back to bed seemed best. When she had been tucked in and reassured, Sarah quietly closed the door.

They conferred in the living room. Carole insisted the sheriff evacuate them in an armored car, if necessary. When Deputy Avila was drawn into the discussion, he pleaded the fifth amendment. He couldn't have them telling the sheriff he agreed.

* * *

Walt Grayson reclined in his black vinyl chair, resisting the urge to desk his feet. Everyone would soon be after his hide, including the county commissioners. By driving a constant patrol, he'd managed to elude the news media, except for a couple of television interviews after the first two killings. Avoiding his own office until late at night, the sheriff depended on his dispatchers to keep him informed. The fog had become his ally, but the opaque mist also concealed the killer. He compared the case to a deadly game of hide-and-seek.

Forensic testing was inconclusive. No blood stains, other than those of Alice Zimmer, had been found at the crime scenes. The killer had left latent shoe prints—a man's size ten. The pattern was an inexpensive brand known to be stocked in quantity by several discount stores. Samples had been express mailed to the nearest hair and fiber lab, but they were slow in responding. That left nothing concrete to go on.

He could no longer ignore the pink phone messages stacked high on his spindle. He looked no further than one from the state attorney general's office. He knew his job was in jeopardy at the county level, his reputation all but ruined. He had to solve this case on his own, without special investigators cluttering up his office. What could they dig up that he didn't already know? Adding to his miseries were the resignations of his undersheriff, captain, lieutenant, and half his detective bureau. They had quit en masse shortly after he had taken office.

He couldn't blot Dana from his mind. If she knew Tamara Merino was still alive, the killer must know too. He'd have to move the comatose woman again, this time out of the county.

Flipping through his card file, he found the hospital number. Checking the time, Grayson realized a phone call could wake sleeping patients, but he had to order the transfer as soon as possible. When someone at the nursing station answered, she sounded relieved to hear his voice.

"We've tried all day to reach you, Sheriff."

"Why didn't you have the dispatcher get a hold of me?"

"We left several messages."

Grayson thumbed through the stack, finding a note from Liz, his blond dispatcher.

"It only says to return your call."

"You left strict orders to be discreet, Sheriff."

"Yes, I did. What's up?"

"I'm sorry, sir, but Jane Smith died this morning."

Grayson felt as though a pacemaker had imploded in his chest.

"To whom shall we release the body?"

"I-I'll get back to you." Stunned, Grayson hunched in his chair. Thank God he'd released her husband that morning with a tail or Merino could have slapped him with a lawsuit. He had only been allowed to visit his wife the night she was strangled. A deputy's report said he'd gone immediately to the hospital. Merino must have been with his wife when she died.

He thought again of Dana. When she learned how he'd botched the case, she would have nothing more to do with him. Dropping the receiver on his desk, he buried his head in his arms. The un-cradled phone buzzed near his ear like a hive of killer bees.

* * *

The multi-car crash was reported front page in every San Joaquin Valley newspaper. Impressed with himself, he reread the papers before switching channels for an eyewitness report. He decided to tape the Sacramento news so he could watch the accident scene whenever he felt low. That wouldn't happen again for days. He had never been on such a high. Planning the retirement village murders was more exhilarating than the others, committed years ago. Killing excited him, especially when his victims struggled.

His failed arson attempt had been a disappointment, as was drowning the Yarborough woman, who reminded him of his grandmother. Her passiveness brought him down too soon and ruined his psyched-up furor. He should have strangled the old broad instead of letting her off so easily. He could quickly kill the others, but it was more fun toying with them. Reliving the killings gave him such a rush. He should have videotaped them, especially the Zimmer woman, who had grappled like a seasoned wrestler.

153

Another firebombing would have been a drag. He'd create exotic scenarios from now on, picking off each victim at his leisure. Kerrie Compton was slated for last. His heart pounded when he anticipated her death. Her beauty earned her very special treatment.

He laughed as he taped the evening news. The fool dog trainer would continue to chase his own tail, no matter how many Sew and Sos were killed. Another look at his list revealed five remaining victims, unless he started taking out deputies. Killing them would be genuine sport, but the village would be crawling with lawmen, searching every inch for the cop killer.

A sudden sense of melancholy settled over him, making his shoulders sag. Sinking deeper into his chair, he rewound the tape and settled back to watch.

Chapter Sixteen

Lana was napping when the bedroom window shattered. The blazing bottle exploded on impact, engulfing the room in flames. Before she could scream, the poster bed ignited, melting her body like sealing wax. She awoke terrified and trembling.

Although she blinked repeatedly, the bedroom was still ablaze. Logic told her she had survived a bad dream, but the nightmare continued. An inner voice screamed "No more." as she groped for a tumbler on the night stand. In the drawer she found the pills. Swallowing the bottle's contents, she drained the plastic glass.

Settling back on her pillow, she envisioned her former home. Cookies were waiting in the oven, their freshly-baked aroma nearly making her swoon. From the window she watched her sons playing football. Stan's certified copies, she thought, as her grinning husband coached them in the yard. A kaleidoscope of memories swept past, ending Lana's euphoria with her husband's death. She saw their retirement home in ashes, along with her belongings. Not even a photograph of her family had survived.

"I'm ready, Stan," she whispered, "Please hurry. Come and get me."

The empty prescription bottle told Carole immediately what had happened. She had looked in earlier, deciding not to wake Lana until the evening meal. When she did, the room was dark and Lana refused to wake up.

The ambulance shrieked from the village, aimed at County General. Paramedics labored to save Lana Nelson, but she failed to respond. Carole had watched her partner slide downhill since the fire. She blamed herself for Lana's death. She should have been a better friend, although they had so little in common. If Lana had been assigned a compatible partner, she might still be alive.

Her friends had rushed over when the ambulance arrived. Consumed with guilt, Carole couldn't bring herself to call them with the news. She found it difficult to meet their eyes. Only four Sew and Sos remained: Sarah, Dana, Micki, and herself. It made her think of Agatha Christie's Ten Little Indians, the mystery novel she had borrowed from Dana. Like the novel characters, she wondered who would die next.

Carole consoled herself when she remembered Lana's unhealthy diet. If she hadn't taken the pills, the sweets would have killed her, eventually. Carole crumpled a damp tissue in her hand. The arsonist-killer had murdered Lana, as surely as if he'd strangled her. How many others were going to die before the sheriff asked for help?

She decided to report the sheriff to higher authorities. But whom? County commissioners? The governor? They should have done something by now. Carole no longer had faith in anyone but herself. She was still stewing when she noticed Kerrie talking at the curb with Beverly Bryant. Realizing the two of them could be friends, Carole stifled the urge to harass the custodian. Kerrie needed the company of someone her own age, although Beverly smoked like a diesel engine. What did those two have in common? Probably more than she and Lana ever had.

Surveying her three remaining friends, Carole considered her next partner. Portuguese women were known for their high-calorie meals, and by the looks of Micki, she was no exception. Carole hoped the dairyman's widow didn't snore.

* * *

"Try my linguisa," Micki said, several hours later. "It's guaranteed to make your stomach happy."

"It's nearly ten o'clock. Eating before bedtime is not a good idea. Do you know the percentage of fat in that concoction?"

"No, but it's tasty."

Carole sighed. Was she the only one in the valley who knew about nutrition? She then remembered Dana. She should have used her traumatic experience with Lana to negotiate a soul mate. At least Dana practiced healthy eating.

Micki was surprisingly healthy for her age and size. Leaning across the oven door, she removed a fresh sheet of brownies. Maybe a little linguisa wouldn't ruin Carole's diet.

"All right, Micki. Cut me a slice of that sausage, but hold the brownies." She couldn't bear to eat chocolate. It reminded her of Lana.

Micki's expressive brows shot toward her hairline. "You will?" She smiled for the first time that evening. "You're not afraid to put some ounces on that cute little body?"

"Cute's not my goal," Carole sputtered. "Healthy is."

"What good is healthy if you're miserable?"

"Miserable? What makes you think—?"

"I watch you sometimes, Carole. You want people to think you're tough."

"Self disciplined, maybe, not tough."

"I know you're scared like the rest of us."

"Of course I'm scared. But I'm also madder'n Hades at the sheriff."

"Sheriff's a nice man. He tries his best to catch the killer."

"Who's been sweet-talking whom, here, Micki?"

"I changed my mind about Sheriff Grayson. He covers his shortages with—what do you call it? Bluster. He reminds me of my husband, Antonio."

Carole fumed while Micki ferried brownies to the living room, offering them to Dalton. The young deputy had probably fallen asleep watching television. Some protection he was. She readied herself to ambush Micki as soon as she returned.

"The deputy likes my brownies," Micki said, taking Carole by surprise.

Carole fired back. "It doesn't matter how nice you think the sheriff is. I need your help to get us out of here."

"You sound like Nola."

"Sew and Sos are an endangered species, in case you haven't noticed. We've got to do something."

Micki licked chocolate from her fingers and sat down heavily in a chair. Carole expected the wooden seat to splinter.

Her dark eyes narrowed to slits, Micki said, "What can we do that the sheriff can't?"

"We can petition the governor for safe haven. We can also demand more lawmen to flush out the killer."

"Sheriff's working on that."

Surprised by her naiveté, Carole insisted, "What the sheriff is working on is digging us all a common grave. If we don't do something soon, we'll be joining our club members in the hereafter."

"I wouldn't mind."

"Well, I would." Carole left her seat to glare at her partner. "Tomorrow I'm filing a petition to have us all flown to Las Vegas. Nobody could find us in the casinos."

Micki clapped a hand to her lips, her eyes round as sausages.

"First, I'll call the state attorney general."

Her partner found her voice in time to wish Carole luck. "Once my Antonio tried to call the agriculture department up in Sacramento. They put him on hold for three days."

* * *

His second shoe landed on its side. Dark trousers followed, producing a muddy nest. Rummaging in the closet for another pair of pants, he paused long enough to admire his souvenirs. He'd limited himself to one per victim, a difficult choice at times. Alice Zimmer's closet held a wonderful outsized silk collection, despite its lack of order. The Yarborough woman's clothing rack had been slim pickings, although he found a wonderful old twenties' fedora stuffed in a trunk on the floor. Fingering each item, he briefly relived their owner's deaths. He had nearly enough costumes now to produce his own play. He should have been encouraged in his theatrical pursuits, instead of ridiculed.

The series of murders had produced more drama than any Broadway Show. Too bad his productions lacked an audience. As playwright-producer-director-starring actor, he doubted Robert Redford could have done any better.

Lana Nelson's suicide was common village gossip. He was furious that she had robbed him of the pleasure of killing her. Perhaps he should kill another villager in her stead. He wouldn't think about that now. There was still too much to do.

* * *

The three of them huddled before the fire, as much for companionship as warmth. No one was hungry enough to prepare a meal, so they snacked on a veggie pack with just enough dressing to satisfy Sarah.

Dana broke the silence. "We can't sit around waiting to be murdered."

"Let's talk about it," Kerrie said, surprised by her mother's outburst.

"Good idea," Sarah agreed around a bite of celery.

"Let's start with Alice Zimmer. Why was she killed first? Surely not because her name spanned the alphabet from A to Z."

"I've given it a lot of thought." Dana's voice was calmer. "Alice was a valley native. There's got to be a logical reason why her scrapbooks were stolen."

Kerrie asked whether the sheriff had investigated.

"I don't think he's given them much thought," Dana said. "The killer must have stolen our membership roster. How else could he kill Sew and Sos alphabetically."

"For what possible reason, Mom? And why not last names, instead of first on his murder list?"

"Maybe Alice told us something," Sarah said, "and he wants to shut us up."

"If that's the case, he's done quite a job. If he did succeed in killing all the Sew and Sos, would he stop there? Would every resident of the village become a target?"

"A mass exodus would occur before that happened. Don't you think, Mom?"

"The moment someone is randomly killed, villagers will stampede to the coast, or into the Sierras. The sheriff's community safety meetings aren't doing much good. Everyone's terrified of opening their doors."

"They'll be headed for Las Vegas if Carole's leading the charge."

"You're right about that, Sarah."

"What could a nice person like Alice have said or done to make a person mad enough to kill her?"

"If we knew the answer to that," Dana said, "we'd know who killed her."

"An old grudge, maybe? Alice liked to gab about the past. You think she blabbed something during a meeting she should have kept to herself?"

"Maybe."

Kerrie asked about Alice's background. Sarah said she was a native of Merced.

"Was she happy there?"

"She loved the place—except for the fog.

"Any enemies?"

"Alice was a sweetheart. A little eccentric, but everybody loved her.

"Wait a minute." Dana scooted to the edge of the couch. "Didn't Alice mention that her best friend had been murdered?"

Sarah's eyes widened. "You're right. Her friend's teenage son killed both his parents."

"Alice's testimony helped convict him."

"It seems he got thirty years to life." Sarah said. "He threatened to kill Alice when he got out of prison, but she knew she wouldn't live that long."

"He couldn't have been released this soon."

"I wouldn't be too sure," Kerrie said. "With prison overcrowding and permissive parole boards, he could already be out on good behavior. When was he imprisoned?"

"Seven or eight years ago."

Kerrie crossed her fingers. "You don't happen to remember his name?"

"That's asking a lot from two mature women."

"Then we need to search the newspaper files. A double murder in a town the size of Merced would have made headlines for quite some time."

"Maybe he was one of those prisoners who escaped not long ago."

Do you remember when it was?" Kerrie fished in her purse for a notepad and pen.

"No, but Walter can certainly find out."

"He must have photos of the convicts," Kerrie said.

"Gals, I think we've cracked the case." Sarah danced a mini rumba while still seated on the couch.

"We might be wrong as Corrigan, but I think Kerrie's right. A visit to the Merced library is in order."

Sarah hesitated. "I once had a bad experience with a microfilm machine. It accidentally chewed up some valuable old film, and the librarians nearly strung me up. I'd much rather stay behind with Carole and Micki. It'll give me a chance to talk to Mr. Dalton."

Kerrie flushed as she glanced at her mother.

"I'm much better with people than machines. I'll do some snooping on my own while you're gone."

Her friends exchanged worried looks. "Don't leave the deputy for a second," Dana warned. "We'd never survive your death."

"Or I either one of yours. Please don't leave till the fog lifts tomorrow."

"We'll take that under advisement." Dana said. "Now that's settled, let's talk about Lana's death. As unpleasant as it is, we need to work through this awful blue funk."

Kerrie asked, "Why do you think she did it?"

"Nothing left to live for. Simple as that."

Dana was inclined to agree. "When it comes right down to it, suicide is preferable to murder."

Kerrie gasped, her mahogany eyes nearly doubling in size. "You wouldn't—?"

Sarah said, "Of course not."

"There are other ways of ensuring our safety, besides the bodyguards. Walter could take us all into protective custody, but I think he's using us as bait." I should have kept that bit of insight to myself, Dana thought bitterly.

Sarah nodded agreement as she dipped the last celery stalk into the ranch dressing.

"Say we're wrong," Kerrie said. "Who else could be the killer?"

Dana rearranged her lanky frame more comfortably on the pillowed couch. Turning to Kerrie, seated next to her, she said, "When you mentioned Alice's name spanning the alphabet, I remembered something from Agatha Christie's ABC Murders. 'Opportunity, motive, and reason' are needed to determine a murderer."

"Someone in the village knows our habits," Dana concluded. "I feel as though I'm constantly being watched, and it's getting to me."

"But who hates Sew and Sos enough to kill them?"

"If it's not the parent killer," Sarah said, "Pat Wilson did it."

"His reason?" Kerrie asked.

"To cover Betty's murder?" Dana cocked an eyebrow. "He's been drinking non-stop since Betty's death, so he's probably incapable of killing a cockroach."

"Some men in their cups are stronger than Hercules and meaner than a bull."

Kerrie pressed. "Any more candidates?"

"Harold hasn't turned up. He could be hiding in the village and watching with binoculars. He might have a cellar with a trapdoor into his house."

Dana groaned. She'd hoped Sarah had changed her mind about Harold. She was certain his body would be found one day.

"Anyone else?"

Dana thought a moment. "John Merino's a possibility, albeit a vague one. He could have killed Tamara and the others for the same reason we assigned to Pat. But John and Tamara seemed reasonably happy."

"He was henpecked," Sarah reminded her.

"Even so…he was in protective custody when—"

"No, Dana, the sheriff let him go. I heard that John was at the hospital when Tamara died."

"Why didn't you tell me, Sarah?" Dana was horrified.

"I thought you knew."

"John's our prime suspect, Mom. Surely the sheriff knows he was there when she died."

"You think he finished her off, Dana? But how?"

"A pillow, maybe. Something inserted in her IV?"

"But she must have had a deputy."

"Jim should have been there." Kerrie was clearly upset.

"He can't be everywhere."

"If it's any consolation, young Mr. Dalton is moping around worse than you. Micki said that he's having 'woman problems.'"

Kerrie brightened. "I wish I could see him."

"Let me talk to him, hon."

"We're not teenagers, Sarah. We should be able to straighten this out, ourselves."

"Sometimes a mediator can speed things along. I'll do my best."

Any excuse to hone your matchmaking skills. Dana smiled. "Speaking of best, which mode of transportation shall we arrange for tomorrow?"

"Deputy Menlo's going along, Mom, so I think we should discuss it with him."

"Good idea. Where is he?"

"Kitchen, I'll bet." Sarah headed in that direction.

Dana knew she would first stop at the refrigerator, regardless of the deputy's location.

They heard Sarah scream. In the kitchen they found her bending over their deputy. Flat on the floor, he was groaning and clutching his stomach. Beside him was a half-eaten brownie.

Chapter Seventeen

Art Menlo's olive skin paled in the overhead light, his breathing measured in gasps. He seemed as helpless as a turtle on its back. Squirming with pain, he held his abdomen as though it might explode.

Kerrie called for an ambulance while Dana tested his brow.

When Kerrie replaced the receiver, her mother said, "Call the sheriff. We need another deputy to take Art's place."

Sarah dabbed at the deputy's face with a wet paper towel. "That's one of Micki's brownies," she said, nodding to the evidence on the floor.

"I'm aware of that. We need a pillow for Art's head."

Sarah muttered something unintelligible as she rushed from the room.

Dana continued to reassure the deputy, although his groans were growing weak.

Glancing at her watch, she wondered aloud when the ambulance would arrive.

"Five minutes," Kerrie said as she knelt beside her.

Sarah was soon back with a pillow, which she placed beneath the deputy's head. "Did you get through to everyone?" she asked.

Kerrie bit her lip to hide a fleeting smile. "Jim and the others are on their way." She seemed more concerned with Jim than she was with the stricken deputy.

Sarah's expression was one of horror. Dana knew what she was thinking. Micki's brownies had arrived that morning. Only one of them had been eaten. Half of that was now on the floor.

They could have driven to Merced and back in the time it had taken for the ambulance to arrive. Or so it seemed. The deputy had stopped groaning, although his pulse was still detectible. Dana's hand rested over his heart, willing it to beat. Her own heart pounded like a kettle drum. A knock sounded seconds before they heard a siren's wail. Kerrie hurried to answer the door, and Dana heard Micki's alto voice echo from the living room. Despite her protests, the small kitchen was soon crowded.

Dana ordered them out. "Paramedics will need this space," she said, realizing how gruff she sounded. She beckoned Jim closer, aware that their earlier confrontation had made him apprehensive. "We're in danger," she whispered when he bent to listen. "The killer has taken out our deputy."

"W-what happened?" Jim Dalton's expression was one of shock. Before she could say more, the ambulance's dying wail cut their conversation short. She knew Jim had seen the brownie and was wondering about the ones he must have eaten.

"Don't let anyone but the paramedics in," she told him. "And be sure to check I.D.s." Dana knew she sounded like a drill sergeant, but someone had to take charge.

The sheriff arrived as the ambulance was leaving. Wiping his sweating brow, he announced the arrival of reinforcements. Neighboring counties were loaning additional men.

"About time," Carole said, with her usual lack of decorum.

"We've got to pull together," Dana warned. "The sheriff needs our help as much as we need his."

While Grayson's expression was one of gratitude, Carole's was sullen anger. When they told him what had happened, the sheriff said he would stand guard until Art's replacement arrived. Kerrie was obviously disappointed, although Jim was ignoring her.

"Now about the brownies," he said, as all eyes focused on Micki. "The rest of them need to undergo some lab tests."

Micki appeared crestfallen. "You don't think that I—?"

"No ma'am," he said courteously. "It's simply routine."

"I don't understand, Sheriff. I baked two pans from the same batch."

"I ate four of 'em last night," Jim said, "Nuthin' happened to me."

Dana watched Grayson's rugged profile, wondering when he had acquired some social polish. Or was he merely trying to impress her? His new image was rather interesting.

"The brownies were tampered with after Dalton ate them, and before the second batch arrived."

"No, sir," Jim said heatedly. "I patrolled most of the night."

"You should have patrolled all night, Mr. Dalton. I'm reassigning you in the morning."

"But, Sheriff," Micki wailed. "Just when I get used to people, you take them away."

Deliberately changing the subject, Dana asked about John Merino.

"Haven't seen him since I let him go."

"So you think Tamara died as a result of strangulation?"

"Coroner's doing an autopsy. We'll know soon enough."

A phone call from the hospital came moments later. After a brief conversation, Grayson announced that Deputy Menlo was suffering from kidney stones.

Micki crossed herself as the other women sighed.

"False alarm," Carole concluded, pushing herself from the chair. "It's my bed time."

"Hold on, Miz Lambert. I'm sure the others want to know his condition." Glancing at each person in turn, the sheriff said with obvious relief, "He's being prepped for surgery. I hope they caught it in time."

Micki said, "We'll say prayers for him." The others nodded.

When Jim Dalton left with Micki, Dana told the sheriff of her proposed trip to Merced.

"Too dangerous," he warned. "If you survive the fog, there's still a chance the perp might follow you down there."

She suggested they take a patrol car.

"If I weren't in charge of the investigation," Grayson said, his voice intimate, "I'd drive you there, myself."

Embarrassed, she briefly looked away. Not now, Walter, her eyes warned. Your timing is terrible.

* * *

John Merino nursed a migraine, the icebag sloshing as he returned it to the freezer. Everything reminded him of Tamara. He would have to redecorate, or eventually move out. A few close neighbors had paid their respects, leaving casserole dishes as condolences. Strange how some of them had looked at him as though he'd killed his wife. Why would they think that? The sheriff had taken him into protective custody. He hadn't been charged with murder.

Betty Wilson's wake came to mind. He wondered if anyone would attend a wake for Tamara. Pat Wilson would. He'd give him a call.

The phone rang long moments before Pat answered. He seemed in no mood to talk, especially to another grieving widower.

"A wake?" Pat growled. "You're not even Irish."

"I need to be with people," John said. "It's so lonely ... I can't stop thinking of Tamara."

"Get used to it, Merino. It ain't gonna get any better."

John felt so low that he searched for his wife's crystal ball. Carrying it out to the patio, he held the transparent sphere between his large palms and repeatedly called her name. It was then he noticed the ball had cleared. Was that a face forming ... or his imagination? Luminous cocker spaniel eyes were staring at him from behind a gauzy drape. Long straight black hair swirled as though driven by an inner wind. The nose lengthened and shortened at will as the face constantly changed its shape. Thick lips were moving. They seemed to be crying "John."

Dropping the glass ball as though it had scorched his hands, he stepped over its shattered remains and retreated to the bathroom, where he locked himself in. The face in the mirror startled him. The stranger peering back was dough boy pale, the black eyes sunken and shriveled. Frightened, he was forming a fist to strike the glass when the telephone rang. Gripping his chest, he feared he was having a seizure.

The phone had stopped ringing by the time he picked it up. When he cradled the receiver, it rang again.

"Merino?" The voice was curt.

"Yeah?"

"About that wake ... you got any Chivas Regal?"

John made his way to the liquor cabinet, the phone cord trailing after him. "Half a fifth," he said, taking inventory. "There's also some Crown Royal, Christian Brothers sparkling burgundy, and other assorted wines."

"That's a start. I'll call some friends. Lay in a good supply of booze and chips. We'll be over within an hour."

John was vaguely aware of Wilson's motives but didn't really care. They could trash the house. Firebomb it. Bulldoze it under. John knew he couldn't live there any longer. When the wake was over, he'd pack some clothes and drive to Sacramento. From there he'd take a flight to anywhere he chose. Australia, Tahiti, maybe even Nepal. Let the sheriff track him down. Grayson couldn't snare a rhino in his own closet.

A generous shot of scotch had already dulled the pain when his first guests arrived. "Let's party," he said. "There's nothing like a good old-fashioned wake."

Chapter Eighteen

Laughter and music woke Dana after midnight. The party wasn't taking place on her street, but sound resonated like thunder in the still country air. Who could possibly find reason to celebrate with villagers being murdered?

Pat Wilson's stubbled face came to mind, and she shook her head to dislodge the disturbing image. He was the most insensitive person she'd ever known. Maybe Sarah's instincts were right. If Pat were the killer, his conscience might be getting the better of him. That could explain his drunkenness. He must be too intoxicated to worry about arrest, and was simply flaunting his guilt. She imagined him taunting the sheriff with thumbs stuck in his ears, his fingers waving wildly.

Poor Walter. He tried so hard to solve the murders. Dana wondered if the sheriff was still awake and worrying. He had probably slipped out of the house to investigate the noise. When she couldn't return to sleep, Dana quietly checked the living room, where she heard the sheriff snoring. Some men could sleep through anything. She decided to heat a cup of milk in the microwave. While she was sipping from her mug, a hand on her shoulder startled her.

"Still willing to make the trip to Merced?"

"Darned right I am," she whispered back, turning to her daughter. "Things are moving much too slowly to wait for due process."

"We'll spend a lot of time behind the machines. I hope you're up to it."

"Try and stop me."

"What about the sheriff?"

"We talked after you went to bed. He's not happy about the trip but agreed, as long our deputy drives. Art Menlo's replacement is due at eight this morning. If he can find us in the fog."

Kerrie drew her close. "Did I ever tell you how proud I am of you, Mom?"

A lump formed in Dana's throat, preventing her from answering. She clung to Kerrie for several moments. When she could trust her voice, she said, "And I'm very proud of you."

* * *

He awoke hungry during the night. Maybe there was still some chocolate pudding in the refrigerator. He would play another round of Nintendo, this time slaying the princess as well as the dragons. Setting the empty container aside, he turned on the set. When his Mario brother fell into a pit, he threw the controller against the wall. He needed newer, more violent games, like ninjas decapitating their victims.

* * *

Slumped in a straight-backed chair, Sarah repeatedly yawned, despite the heavenly scents of freshly-baked biscuits, country gravy, eggs, hash browns, hotcakes, and linguisa. Micki was busily preparing breakfast for her guests at five a.m. The noise from the all-night party down the street had awakened Sarah sporadically throughout the night. She wasn't sure whether she was awake or in the midst of an aromatic dream.

"Who's making all that noise?" She failed to suppress another yawn. "And why haven't the deputies broken it up?"

"Party's at the Merino house," Micki said, pouring another batch of flapjacks on the griddle. "Pat Wilson and his friends are having another wake."

"You think that's why he's killing all our friends—?"

"That man doesn't need an excuse to party."

Micki placed a steaming plate of hotcakes on the table. "He drinks all the time."

"He never did when Betty was alive."

"She would not allow it."

Micki banged Jim's plate with a tablespoon. The young deputy had fallen asleep in his chair, his handsome head hanging at a distressing angle. He awoke with a start, his hand instantly on his gun.

"Good heavens, Micki, you're going to get us killed. Don't you think he needs more sleep to do his job?"

"You can both take siestas after breakfast. I'll stand guard with Antonio's hunting rifle."

"You know how to use that thing?"

The large woman lowered herself into the nearest chair. Leaning forward she said, "Who do you think shot the game meat for our freezer all those years? Antonio couldn't hit a haystack if he was standing next to it."

"Oh."

"You won't tell anyone, will you?"

Sarah shrugged. "What if the killer strikes while Jim's nodding off?"

"I'll hit him with a frying pan." Micki indicated a neat row of hanging cast iron skillets.

"Maybe we should sleep in shifts, like Carole and Lana."

"Sounds like a good idea to me." One of Jim's red-rimmed eyes was partially hidden with dark, tousled hair. The other drooped at half mast. His uniform was as rumpled as cotton pajamas.

"Who will take the graveyard shift?" Micki asked as she drained the linguisa.

The mention of a graveyard made Sarah shiver. "Jim should take the night shift. You can relieve him at four."

Jim winked, mouthing "Thank you." as Micki retrieved biscuits from the oven.

"No problem," Sarah said. "By the way, there's something I'd like to discuss with you, privately."

"Uh … like what, ma'am?"

"After breakfast," she said.

Jim shot her a strange look. Before he could question her further, she rose from the table, saying, "I'll help you finish breakfast, Micki. You've cooked enough for a haying crew."

Micki's shiny face smiled. "It's good to have a partner who appreciates my cooking. Carole makes me feel like a shoat."

"A what?"

"A pig. She says I eat too much."

"Carole weighs ninety-seven pounds. Doesn't it make you want to hate her?"

"No, she doesn't enjoy the good things—like food."

"Is Carole still sleeping?"

"She snarled like a bear when I tried to wake her. She wants to sleep till six o'clock when she does her Yogi exercise."

"I think it's called Yoga, Micki."

"I was making a joke."

Sarah smiled.

"I'm glad you decided to stay while Dana goes to Merced. But how can she find the murderer in one of those library machines?"

Sarah explained the process. She then asked Micki if she recalled the boy's name who killed his parents.

Micki's ladle halted mid-air, chalky white gravy spotting the range surface. "I'm sure it was Robert."

"His last name, Micki?"

"I don't remember."

"Well, that's a start."

* * *

Kerrie stood at the window, intently studying the fog. "You can't see across the street, Mom."

"I'm glad the deputy's driving. He should be here any minute."

Kerrie closed the drapes and retrieved her purse from the coffee table. She pulled out various items, listing them aloud: "Note pads, pencils, pens, crackers, and quarters for the vending machines."

The doorbell sounded a moment later. The sheriff stepped from the kitchen, wiping syrup from his chin with a napkin. "Let me get that," he said, smiling at Dana. "Must be your new deputy."

She followed him to the door.

A young woman with cropped red hair stood at attention on the porch. Her uniform hugged a well-endowed body.

"Officer Murray reporting for duty, sir."

Surprised, the sheriff sputtered, "You've got the wrong house. I'm expecting a deputy named Harlow."

"Serious mountain flu epidemic, sir. He'll be guarding his bed for days."

"How'd you find this place in the fog?"

"Your dispatcher drew me a map, and I was lucky."

The sheriff asked for her length of service. She replied that she had graduated from the academy the previous spring. "Top marksman in my class, sir."

"Well, that's something." He stepped aside, allowing the deputy to enter.

The phone rang as Dana was pulling on her flannel-lined trench coat. Sarah's excited voice was on the line.

"If the newspaper hadn't been tossed on the curb, I wouldn't have seen John drive by. His suitcases are strapped to his ski rack."

"You're sure?"

"He must have seen me standing there, because he took off like a bullet."

"How long ago, Sarah?"

"Not more than two minutes."

"Which direction?"

"He headed for the highway. Fog's too thick to tell which way he turned."

Dana pulled the phone from her ear to inform the sheriff. He immediately left in his patrol car.

"I've got information that might help find the parent killer. Micki remembers the young man's name is Robert."

"No last name?"

"No, but how many kids kill their parents?"

"I can think of several. We'll ask the librarians about the case. They should be able to narrow down the time frame."

Dana finished pulling on her coat, the telephone wedged beneath her chin. "Our new deputy's here. Nancy Murray was top marks woman in her class."

"A lady deputy?"

"You'll be meeting her soon."

"I wish you'd wait till the fog lifts, Dana. It's dangerous out there."

A few minutes later Dana sat in the rear of the patrol car, relieved that a wire screen didn't separate her from the others.

"Wettest fog I've ever seen," Kerrie said, turning in the seat to glance at her mother.

"I'm already a bundle of nerves."

"Relax, Mom. We're going to solve the murders for Sheriff Grayson."

The deputy laughed. "This assignment was supposed to be routine."

"Nothing routine about it, Nancy. Someone's stalking Sew and Sos like game animals."

The deputy pulled slowly from the curb. "I should have brought along some flak jackets."

We'll need more than that. Dana stared through the clouded rear window. No one seemed to be following. With any luck they would make it to Merced without mishap. By the time they reached the highway, the fog seemed impenetrable. Kerrie rolled down her window to listen for oncoming traffic.

Dana thought she might be hyperventilating. "You all right, dear?"

"The fog's so thick, I can't hear a thing."

For all her bravado, she's as frightened as I am.

The interior of the car was suddenly filled with muted light. "Uh-oh," Kerrie said. "A car pulled in behind us."

Dana turned in her seat, but could see nothing more than headlights.

"Don't panic. Someone probably has an early doctor's appointment."

"How can you be sure?"

"We're not being followed," Dana said, although she wasn't convinced, herself.

"What if he staked us out?"

"Nonsense. We're just being paranoid."

"I'll make a right onto the highway," the deputy said. "It's safer than a left."

Dana held her breath as the patrol car lurched forward. Straining to peer through the windshield, she realized visibility was practically nil. What had they gotten themselves into?

"That car's on our bumper." Kerrie's voice was strained.

"Too bad we're not following taillights." Dana tried to sound lighthearted. "There's an old San Joaquin Valley joke about following someone into their driveway. It could certainly happen this morning."

Nancy said nothing, but Dana noticed her constant glances in the rearview mirror.

"I'll make another right when we come to the next street," she said. "Drats. Didn't see that one in time."

Seated sideways, Dana's head swiveled from the windshield to the rear window, as though watching a tennis match.

The deputy held the speedometer at twenty-five. "We don't want him running into us. I've half a mind to pull him over for tailgating."

Dana suggested they wait for a streetlight.

"One's coming up. You have any idea where we are?"

"Must be Bennington Drive. Turn right and then another right at the next road."

"We'll be heading back to the retirement village, Mom."

"But we'll know whether that car behind is following."

"And if it is?"

"I'll take care of him," the deputy said, sounding confident. When she slowed to negotiate the turn, brakes squealed as the other car followed.

Signaling a few feet from a side road, Nancy sharply cut the wheel. The headlights stayed with them.

"Now what, Mom?"

Dana leaned forward, placing her hand on the deputy's shoulder. "Pull over and let him go by."

"I wish I was in home territory."

"Signal, Nancy, then slow down and ease off the pavement."

"He might run into us."

"Take your time, let him know what you intend to do."

The deputy did as Dana asked. When the patrol car came to a bumpy halt on the shoulder, they waited for the other car to pass, but it pulled in behind.

"Oh, no," Kerrie whimpered, as the deputy sprang from the car, leaving the engine running.

"Sarah was right," Dana admitted. "We should have waited for the fog to clear."

"Then anyone could have followed."

"I hope Nancy's as good as she says." The wait seemed interminable.

"We're sitting ducks if something happens to her."

"Make sure the doors are locked, Kerrie, and keep your eyes on the rearview mirror. If anyone other than Nancy approaches the car, take off."

"What about Nancy?"

"If she doesn't come back, she's probably dead."

They heard vague voices and a car door slam. Dana shifted in her seat to glance through the rear window. A large form passed in front of the headlights, walking in their direction.

"A man's coming," Dana said. "Let's go."

Kerrie quickly slid into position and shifted into gear. She jammed her foot on the accelerator, causing the tires to spin. The patrol car fishtailed onto the pavement, the left front tire slipping onto the narrow shoulder of the two-lane road.

"Easy," Dana warned. "Cut the lights, then turn right at the next road." Her breath ran out before she could tell Kerrie to stay off the brakes.

Chapter Nineteen

"Where are you going?" he yelled at the departing patrol car. He turned to glare at Deputy Murray.

"They're scared, Sheriff. We didn't know who was tailgating us."

Slapping dust from his uniform, he said, "I had to make sure they made the trip okay." He refused to meet her eyes.

"If we'd known—"

"Get in the car, Murray. We'll have to catch 'em before they get themselves killed."

It was half past eight and fog still hugged the ground, denser than any sauna. Grayson slowed to fifteen, attempting to stay in his lane. The women weren't that far ahead, although their taillights had vanished.

Keying his microphone, he said, "Pull over ladies. Sheriff Grayson's in the car behind you. Don't be frightened. Deputy Murray's with me."

"Sheriff?"

"What is it, Murray?"

"My radio stopped working during the trip down the mountain. It's been acting up lately."

"What?"

"County tech was supposed to fix it yesterday before I left, but he called in sick with the flu."

The sheriff groaned.

"Did the perp you were chasing get away, sir?" she said, breaking an eerie silence.

He said nothing, knowing she was trying to distract him.

"Don't feel bad, sir. He had a head start."

"There's an APB out on Merino," he grumbled. "If he's headed for Frisco, they'll pick him up at the bridge. Airports, Amtrak, and the bus depots are alerted. If he's traveling the ninety-nine, north or south, it won't be that easy. But if he stays in his car, we'll collar him. Eventually."

"You sure he's our man?"

"Why else is he running?" His side glance was deliberately contemptuous.

"I don't know, Sheriff. I feel like I walked into the middle of a horror movie."

Grayson slowed to ten miles an hour, scanning both sides of the road. "Where the hell are they?"

"Heading for the library, sir. Couldn't someone from the department have gone there instead? Or one of the librarians check out the lead?"

"Who's running this investigation, Murray?" He heard her gulp. She must have realized she'd overstepped her bounds.

In a small voice she said, "I thought you might call and leave Mrs. Logan a message."

"If she gets there."

Grayson peered through the windshield, afraid he would leave the pavement. He'd treated the deputy badly, and decided to be more civil.

"Where're you from, Murray?"

"On loan from Calaveras County, sir. Sheriff got your message and sent me down the mountain in the fog. I should be getting hazard pay."

"Calaveras? Are they still holding that frog jumping contest Mark Twain started with the short story of his?"

"Every year I know of," she said. "Those big imported jumpers need pogo sticks to compete with our California bullfrogs."

"Maybe they had jet lag. Ever think of that?"

"Probably the thin mountain air, sir."

Grayson kept his thoughts to himself until they reached the 99. He needed eyes like a fly and enough concentration to avoid potential death traps. But all he seemed to be doing was slowing down traffic, which had nearly reached a crawl. The six-car pileup kept running through his mind. If Dana and Kerrie were involved in a crash, he'd never forgive himself.

"Be alert for your patrol car, Murray. And while you're at it, John Merino's sand-colored Mercedes."

"Hard to make out colors in the fog, sir, let alone the brands."

Grayson continued muttering to himself. If he had to accept outside help, why wasn't it somebody who was vehicle savvy. Murray probably couldn't tell a Volkswagen from a Porsche."

He was adamant in his decision to never run again for sheriff.

* * *

When the headlights disappeared, Dana insisted they wait before turning back. They had to report their deputy missing.

"But we don't know where we are." Kerrie bit her lip to keep from crying.

"When we find Bennington Road, turn south."

"Easy as finding the north pole, Mom."

"When we get there, we can call from the library."

"From the library? What if the killer's waiting?"

"How could he know?"

"Your phones might be tapped." Kerrie stopped the car and turned to stare at her mother in the back seat.

Dana opened her door and hastily climbed in beside her. "How in heaven's name could that have happened?"

"Remember when you called the sheriff because someone had broken in?"

"You think my phone line was tapped?"

"Anything's possible, Mom."

"But that cord the killer dropped in the kitchen—"

"Protection in case someone was in the house?"

Dana's hand moved to her throat. "You're right. He could be lying in wait."

"If the library's as large as I remember, there are plenty of book aisles to drag us into."

"Sarah and Walter were right about us traveling in the fog. Head for home so we can report Nancy missing."

"We're lost, Mom. Which way?"

"Call for help on the radio."

"The police car's stolen."

"Get in touch with Walter." Dana slid across the seat to peer at the dashboard. Flipping switches, she managed to activate the siren as well as the overhead lights.

"Turn them off," Kerrie shrieked. "He'll hear us."

Dana flipped switches until the siren stopped warbling. "Use the radio, Kerrie. We can't just sit here waiting for him to find us."

Kerrie retrieved a long-handled flashlight from its holder in the door. Aiming the light at the control panel, she found the radio switch. Reaching for the microphone, she depressed the side button. Voice trembling, she said, "Calling Sheriff Grayson. Come in."

They heard nothing but static.

"Try another station," Dana urged. "Nancy's not from this county."

Kerrie worked for several moments without success.

"We might run the battery down," Dana said. "Let's get back to the village."

"What about Nancy? Shouldn't we check the place she disappeared? He might have dumped her body along the road."

"If she's dead, it's my fault, Kerrie."

"She was just doing her job."

Kerrie eased back onto the narrow roadway, creeping until they reached an intersection marked with a stationery stop. Doubling back, they reached an approximate location of the deputy's disappearance. Kerrie was afraid of driving over Nancy's body in the fog.

Dana suggested they walk.

"And if he comes back?"

"He'll need radar to find us. We'll take the flashlight for protection.

Once they left the car, Dana knew they wouldn't be spotted until the fog dissipated. Adding theft of a patrol car to her growing list of felonies, she activated emergency lights to prevent a rear-end collision. Gripping Kerrie's arm, she used the flashlight to search for tire tracks.

The silence was eerie and the heavy mist claustrophobic. Dana found herself gasping for breath, which frightened Kerrie even more. Turning back they realized the patrol car's blinking lights were no longer visible. The battery must have lost its charge, or they had strayed off the shoulder into an unplowed field.

"We're lost, Mom."

"We can't be. We're just turned around."

"You never had any sense of direction."

"Now's not the time to list my many inadequacies, dear. Let's stand here a moment and listen."

"For what?"

"A vehicle of some kind. Maybe even a tractor."

"This time of year?"

"They must grow something during late fall."

"If we yell, someone might hear."

185

"The killer, maybe?"

"What if Nancy's still alive, laying here somewhere?"

Dana turned toward her daughter's hazy figure. Her heart lurched as though she'd glimpsed an apparition. Perhaps their spirits looked this way when victims had been strangled. Confused and disoriented. Pulling her trench coat tightly about her, she couldn't prevent the damp chill from entering her very bones.

"Go ahead and yell.

"Nancy," Kerrie screamed.

They waited.

"Nancy," they shrieked together.

Still no other sound.

It seemed an alien force had lifted them into a cloud, suspending them indefinitely.

"What can we do?"

"Wait until the fog lifts. We might be walking in circles, or farther away from the car."

"We could stand here for hours, Mom."

"You're right. We've got to keep moving." Dana swung her flashlight horizontally, sweeping the uneven ground. It wasn't a cultivated field, which was rare in this area. Where in heaven's name were they?

She noticed the limb a nano second before it tripped her up. Landing hard on her elbows and knees, Dana lost her grip on the flashlight. It landed on a rock several feet away, glass breaking on impact.

Kerrie immediately knelt to help her.

"Wait." Dana gasped. "I think I've broken something. The pain—" She rolled onto her side, groaning.

"Can you move your arms?"

Dana carefully straightened each elbow. "They're still working."

"Thank goodness. How about your legs?"

Groaning, she tried to lift one. Damp earth clung to the knees of her jeans and the edges of her trench coat.

"I'm not sure about these knees. They were creaking before I fell."

"I guess all we need is an oil can." Kerrie grinned through her tears. "You can't just lie there. You'll stiffen up."

"And rust. Give me a hand and we'll estimate the damage."

Carefully helping her mother to her feet, Kerrie supported her as she took a tentative step. Dana limped a few feet, gritting her teeth.

"Everything's working. But what I wouldn't give for my king-sized bed with the comforter pulled up to my chin."

"As soon as the fog lifts, Mom. I promise."

With Kerrie's help, Dana hobbled several hundred feet. Stopping to rest, she realized the ground had been leveled. Carefully nudging pea gravel with the toe of her boot, she said, "Looks like a dirt road. Where do you suppose it leads?"

"Hopefully back to the highway."

"We need a compass, for all the good it would do in the fog. Which direction are we going?"

Kerrie stopped to calculate. "I think we were going west when we stopped, then north away from the highway. We're probably walking the wrong way."

"I think you're right. Let's turn around and try to stay on this road. It must lead somewhere."

They walked some distance before squinting at their watches. "Ten-fourteen," Kerrie said.

"The fog's thinning, dear."

"You sure that's not wishful thinking?"

"No, look over there."

A vague square shape loomed to their right.

"A house?"

"Probably a mirage."

"No, it looks like an old farm house."

Kerrie helped her limp to the building. Running her hand along the decaying exterior, she yelped. "I've got a splinter."

Dana mumbled, "Two wounded and one possibly deceased."

"Let's find the door."

"Careful of that front porch, Kerrie. It could crumble under your weight."

"I know I've gained a few pounds—"

"You have a beautiful figure, dear. I'm worried about rotting wood."

Kerrie gingerly placed a tennis shoe on the bottom stair. It creaked but stayed intact. Gripping the splintered railing, she took another step.

"Nothing to it," she said. Turning, she extended her hand. When Dana hesitated, Kerrie insisted the steps were solid.

"Stay to the outer edges," her mother warned. "The middle's are always the weakest."

They edged up five steps and stood on the narrow porch. The wooden door hung at an angle, supported by a single, rusty hinge. If they tried the door, the hinge would no doubt break.

"Now what?"

"We regroup."

"Meaning?"

"The back door."

"Stand where you are. I'll look around."

"Careful you don't fall."

"Look who's giving advice."

Dana laughed in spite of her pain. "Sorry," she said. "I can't stop being your mother."

"I'm glad you are." Kerrie kissed her cheek before leaving to negotiate the steps. The wood groaned, but none of the stairs gave way.

"Take your time," Dana called after her. "We don't need any more injuries."

The heavy mist didn't feel quite so cold. Or wet. Even her frozen fingers seemed to have thawed. Was it her imagination, or had an inner warmth radiated to her extremities? Dana hugged herself, smiling inwardly. Before she allowed fear to creep back in, she'd retain her closeness with Kerrie for as long as possible.

"Mom." Kerrie's plaintive voice slashed through Dana's euphoria. "A man's body. I saw it through the window."

"Where?" Dana felt as though she would lose her precarious balance.

"Back room. But I don't think you should—"

Dana insisted: "Help me down these stairs."

Kerrie hesitated before offering her hand. When they had crossed the littered yard, she helped her mother onto the decrepit back porch. The tattered screen door squeaked as it swung outward.

"Where?"

"In this room." Kerrie pushed the door wide so that Dana could look without entering. The stench was intolerable. A large man lay on his back, tied with a frayed rope. He didn't appear to be breathing.

Dana edged closer, a feeling of familiarity drawing her into the room. No curtain hung from the dirty window, its lower pane cracked in a spider web design. Torn and colorless linoleum covered the center floor where he lay, the outer edges aging wood. The room was as barren as an abandoned storage shed.

Kerrie's cry of alarm didn't stop Dana from kneeling on bruised knees to inspect the body. Holding her breath, she placed two fingers on the man's jugular vein.

"It's Harold. He's still alive." He was wearing the same wrinkled, mismatched clothing as the night he disappeared, and that awful mustard jacket.

"The missing neighbor?"

"The same. We've got to get him to a hospital."

"How, Mom? He's too heavy to carry and he smells like an outhouse."

Dana's memory flashed back to the night of Sarah's dinner. How they had lifted Harold into the wheelbarrow she'd never know. Adrenalin and necessity, most likely. They now had no wheelbarrow, and Dana herself could barely walk. Another thought was even more frightening. The killer must have kidnapped Harold while he was still in a stupor, leaving him there to die.

But why? And what if the killer returned before they could rescue Harold.

"Kerrie, we've got to find the car and get him out of here."

She looked as though her mother had lost all reasoning.

"Untie him so we can bring him around. But first let's open that window."

Kerrie held her nose.

"Check the other rooms for a blanket and something to cut the ropes."

"I never realized what an optimist you are, Mom."

"Please do as I ask."

"Let me help you up before you rust in that position."

Dana made a face and waved her off. "Hurry. No telling when the monster will return."

Kerrie inspected the other bedroom, finding nothing more than muddy footprints and a rickety wooden chair. The kitchen cabinets were ajar and empty. In a bottom drawer she found a dull butcher knife. Hurrying back, she offered the chair to Dana, saying, "Nothing to cover him with, but we can take turns sawing through the ropes."

Dana sighed. "I've been trying to raise the window, but it refuses to budge."

Kerrie squeezed her nostrils together. Taking the dull knife blade in her hand, she smashed the shattered lower pane with the wooden handle. When the webbed glass gave way, a cold breeze snaked into the room. Turning back she noticed Dana covering Harold with her trench coat.

"Mom, you'll freeze. And you'll never get rid of that smell."

"It's my fault he's here. Mine and Sarah's."

Kerrie quickly removed her ski jacket, placing it around Dana's shoulders. Before her mother could protest, Kerrie yanked at the neck of her Irish fisherman's sweater. "I'm burning up from all this exertion."

As they stood deciding how to rescue Harold, a creaking step startled them. Reacting swiftly, Kerrie pulled her mother into the bedroom closet. Each held her breath as the door closed with a squeak. Shivering, they heard footsteps on the porch and the door banging closed. Gripping the butcher knife, Kerrie nudged Dana deeper into the closet, behind her. It was then she remembered that Harold was under her mother's coat.

Chapter Twenty

Jim Dalton seemed wary when she approached him after breakfast. Micki's bountiful meal, following little sleep, had left him lethargic. He managed, however, to stand when Sarah entered the room.

"I must have gained ten pounds," she complained when she had seated herself on the couch.

"A couple more days of Miz Lugundos's cookin' an' I'll be buyin' bigger uniforms." He raised a questioning brow, his lopsided grin gone serious.

"Ordinarily, I wouldn't meddle," she said, prefacing her remarks in terms she thought he would understand. "But two people I admire are in torment, and I'm obliged to help them settle things. You understand what I'm getting at, Jim?"

He blinked, apparently puzzled. He wasn't making it easy for her.

Clearing her throat, she said in a rush of words, "I'm very fond of Kerrie—as you are, Jim—but when people are drinking…"

Jim raised a hand, warning her not to continue. "I don't wanna get into this, ma'am. Miz Compton and I've parted company."

He excused himself and left the room. Stunned, she realized how deeply hurt he must be. This wasn't a problem

Saharh Cafferty, resident peacemaker, could easily solve. It would take a king-sized bandage to patch that wound. Men's egos were so fragile, and his could be shattered beyond repair.

Friends had always said she'd missed her calling. She should have been a marriage counselor or working class diplomat. Sarah was beginning to doubt their collective wisdom. She was no longer the sage counselor of Bointon's Bluff, Nebraska. Times had changed and relationships were complicated. Well, she wouldn't give up. A morning's nap would improve her concentration, and she might awake with the answer. Gazing through the misted window, she told herself, "You haven't lost it yet, old girl."

The doorbell woke her later that morning as she was napping on the couch. She found a grim-faced sheriff standing at parade rest. A young woman in uniform was partially hidden behind him. Stetson in hand, he asked if she'd heard from her friends.

"No," she said, alarmed. "Have you tried the library?"

"They never made it." Glancing at himself in the shiny toes of his boots, he apparently didn't like what he saw.

Breath caught in Sarah's throat when she glanced at his companion. "Aren't you their deputy?"

"Yes, ma'am."

"How in heaven's name did you lose them?"

Long story," the sheriff said. "Mind if we come in?"

Trembling, Sarah stepped aside.

They were still in the foyer when Deputy Dalton appeared. Noticing Nancy he stopped, his chin rising noticeably. Nancy's chin was also elevated, her eyes riveted to Jim's. Sarah could almost smell the chemistry. They seemed oblivious of anyone else in the room. Although she was frantic with worry, she took mental note of this new complication. How was she going to tell Kerrie? If she saw her again.

"The ladies are missing," Grayson informed her. She detected a quaver in his voice. "Dispatcher's broadcasting a missing persons' bulletin, but the fog's got every available patrolman working accidents."

"How'd they get separated from their deputy?" Sarah demanded to know.

Nodding toward the living room, he said, "Let's have a seat and I'll explain."

Before he finished, a voice dipped in acid cut him short: "Nice work, Grayson. You've screwed things up again." Carole leaned against the kitchen door, small fists clenched at her side.

The sheriff's gray eyes rolled toward the ceiling. "Why don't you run for sheriff, ma'am? The position will be open soon."

"I'd do a better job—" The door opened behind her, putting an end to Carole's tirade. Looming like a giant spider, Micki collected her prey.

"I need your help in the kitchen." she said, her rich voice resonating. When Carole protested, she was dragged from the room.

Embarrassed smiles were exchanged as the sheriff rose to leave. "If you hear from Miz Logan," he said, "call my dispatcher immediately."

"What about Deputy Murray?" Sarah groaned as she got to her feet. "Shouldn't she go along?"

"I could use some help here," Jim said sheepishly.

Sarah glared at him. "The sheriff needs the deputy's help more than you, young man."

"You're right, Miz Cafferty." Beckoning to the deputy, Grayson replaced his hat. As they were leaving, Nancy turned to wiggle her fingers at Jim. The young man blushed and wiggled back.

I'm sorry, Kerrie, Sarah thought mournfully. *Jim seems to fall in love as often as he changes underwear.*

⋈ ⋈ ⋈

The keyhole provided a limited view. Seated on her haunches, Kerrie still gripped the butcher knife. Squinting, she noticed dusty black jeans and matching running shoes.

One foot unexpectedly kicked at something—probably Harold's ribs. Ear against the door, she could hear no cry of pain. Thank God Harold's out of it. The killer must think he's dead.

Before she could blink, the chair was wedged beneath the doorknob, completely blocking her view. She thought she heard a snicker as the barricade was tested. Dust motes threatened to make her sneeze as she gripped the frame to steady her trembling legs. Placing an ear against the closet door, she heard fading footsteps.

"What's happening?" Dana breathed in her ear.

"He's leaving."

"He knows we're here, Kerrie."

"I know. He must be getting something to finish us off."

"That rickety chair might fall apart if we push hard enough."

Both women repeatedly fell against the decaying wood, but the flimsy barricade held.

"The knife, Kerrie. See if you can loosen the screws."

"Hinges are on the other side."

"The screws holding the doorknob. Or pry it loose from the wood."

"I'll try but I can't see." This knife handle's heavy enough to crack a coconut. Just let him stick his head in here.

"He probably has a gun."

"Not his modus operandi." Kerrie dug into the wood, attempting to dislodge the knob. She found the blade too thick to be effective.

"Try the screws."

"They won't budge. Must be cross-ended."

"Then we need a Phillips' screw driver."

"There's a nail file in my purse, but that's in the car."

"I wish we had the flashlight. We could use it as a weapon."

"It's in there with Harold."

Dana sighed. "I pray he's still alive."

196

"Of course he is." She couldn't tell her mother he'd been kicked. From the smell of him, the killer probably thought he was decomposing.

Dana straightened and banged her head on the shelf. While rubbing the pain she noticed dim light coming from the ceiling.

"Kerrie, look."

"Trap door?" Reaching for the square of light, she stood on her toes, her fingertips shy of touching the hatch.

"Great," Kerrie said, "I wish we had the chair."

"You can stand on my back."

"No, Mom. You've been hurt enough."

"We'll be worse than hurt when he comes back."

Dana knelt on throbbing knees as Kerrie gripped the shelf for support. Carefully placing a tennis shoe on either side of her mother's spine, she drew herself upright. Pushing against the trap with her hand, she braced her back against the wall. If he comes back now, we've had it."

"It's stuck, Mom. I need the butcher knife." Kerrie ran her hand along the shelf, the weight shift causing Dana pain.

"It's here," she whispered as her hand closed around the blade. "Thank God it isn't sharp."

Using the handle as a hammer, Kerrie tapped the small hatch until it loosened. She slid the knife into her back pocket. Pushing hard to raise the trap, she was unprepared for the dust and debris that rained down on her. Shaking her head and coughing, she managed to open the hatch.

"I heard something," Dana warned.

Kerrie stopped breathing long enough to listen.

"Harold." Dana whispered. "If only he'd untie himself."

Kerrie heard a moan. The unconscious man must be coming to. She doubted he would move with broken ribs.

"I'll pull myself through the opening," she said. "Hold steady as you can."

Gripping both sides of the frame, Kerrie lifted her long legs, wedging them against the opposite wall. "Thanks for passing on your height," Kerrie whispered. "I never appreciated it till now."

Reaching for a handhold on the floor above, she felt feather light feet scamper across her hand. Jerking convulsively, she nearly lost her footing. Recovering, she found a crossbeam and tested its strength. Satisfied it would hold her weight, she used her dwindling energy to pull herself upward. Scraping her arms and neck on splintered wood, she was halfway through the opening when she realized her hips were stuck.

"Darned big butt," she muttered, resting her forehead against the littered subflooring. Squirming, she managed to pull the knife from her jeans.

Balancing weight on her elbows, Kerrie lowered her body enough to stand again on her mother's back. She then attacked the rotted wood on either side of the opening, carving a large enough hole to slide through.

As she worked, Kerrie listened for the sound of a car. She wondered if the killer was hanging around, laughing at their futile attempts at escape. Anger provided renewed strength, and she pulled herself into the attic. The smells of dirty, rotting wood and mold assailed her as she rested on her knees, quietly surveying her surroundings. Rustlings from the darkest corners of the loft convinced her she had invaded a colony of mice. She prayed it wasn't their larger cousin, the rat.

A shank of dim light shone halfway up the slanting roof and had her full attention. With any luck she could enlarge the hole enough to crawl through, but first she'd use the peep hole to reconnoiter the yard.

Leaning to look at her mother through the hatch, she said, "Don't get too comfortable. I found a way out."

"Stay on the beams," Dana warned, "or you'll fall through the ceiling."

Kerrie tried to stand, but banged her head on a beam. She had to be along the outer wall where the roof sharply slanted. Crawling slowly along the ceiling joists, she carefully avoided what was left of the plasterboard. So much debris littered the attic; she stopped to wipe her hands on her jeans. If only she had a pair of gloves.

If I'm going to wish for something, make it my cell phone. Why didn't I bring my purse with me?

The hole in the roof was several feet away when a sticky, bitter substance attacked her face and hair. Gagging, she tried to wipe the web away, but it stubbornly clung to her hands. Nauseous, she imagined eight-legged creatures with red underbellies crawling over her body. Rivulets of sweat dripped into her eyes, temporarily blinding her.

"Kerrie, what's wrong?" Dana's worried voice echoed in the attic.

Wiping her mouth with the back of her hand, Kerrie said, "Nothing. I'm almost to the hole."

Crawling forward she rose on her knees to peer through the opening to scan the overgrown yard. Squinting, she realized the fog had finally begun to dissipate. When her eyes adjusted to the light, she noticed countless rows of leafless trees beyond the house. An orchard. They've got to be nut trees, she thought, nearly giggling at the irony. A psychopath burying his victims in a walnut orchard. Briefly closing her eyes, she told herself, "Get a grip, Kerrie. Now's no time to crack."

The hole was large enough for her head and she craned her neck to look for a car. No tire tracks were visible. Unless he parked out front, she saw nothing to suggest he was still around. A closer look revealed damp weeds crushed under someone's feet, leading toward the orchard. Or was it the other way around?

Kerrie drew a ragged breath before pulling the knife from her jeans. Hacking noisily at the rotting wood and shingles, she enlarged the hole. The roof's slant was steep, ending in a broken gutter. If she could slide to the edge, she might be able to drop to the ground without injury.

Edging from the attic, one leg at a time, she sat motionless on the roof, dizzy from the height. Digging her heels into the faded green shingles, she scooted an inch at a time, her back pockets catching on the roof's rough surface. Dampness from the fog caused her hands and heels to slip, losing purchase. Several feet from a missing section of gutter, her legs dropped over the edge. Falling onto her back, Kerrie gripped the ragged edge of the roof and jerked both knees to her chest to stop her forward motion. Breath bunching in her lungs, she looked skyward, aware of the sun's faint image.

"What now?" she wondered aloud. Was the ground soft enough to absorb her fall, without breaking her legs? She was afraid to raise her head to gauge its composition. Breathing shallowly, she decided on a gymnastics move she'd learned in college. Rehearsing the movements, she flexed muscles in her hands and arms, then smoothly jerked her upper body into position. As the support beneath her fingers buckled, she pushed away from the roof.

A woodpile broke her fall.

Chapter Twenty-One

The fools were literally falling at his feet, spoiling his stalking pleasure. He disgustedly likened the change of events to spearing goldfish. He wondered again how the women had found the farmhouse. It didn't matter. They weren't going anywhere. The old farmhouse would make an excellent crematorium. Removing his soiled clothing, he kicked off muddy tennis shoes, flinging his socks at the wall. Walking barefoot to the sink, he rinsed a stained water glass. Three fingers of scotch should warm his innards nicely. They might even stave off another anxiety attack.

* * *

Dana envisioned every possible scenario. Kerrie had been gone too long to have survived a jump from the roof. She must have fallen and injured herself. She could be lying on the ground, bleeding. Or the killer captured her. Dana wouldn't allow herself to consider her daughter's death. Kerrie was a survivor.

The floor was cold and drafty where she sat, back against the wall. Her knees ached, as did her hands where she had scraped them. Although the gritty sand and dust made her sneeze, they cushioned the splintered flooring. She was beyond caring what she looked like.

Straining to listen, she thought she heard the sound of footsteps hesitantly climbing stairs. Had the killer come back to finish them off? A hinge's squeak brought fleeting memories of "Inner Sanctum," the radio mystery drama that had frightened her as a child. A remembered victim's heart was pounding again beneath the assassin's floor, her own heart keeping pace. She heard nothing for several moments. She worried that the killer was quietly strangling Harold. Before she could get to her feet, the door was wrenched open. Light from the bedroom blinded her as a hand reached for her throat.

Dana tried screaming but only succeeded in sucking air. The hand missed its mark and grasped her upper arm. A familiar voice was saying, "Let's get out of here."

"Kerrie?"

"Hurry."

Dana's legs nearly buckled, but with Kerrie's help she managed to leave the closet. When her eyes adjusted to the light, she took a closer look at her daughter. Kerrie was filthy, from the cobwebs in her hair to her shredded tennis shoes. Her face and hands were scratched and bleeding.

"I'm fine, Mom," she said, wincing. "What about your friend?"

Harold still lay motionless on the floor, his eyelids vaguely fluttering. Her heart lurched as his face distorted with pain.

"Dana," he said feebly when she knelt to grasp his hand. His face lighted as though he'd seen an angel.

Surprised, she said, "His rope's been cut."

"I found a hatchet buried in the woodpile. I couldn't leave him totally defenseless. The killer might return before we get him out of here."

Harold moaned, attempting to raise his head.

"If we support you, can you walk?" Dana asked.

"Too weak . . . Get help."

"As soon as possible."

202

"Take your coat." He attempted to lift the collar from his chest.

"No, Harold, you need to stay warm."

Kerrie assured him the outside temperature had risen, and they would soon be bringing help. When Harold closed his eyes, Dana planted a kiss on his forehead. Kerrie grimaced as though she considered Dana's show of sympathy excessive. Despite fresh air pouring through the broken window, the room still reeked of sickroom waste.

"Let's go."

Dana reluctantly accepted Kerrie's hand. When they descended the back steps, Kerrie gestured with the axe to a trail leading into the orchard.

"While I was lying in the woodpile, afraid to move, I calculated directions we've taken since leaving the house. The village may be on the other side of these trees."

Dana glanced toward the orchard. "Apricot trees." she said, smiling. "You're right. I know you're right."

"Not walnuts?" Kerrie laughed. "So much for my psycho nut tree theory."

The trail led between a lengthy row of trees. Footprints visibly overlapped one another, leading in both directions.

"Looks like he's been here on a regular basis."

Kerrie grimly shouldered the hatchet. "He's in for a surprise if he comes back now."

Dana cringed, hoping they would not have to face him until they testified at trial. Getting Harold safely to the hospital was her main concern. Let Walter worry about catching their serial killer. She was weary of playing detective.

When they reached the edge of the orchard, a four-lane highway loomed ahead. Their highway. The fog had lifted sufficiently to reveal the village on the other side. Micki's house was less than a block away.

When Deputy Dalton answered the door, Kerrie seemed bewildered by his reception. Dana knew she'd willingly fall into his arms, but he apparently didn't recognize her. Stony-faced, he continued to stand and stare.

"We escaped, Jim." she said. Her hands then flew to her face. Kerrie must realize how she looks, Dana thought, wanting to shield her from further pain. Cobwebs, dirt, and scratches. She wasn't a pretty sight.

Before he could respond, Sarah shrieked from somewhere behind him. "My Lord, deputy, let them in."

As Jim moved aside, Sarah rushed forward to embrace them. She gasped when she noticed their condition.

"We found Harold." Dana said before Sarah could ask what had happened. "Call an ambulance."

"Where?"

"In an old farmhouse not far from here."

"It's true," Kerrie confirmed when Sarah glanced in her direction. She dusted her backside and collapsed on the couch.

Dana took the receiver. "I'll give the dispatcher directions. Then we'll call the sheriff."

"So now it's the sheriff. What happened to Walter?"

Dana ignored Sarah as she talked to an ambulance driver at County General." They're coming here first," she said, hanging up. She immediately called the sheriff's office.

"Sheriff Grayson's worried about you," the dispatcher said. "I'll try to patch him through."

Dana listened to static before Walter's baritone voice came on the line. She told him their deputy was missing, and that they had found Harold Samuels. "He's alive but I'm not sure about Nancy."

"Murray's with me. Be there soon." Static replaced his voice.

Dana gave them the news as she sat beside her daughter. Kerrie was obviously relieved that Nancy had been found, but Jim Dalton's chilly reception had obviously made her miserable. Dana reached to take her hand. She had never seen Kerrie so dejected or disheveled. She resembled a battered young bag lady. "What's wrong, dear?" she said, attempting to hug her.

"He hates me." Kerrie glanced briefly at Jim, who stood at the window with his back to them.

"Give him time to absorb what's happened."

"He's too stubborn to listen."

Dana stood, saying, "Let's clean up before we see a doctor." When the ambulance arrived, Dana accompanied paramedics to the farmhouse. Moments after they left, the sheriff and his new deputy arrived.

"Nancy." Kerrie bolted from the couch, but the deputy only briefly acknowledged her. After a fleeting smile, Nancy turned her attention to Jim. Kerrie stopped short, noting the exchange between them. They seemed like old and intimate friends. How had that happened?

* * *

Sitting bedside, Dana cradled Harold's limp hand. Paramedics said he had slipped into a coma. If he died, she shared the blame with Sarah. She understood her friend's desire to swim in her husband's wake, but they had nearly drowned in their own ineptness.

She anxiously watched the heart monitor, briefly scanning liquids running into his wrists. Everything possible was being done, but was it enough?

"Talk to your husband," an aging nurse said from the doorway. "It could help bring him around."

"Oh, he's not my…" Dana hesitated, wondering whether she could bring him out of his coma. Harold had shown a more than a passing interest in her. Maybe, just maybe…

Leaning to kiss his cheek, she breathed in the scent of hospital disinfectant, a distinct improvement over his previous condition. "You've got to hurry and get well, Harold. Our wedding's tomorrow, remember?"

When he didn't respond, she said, "You've got to be fitted for your tux. You wouldn't leave me waiting at the altar, would you?"

She searched for a sign that he was regaining consciousness, but she wasn't sure he was even breathing.

Desperate, she said, "I love you, Harold. Please come back to me."

The heart monitor continued its passive bleeps, but... was it wishful thinking, or had the electronic spikes jumped higher on the screen.

"Love you, too," he murmured, his eyes still closed. A faint smile tugged at the corners of his lips.

Thank God he was coming around, but would he remember what she had said.

"Tomorrow's a bit soon, don'tcha think?"

"What?"

"The wedding, sweetheart?" His eyes were open and searching for her. "How about day after tomorrow?"

"But Harold..."

"Okay," he said, reaching feebly for the hand rails. "If you can't wait, we'll call in a preacher to marry us right here."

Dana's chin sank to her chest. "I-I'm not feeling well, Harold. I fell and injured myself before we found you in the farmhouse."

Attempting to pull himself into a sitting position, he said, "Whenever you're ready, Dana. You saved my life so I belong to you now."

She had never seen him so happy. How was she going to get out of this?

The silence was broken by a familiar voice behind her. "You're getting married, Dana? How wonderful. But don't you think it's too soon?"

"Yes, Mom." Kerrie appeared thunderstruck. "It seems we were having a similar discussion not long ago. I hope your engagement lasts longer than mine." Bursting into tears, she rushed from the room. Dana immediately left her chair to limp after her.

"Oh, my," Sarah said. "Looks like I cracked another egg." Taking the seat Dana had vacated, she leaned to whisper, "You wouldn't hold her to it, would you, Harold? Dana's so full of guilt, she'd marry the Hillside Strangler."

"She loves me, Sarah. She told me so herself." A small tear escaped the corner of his eye.

"But wasn't rescuing you enough?"

"No, ma'am. I hold people to their promises. I aim to get hitched."

The red-haired nurse returned to hustle Sarah from her chair. "You'll have to wait in the hall while I attend to this nice looking man."

"You think he's—?"

"Indeed I do. Why, if he wasn't married..." she whispered at the door.

"Good news," Sarah said, smiling. "He's divorced and looking for a wife."

"Really? But I thought..."

"Delirium. Don't believe a word he says for the next twenty-four hours. I wouldn't lie. He's all yours."

Chapter Twenty-Two

Pat Wilson staggered to his vintage TV set, a fifth of Chives Regal in his hand. Missing the volume control, he overshot the console and sprawled across the set. Scotch poured through rear cooling vents, sparking a pungent odor of shorted wiring. So much for the wrestling match. Tossing the bottle aside, he decided to replenish his supply. The telephone rang as he pulled on his shoes over mismatched socks. The phone was buried again and he gave up looking for it.

He dropped his car keys in the foyer. When he stooped to retrieve them, he fell forward, banging his head on the door. Before he could right himself, someone knocked.

"Wilson?"

He found the sheriff leaning against the frame when he managed to open the door. Grayson's massive arms were folded across his chest.

"Whatta ya want, Sheriff? I'm goin' ta the store."

"Have it delivered, or I'll pull you in for DUI."

"Canna man grieve in peace?"

"Not when it endangers other lives." Grayson straightened to his full height, half a foot taller than his prime suspect. When the sheriff stepped into the foyer, Wilson instinctively shuffled backward.

"Police brutality," he muttered, falling into a chair.

The sheriff sniffed the stale air. Recoiling, he surveyed the mess. "Burn your lunch, Wilson?"

The suspect threw a flabby leg over his arm chair. A lopsided grin distorted his stubbled face. "I drank it, ya damn fo'."

Noticing his mud-encrusted soles, Grayson asked about his shoe size.

Bouncing his leg to have a better look, Pat said, "Ten an' naff."

"Where were you this morning, Wilson?"

"Why sho' I tell you?"

"You're under arrest, if you don't."

Wilson muttered to himself. "Din' git out a bed till noon-thirty."

"Prove it."

"Gen'lemen don't kish an' tell."

"Outdated chivalry, Wilson. Won't hold up in a murder investigation. Now, either give me her name, or we're going to jail."

Wilson tried to scratch his head but failed. "No good at names. It was–uh–uh–Nola."

"Let's go." Gripping his arm, Grayson pulled him from his chair. "There's a think tank at the station to help refresh your memory."

He half-carried him to the hall closet where he helped him into his coat. He then dragged him out to the patrol car.

"Police brutality, my foot," the sheriff grumbled. "You're gonna dry out in jail until I can prove you're guilty. You're so soused, you can't remember who you whacked."

Wilson was snoring when Grayson slid behind the wheel. He'd stash him in protective custody until the lab results were in. Too bad Samuels couldn't identify his abductor. He hadn't even heard his voice.

In the meantime, there would be fewer bodies cluttering up the county morgue.

* * *

Kerrie buried herself in blankets, crying until exhausted, but the disturbing scene continued to replay. Jim deliberately ignored her while sliding an arm around Nancy Murray. Kerrie thought he might have given Nancy a full bear hug if the sheriff hadn't been standing there. As it was, Grayson grumbled something about unprofessional conduct.

I'm the one who's been through hell. Why's he hugging her?

Voice quavering, she touched Nancy's sleeve. "Looks like you two are old friends."

"More like new friends," Nancy replied.

How could she have been so wrong about Jim? He seemed like such a gentleman. Had he always been a Jekyll and Hyde? Maybe his shyness was an act, Kerrie thought, a fresh lump forming in her throat.

She managed the ride home with Nancy, who was now patrolling her mother's house. Pride prevented her from telling Nancy about her relationship with Jim, but she must know something was wrong. Kerrie stormed into the bedroom and slammed the door as soon as they were home.

To make matters worse, her mother promised to marry that smelly old man in the hospital. Life's not only unfair, it stinks as bad as Harold Samuels.

After a shower and brief trip to the hospital, Kerrie returned to take a nap. She awoke angry. Not just angry—furious. She wouldn't stay in the village longer than to pack her clothes and leave. Tossing bedclothes aside, she hastily pulled on rumpled jeans and a faded college sweat shirt. Taking her red nylon suitcases from the closet, she collected her clothes from the bureau.

Her mother was still at the hospital with Harold, so she'd simply leave her a note. Hastily scribbling: "Thanks for letting me stay. I'll let you know when I'm settled," she tore a sheet from the pad and left it on her pillow. Donning her jacket, she picked up both suitcases and placed them near the door.

Easing the bedroom door open, she listened for Nancy's whereabouts. Hearing water running in the bathroom, she snatched up her luggage and hurried to the foyer. Leaving her key on the entry table, she quietly closed the door. She had no destination in mind, just away from there.

The sun had dropped to palm tree level when she sprinted from the house. Remembering she had forgotten to call a cab, she patted her pocket for her cell phone. It was still on the charger and she couldn't risk going back. There was a pay phone at the recreation hall so she headed in that direction. She'd leave the village before anyone discovered her missing. Nancy thought she was asleep, and her mother wouldn't return until visiting hours were over.

Crossing the street diagonally, she cut across the center lawn. Few people were out-of-doors, none of them familiar. Within minutes she set the suitcases down and fished in her purse for some change.

"Going somewhere?" a melodious voice asked before she could lift the receiver.

Kerrie turned, noticing the custodian.

"I'm calling a taxi."

"Cost a fortune from here to town," Beverly Bryant said, leaning on a broom handle. "I get off in five minutes. Why don't I give you a lift?"

Kerrie hesitated. "Sure you don't mind?"

"Of course not. You're not leaving us for good, are you?" Her full lips drooped mournfully.

"As a matter of fact—"

"Where're you headed?"

"I'm not sure."

Beverly smiled. "Let's have an early dinner before I take you to the station."

"Oh, I couldn't impose…"

"Don't be silly. We're friends. I'm disappointed you'd leave without telling me."

Glancing away, Kerrie jingled coins in her hand. "Sorry, things haven't worked out."

"No wonder, with the murders and all. I'm considering leaving, myself. God knows who the next victim might be?"

"Oh, you needn't worry. The killer's concentrating on Sew and Sos."

"What about the man from Texas, visiting his brother?"

Kerrie left the telephone to close the gap between them. "He was killed because he left with Nola Champlain."

"An innocent bystander, you mean?"

"Something like that."

The setting sun cast a harsh orange glow on Beverly Bryant's skin. Kerrie noticed a heavy layer of makeup covering her attractive face. The cologne she wore was sickeningly sweet. Repelled, she backed away.

"What's that scent you're wearing?"

"Oh, you must mean the cleaning solvent." Beverly's smile dissolved. "By the way, how'd you get those scratches on your face, Kerrie?"

"You'd never believe—"

"Try me."

"I cut myself shaving."

Beverly laughed. "You remind me of my mother."

"How's that?"

"Sense of humor. You're a younger version of her." Beverly squinted at her watch. "I'll toss this broom in the supply closet, and we'll be on our way."

* * *

Sarah was surprised by Grayson's second visit.

"Miz Logan here with you?" he asked.

"Dana's still at the hospital, Sheriff."

Fidgeting with a sheath of papers, his expression was exceptionally glum. "Just got a fax from the library, ma'am. Thought you'd both want to see it."

"Dana won't mind if I look first."

213

Grayson reluctantly followed her inside. Once seated, he gave her the report.

Briefly scanning the pages, she crowed, "We were right."

"Looks that way. The young man who killed his parents escaped from prison last month."

Sarah ran a finger down the first page. "Robert Bailey. That's the name. Is there a recent picture of him, Sheriff?

His hat brim twisted slowly in his hands. "Just the fuzzy fax copy. Last page. I'm expecting an eight by ten wire photo soon."

Sarah flipped to the final page, turning the copy toward the nearest light. "He looks familiar, but it's hard to tell."

"I thought the same."

She shivered. "Why didn't he just kill Alice and be done with it?"

"He's obviously insane. Should've been committed to Atascadero, instead of Folsom Prison."

"Some misguided psychiatrist might have turned him loose."

"Moot point now. He's out there and I've got to find him."

"Mind if I show this to the girls?"

"After I leave," he said, getting to his feet. "By the way, I'm grateful to you ladies for recalling eight-year-old murders."

She followed him onto the narrow porch. "Is it true you arrested Pat Wilson?"

The sheriff nodded, refusing to meet her eyes. "Protective custody's what he needs. Keep him from drinking himself to death."

"Amen, Sheriff. But we both know he'll be out as soon as he sobers up."

* * *

Harold had been given a sedative. Excited about his forthcoming marriage, he fought the drug until Dana feared a relapse. She would have to wait until he recovered to confess she couldn't marry him. The red-haired nurse had recently gone off duty following a number of trips to Harold's room. Dana wondered why she'd been so sympathetic when he talked about the wedding. When Harold at last drifted off, the nurse patted Dana's shoulder.

"He's anxious to get married, isn't he?" Her smile was reminiscent of Dana's mother's.

She nodded, sighing wearily.

"Don't you worry, dear," she whispered. "Male patients often fall in love with their nurses."

"Yes, I've heard that." Dana glanced into her gentle gray eyes. She and Harold were about the same age, and Nurse Thompson was still an attractive woman.

"You like him, don't you?"

"Yes, indeed. He reminds me of my late husband, Carl."

So that was the attraction. A small ray of hope burst into a cathedral filled with sunlight.

"Do you like camellias?"

"Gardening's my only hobby."

"Perfect."

Dana left the room in high spirits. Sarah would be proud at her matchmaking skills, if Harold would only transfer his passions to Nurse Thompson. Her plan was to become as contrary as possible, her visits increasingly short. The nurse's kindness would hopefully make the difference.

It had to work.

The sheriff was waiting in the lobby. Dressed in a suit and tie, he resembled a business executive.

"Walter. How nice of you to escort me home."

"I have something to show you," he said, offering her a slim manila envelope.

"What's this?"

"You're a good detective, Dana. You may have solved the case."

He stepped aside to offer her a chair. Seating himself beside her, he refrained from comment until she read the report.

"Robert Bailey. Thank God, Walter. But how will you find him?"

The sheriff's brow wrinkled. "I won't sleep until I do. That's a fact."

"But…"

"Have you eaten? We can discuss this over dinner."

Dana hesitated. "If you don't mind checking in on Kerrie first. She left here terribly upset."

"She's a lovely girl, Dana. So much like you."

Dana lowered her eyes. "Please don't complicate things, Walter."

The sheriff stiffened. "Whatever you say, Miz Logan."

She placed a tentative hand on his arm. "I'm struggling under enough weight to crush this building. Please give it some time."

* * *

The doorbell rang at a quarter till eight. The porch light flicked on, illuminating a young, tow-headed boy holding a priority envelope. When Nancy opened the door, he shoved it at her. Swiveling on new tennis shoes, he quickly turned to leave. She noticed an older man standing on the sidewalk, watching.

"Wait a minute. What's this?"

"Grandma said they delivered it to the wrong house. I didn't know a cop lived here."

"Patrol woman, sonny. And I don't."

"You'll give it to the lady who lives here, woncha?" The boy frowned, rubbing freckles on his nose.

"Sure, but why so late?"

"Gramps took us to town," he said, grinning. "We just got back from McDonald's."

She waved him goodbye, then closed the door and squinted at the envelope. It was addressed to Kerrie Compton. Her watch said Kerrie had slept long enough. A talk about her temper tantrum was in order. She knocked and waited. When Kerrie didn't answer, she eased the door open. Groping for the light switch, she noticed the rumpled blankets and empty bed. Tossing the envelope on the bureau, she left to search the house.

Her first guard job and she'd blown it. Heart sinking, she decided to wait. Kerrie might return and no one would be the wiser.

Chapter Twenty-Three

"I'm not very hungry," Kerrie said as she struggled with her seat belt.

"We'll stop by my place then, so I can change clothes."

"Why not grab a burger on the way to the station."

Beverly pursed her lips. "I thought we'd have a quiet meal at one of the nicer restaurants."

Kerrie glanced at her warily from the corner of her eye. "You have a boyfriend, Beverly? I don't recall you mentioning one."

Beverly jammed the Volvo into gear. "Don't date much."

"You're not gay or anything?"

Clearing her throat, she pulled from the lot onto Strawberry Lane. "Why'd you ask?"

"I thought it might explain—"

"My interest in you?" The janitor laughed, a deep, rich baritone that startled Kerrie. "I'm attracted to your creativity. We're birds of a feather. Forgive the cliché."

"How so?"

"You're a newspaper correspondent. I write plays and act."

Kerrie flushed. "Really? I should have known you were more than a…"

"A janitor?"

"Well, yes."

"I am, but Broadway and Hollywood have failed to discover my talents."

"It must be tough getting started."

"Worse than that. Especially if your family doesn't support you. And I don't mean monetarily."

"I know what you mean."

"You do? I just assumed that your mother—"

"It wasn't her fault. I was a rebellious teen."

"So was I. We have a lot in common, Kerrie. How old are you?"

"Twenty-five."

"So am I."

"You're kidding."

Beverly laughed again, an octave higher. "Theatrical makeup does age one."

"Then why?"

"A bad case of acne left me scarred."

"I didn't notice."

"I'm an expert at disguises, Kerrie. It's a part of role playing."

"Theatrical, you mean?"

"Of course. I practice my craft daily."

"You must be good."

Beverly smiled. "Too bad you're not a casting agent."

Kerrie shifted in her seat, intrigued. "Have you been to many auditions?"

"Hundreds of cattle calls, but they all seem to think I'm too intense. I've probably been black-listed for telling them what I think."

"Then why are you here, of all places?

"I'm a character actress. Not pretty enough for leading roles…"

Kerrie glanced at her appealing profile. Despite the chill in the air, perspiration had formed on Beverly's brow. Small beads were escaping down the side of her face.

"…so I came to the valley to study older women. To learn their habits and mannerisms."

"To play them on stage?"

"Exactly."

"So that's how it's done."

"I believe you'd call it research."

When they reached the highway, Beverly stepped down hard on the accelerator. Changing lanes, the shiny black Volvo soon outdistanced other cars.

"I'm in no hurry to leave the valley," Kerrie said, bracing her feet against the floorboard.

"Sorry. This baby loves to run."

"How can you could afford a car like this?"

Beverly's eyes narrowed. "My grandmother died a few months back. Left me a bundle."

"I'm sorry."

"I'm not."

"Then why are you working as a janitor?"

"Research, as I said before."

Kerrie felt her scalp tighten. "Why don't you drop me off at Amtrak. I don't want to inconvenience you."

"I was hoping you'd read my play."

"I'm not really into plays. In my line of work, I only deal with facts."

"The play's about a news reporter, Kerrie."

* * *

Dana's deputy was on the phone when she arrived at home. Receiver in hand, she hesitantly told her that Kerrie had disappeared. The crumpled note rested on the table beside her.

"What were you doing, Murray?" the sheriff demanded. "Sleeping on the job?"

Dana took the receiver from the deputy's hand. She found Jim Dalton on the line.

"I'm sorry, Miz Logan," he said. "I had no idea that Kerrie would run off like that."

"She's been through a lot, Jim. What did you expect?"

"I just wanted to teach her a lesson."

Dana's hand trembled. You may have gotten Kerrie killed. "We'll get back to you," she said evenly, disconnecting the line.

* * *

Did you tell your mother you're leaving?" The Volvo pulled onto a gravel lane.

"I left her a note."

"Good. You wouldn't want to worry her."

"Why do you care?"

"I never really knew mine. She worked from the time I was born. My grandmother took care of me."

"Oh." Kerrie felt a rush of sympathy for her sad-faced friend.

The lane narrowed and visibility was obscured by a once-light mist now thickening rapidly. Kerrie's skin prickled with anxiety. "Where's your mother now?"

"My parents died some years back."

"I'm sorry. How'd it happen?"

"They were murdered."

"By whom?" Kerrie swallowed hard, a chill raising bumps on her arms.

"If you don't mind, I'd rather not talk about it."

The Volvo skidded to a stop several yards from a decrepit two-story house. Weeds had replaced the grass. A drooping eucalyptus stood near the door, its dry leaves littering the yard.

"Why don't I wait in the car?"

"Come on in. I want you to read my play."

Tense, Kerrie took her time with the seat belt. "I hated Shakespeare in college. I can't critique something I don't understand."

Beverly reached to help unlatch the belt, her red acrylic nails clicking on the metal. "I'm not crazy about the work from Stratford-on-Avon, myself. My plays are contemporary. What I need is an opinion on my news reporting."

"But I need to catch a train."

"I'll get you there in plenty of time."

Kerrie glanced into her light brown eyes. The urgency in her voice made her balk.

"What's wrong?"

"I-I guess it's this place, so far from anywhere."

"I love it here. So quiet and no nosy neighbors."

Kerrie continued to stare at the house.

"Shall we go in?"

Out of excuses, she unlocked her door and slowly pushed it open. When she stepped from the car, Beverly gracefully swung an arm toward the house. Although fog partially obscured her view, Kerrie noticed peeling paint and shutters in need of repair.

"Needs some work," her companion said. "Haven't had much time. Just moved in a week ago."

"Where'd you live before?"

Beverly frowned. "With my grandmother."

"But you said…"

"It's cold out here. Let's talk inside." Placing a hand on Kerrie's back, she nudged her toward the door.

Misty twilight made the house seem as uninhabited as the abandoned farmhouse. Trembling, she turned to locate the janitor, whom she sensed had fallen behind. Instinctively raising her forearm, she saw the board too late. A splintered beam struck her temple, knocking her to her knees. Brief fireworks faded into blackness.

* * *

When the sheriff arrived at his office, Joley, his night dispatcher, seemed amused to find him out of uniform. "I almost didn't recognize you, Sheriff. Been on a date?"

"As if it's any of your business, Miz Sheppard." He liked the dispatcher, considered her a friend, but tonight was not the time for idle chit-chat.

Joley pretended to pout. Ruffling her graying hair with one hand, she carelessly flicked ashes into an empty coffee mug.

"Wire photo just came in. Thought you'd wanna see it."

"Where?" Grayson almost shouted.

"Whoa, Sheriff. Not my fault your date was a dud."

"Hand it over."

Whipping the photograph from her "in" box, she playfully tossed it on his desk.

Walt Grayson's sweaty hand picked it up. The image was sharp and defined. Bailey's face had a haunted quality, instead of the crazed expression he'd expected. Deep set light eyes seemed luminous on either side of a straight nose. His lips were wide and full, his light hair cut as short as a boot camp marine. The black-and-white photo should have been in color, he thought, although the portrait was striking.

"Ever seen this guy?" he asked.

"Caption says he's a convict. Where would I have seen him?

Ignoring the chance to tease her, he said, "Run me some copies. I'll circulate them tonight."

"Tomorrow's soon enough, Sheriff. You're in bad need of sleep."

"Not while Kerrie Compton's missing. Any reports in on her?"

"Only the cab company and village resident interviews. Nobody admits to giving her a lift."

Half an hour later he arrived back at Dana's. Nancy Murray opened the door. Obviously chagrined to see him again that night, she stepped aside with her head lowered. Dana appeared a moment later dressed in a long dark robe. Her face was drawn, her eyelids swollen.

"Have you found her, Walter?"

"No, but I've got the wire photo."

She squinted when he handed her the photo. "I need my reading glasses."

He remained standing until she returned.

"This looks enough like Beverly Bryant to be her brother," she said, waving the photo as she rushed back down the hall.

"Who's Beverly Bryant?

"The new custodian."

The name then registered. "You sure?"

"I'm positive."

"Jim Dalton interviewed her, as I recall."

"Then let's get over there."

They were on their way to Micki's house in less than five minutes. Jim Dalton let them in, his young face haggard. Mumbling, he averted his eyes.

"Janitor told me she just did her work. Didn't know anybody."

"She knew Kerrie," Dana said. "She made a point of talking to her every chance she got. I thought it was because they're the same height. Tall women seem to gravitate to one another."

The sheriff glanced at Dana. "That settles it. We've got to locate Bailey."

Micki and Carole had gone to bed, but Sarah was finishing her tea. Setting her cup aside, she embraced Dana the moment she entered the house.

"I've packed my bag, Sheriff. Dana needs me."

Grayson shook his head as though to clear it. "I should have taken you there." Withdrawing a picture from an inside pocket, he said, "Have a look at this

Sarah studied the photograph. "Face looks familiar but…"

"Imagine shoulder-length, light brown hair, mascara, and lipstick," Dana coaxed. "Then add a broom."

"The janitor," she shrieked.

Awakened by Sarah's voice, the others appeared in their night clothes: Micki yawning, Carole glaring.

Distressed that Kerrie had not been found, they inspected the photograph.

"It's that snooty janitor, all right" Carole said. "I knew she was trouble."

Jim admitted, "She did seem strange."

Grayson asked where she lived.

A lot of head shaking, but no one seemed to know.

"Who hired her, him?" Carole demanded.

"Personnel." Dana gripped the sheriff's arm to steady herself. "How can we get an address this time of night?"

"Don't jump to conclusions," Grayson said. "We're not sure Kerrie's with him. She might be riding an Amtrak train this very minute."

"She's with him all right. No cab picked her up, and no one gave her a ride. You told me so yourself."

He had to keep a tighter rein on his mouth. He had needlessly worried Dana.

"Who owns the retirement village?" Sarah asked.

Carole knew. "Somebody named Andover."

Micki placed both hands on her ample hips. "My son went to school with their daughter."

"Then get on the phone, even if you have to wake them."

Dana left the sheriff's side to escort Micki to the phone. Trembling, she sank into the couch. Were they already too late to save Kerrie? And would the custodian show up for work in the morning, if they failed to locate him tonight? If only Tamara were alive. They desperately needed her crystal ball.

Chapter Twenty-Four

The porch light was on, as was another in a second story window. Checking the time, he was surprised that anyone was still awake.

"Stay in the car," he said, immediately regretting his tone.

"I'd rather go with you."

"Official business. I shouldn't have let you come."

"But, Walter…"

Gentling his voice, he said, "You can monitor the radio while I'm gone."

Dana agreed but still seemed disgruntled.

The house was an English Tudor, its dark trim vague in the fog, like timbers stacked on air. Leaves had been raked into piles and scattered by the wind. They crunched beneath his feet as he made his way up the steps. Margaret Hastings, a stout woman in her late fifties, was waiting for him. She reminded him of his stern algebra teacher.

"Mr. Andover called," she said briskly, ushering him in.

"You have Beverly Bryant's address, ma'am?

"The file's at the office. You didn't expect me to retrieve it tonight in the fog?"

"Then I suggest you grab a coat and come with me."

"At this hour?"

"A young woman's life's at stake."

Grumbling, she retrieved a fur coat from its special closet. She took her time removing it from the cloth wrapper. "County supervisors will hear about this, Sheriff."

"Tell them with my best wishes."

Taking her arm, he led her down the steps. The fog was so intense that he was briefly disoriented, and had trouble locating his car. When he stumbled from the curb, Dana's face was framed like a ghost in the windshield.

"Where am I going to sit?" Margaret Hastings whined.

He opened the rear door. Let the old bat fume behind the wire screen. That should give her something to complain about to the county commissioners.

Half an hour later, Hastings unlocked the personnel office, a stark, white, windowless box. Switching on the overhead light, she grumbled about the fog and the "life-threatening danger" the sheriff had placed her in.

"I'll see you defeated next election," she threatened.

"You'll be wasting your time, ma'am. I'm not going to run."

"You're not?" Dana seemed shocked by his statement.

He nodded. "Now, Miz Hastings, where's Bryant's address?"

The older woman took her time rifling through the files. When she finally pulled the Bryant folder, she said the information was missing. He noticed Dana's facial muscles contort, half expecting her to slap the old biddy.

"My daughter's life's at stake. You must have filed it, somewhere."

Hastings lifted a yellow sticker from the employment application. "It says here that Miss Bryant was living with her grandmother, but she was planning to move into an apartment. She said she'd furnish us an address the following day."

"And you didn't follow up on it?" The sheriff refused to hide his sarcasm.

"What about her references?" Dana attempted to read over the woman's shoulder.

Hastings flipped to the second page. "A Sacramento address."

"I need that folder, ma'am," he said, reaching for it.

Hastings snatched the folder away. "This is highly irregular."

The sheriff pulled handcuffs from his belt. "Withholding evidence is obstructing justice."

The woman looked incredulous, as did Dana.

"Walter."

Hastings gave up the folder grudgingly.

"Call a cab," he told the woman, "and send me the bill." He steered Dana around the desk and through the office door. Enough time had been wasted.

"No other addresses," Dana said when they were seated in the patrol car.

"I'll call my dispatcher. Have her check with Sacramento."

"What now, Walter?"

"We wait."

"There must be something we can do."

"Not unless you know where Kerrie's headed."

"I have no idea where she's gone."

"Why'd she leave, Dana?"

"Jim Dalton, primarily, and possibly Harold Samuels." Dana seemed to be glancing at her hands, although they were hidden in darkness.

"Dalton, I understand. But Samuels?" Dana was silent for several moments. Staring through the windshield," she said, "Kerrie thought I was marrying him."

"Who gave her that idea?"

"I did."

Grayson open-palmed the steering wheel. "So that's the reason—"

"No, you're wrong." Dana decided to tell him the entire story. Before she finished, the dispatcher's voice reverberated through the patrol car. "No forwarding address, Sheriff. Looks like we hit a stone wall."

"Get someone there to investigate. Call me soon as you hear," he said, signing off.

Dana was sobbing, her shoulders heaving as though she were ill. Grayson hesitated, then draped a cautious arm around her.

"Kerrie might be dead."

He couldn't argue with that. Before he could figure a discreet way to comfort her, Dana sat bolt upright and abruptly blew her nose.

"What about Beverly? I mean Robert's car?"

"Last seen driving a late model Volvo, but no driver's license has been issued to a Beverly Bryant."

"What about the grandmother?"

"What about her?"

"Where does she live?"

"If we had a name—"

"Folsom Prison must have her listed as next of kin."

"You're right, but we won't be able to get that information until the office opens tomorrow morning. I can't drag the staff out of bed like I did Margaret Hastings."

"She's going to make trouble for you, Walter."

"Ask me if I care."

"You're a good man, Walter Grayson. I know you care."

* * *

Kerrie regained consciousness face down on a rough wooden floor. She was covered with something smelling of mildew. The room was dark, with no detectable light source. When she tried to move, she realized her wrists were taped behind her back. Her ankles had been tied with cord, one crossed over the other. The floor felt like burlap beneath her face. Lifting her chin caused pain to radiate upward from her collar bone. She gasped and lowered her head until the pain subsided.

She was momentarily disoriented until the past came roaring back. Beverly had hit her with the board she'd picked up in the weeds. But why? If Beverly was the killer, what could possibly be her motive?

With considerable pain and effort, she wrenched herself to her side. A damp draft seeped in from somewhere, causing her teeth to rattle. She still wore her jacket, but the dirty quilt had been left behind when she managed to roll away. Struggling with the tape that bound her wrists, Kerrie exhausted her energy. A lump rose in her throat, threatening to throttle her. She wouldn't allow herself to cry. Instead, she gave full rein to her anger.

"Stupid. Stupid. Stupid." What had possessed her to run off like that? Her mother and the others must be frantic, although Jim didn't care. She deserved whatever fate Beverly had in store for her.

Where was Beverly? Straining to listen, she heard nothing. Not even the sound of crickets. Fog seemed to have a deadening, insulating effect like prescription bottle cotton. Tugging at her wrists, she experienced a flash of déjà vu. Someone else had been lying on the floor, tied like an aged steer.

Harold.

How and why had Beverly kidnapped him? She envisioned the young woman's muscular arms. When asked about them weeks earlier, Beverly said she worked out regularly. She planned to compete as a body builder.

How long had she been on the floor? Her left temple throbbed. There must be a billiard ball-sized lump, her hair plastered with blood. Kerrie's strength seemed to have leaked out into the floorboards, leaving her weak and disoriented.

If she could only reach her ankles, she might be able to untie them. Bending her knees, she pulled her feet as close to her body as possible. Stretching, she was able to touch her heels with her fingertips. She scissored her ankles, getting cord burns for her trouble.

Kerrie craned her neck, searching for a window. If she could roll to the wall, she'd raise her feet high enough to break the glass. A dim square of light seemed to beckon from the direction her feet were angled. Struggling, she managed a ninety degree turn. Progress was slow, but the light square seemed to have gotten larger. She lifted her head and rolled over twice. Her shoulders ached as though she had pressed a thousand pounds. Accessing the remaining distance, she decided three more revolutions would place her beneath the window.

The sound of footsteps startled her. Holding her breath until her lungs ached, she heard a door creak open behind her. A single overhead bulb exploded with light above her head, effectively ending her escape.

"Looks like you've been busy," Beverly's voice said. When Kerrie glanced over her shoulder, she noticed a man standing just inside the door. Lanky, like Beverly, but with light brown, short-cropped hair. The pale brown eyes were also hers, the face looking scrubbed without makeup. He had changed into a blue jogging suit.

"Ohmygosh."

He walked over to her, smirking. "Figured it out yet, Miss News Reporter?"

"Great impersonation, Beverly. But what did you do to your hair?" Keep it light, Kerrie. Keep him talking.

"Oh, come on. You must know by now."

"I thought we were friends. Why'd you—"

He nudged her in the ribs with his shoe. "Next time I'll drop kick your spleen."

"What do you want from me?"

"Watch you die."

He sat beside her, crossing his arms and legs, resembling a scrawny Buddha. His eyes appeared glazed, reflecting the overhead light.

"Why?" She couldn't control her voice tremor.

"Why not? I planned to do you last, but you ran right into my arms."

Kerrie closed her eyes, hoping she'd soon wake up. Reopening them, she noticed he'd taken a small, brown box from his jacket pocket.

"Ants," he said, removing the lid and sprinkling them in her hair.

* * *

The sheriff walked her to her door, insisting she get some rest. Promising to call the minute he had some news, he leaned to kiss her cheek. Dana didn't resist.

When Nancy bolted the door behind her, Dana immediately invaded Kerrie's room. She had briefly looked in earlier from the doorway, too upset to even make the bed. Now she longed for Kerrie's scent, something to hang onto. Closing the door, she noticed a large, colorful envelope lying on the bureau. Priority mail. When had it arrived?

Turning the envelope over, she noticed Kerrie's name. Her reporter friend had mailed the packet from Bakersfield. Ripping it open, she read the accompanying note:

Dear Kerrie,
The enclosed morgue copies, as per your request,
are of the Bailey murders. Sorry I couldn't get a
line on your earlier inquiry about Nola Champlain.
I hope this will suffice. Keep in touch. We miss you.
Sally

Dana scanned the pages rapidly. Robert Bailey's grandmother was mentioned near the bottom of the first news article, dated eight years earlier: Roberta Hendrix, address listed in Sacramento. The final page featured the woman's obituary. She had died four weeks ago. The woman had been strangled. Dana searched for an address. None was mentioned except that she'd been a county resident.

"Nancy."

The deputy rushed in, her gun drawn. "Ma'am?"

"Call the sheriff."

"He just left."

"I think I know where Kerrie is."

Nancy hesitated when she noticed the envelope in Dana's hand. The deputy's face fell as she must have contemplated her fate. Before Dana could yell at her again, she holstered her revolver and sprinted for the phone.

* * *

"You bastard," Kerrie screamed, rocking and tossing her head to dislodge the ants. One had bitten her right ear.

Eyes widened, his expression was one of disgust. "Watch your mouth," he scolded her.

She stopped moving, aware that his voice had changed.

"Wait till you see my spider collection, Mommy."

Chapter Twenty-Five

Traveling in the fog had been difficult and slow. The sheriff was only two miles from the village when Nancy Murray was patched through to him. Activating his overhead lights, he cautiously turned back north. The fog was as dense as he had ever experienced, an opaque wall of mist that seemed to have swallowed the earth, leaving him capsulated in his patrol car. With his window down, he kept one eye on the center white line, hoping he had the road to himself.

Dana was waiting for him. Dressed in ski pants and parka, she strongly resembled her daughter, Kerrie. The sheriff felt his heart lurch. Stubborn woman. Didn't she know he was in love with her? Apparently not. She was more concerned with Samuels' feelings than she ever was with his.

"We've got the address," she'd said, as soon as she opened the door.

"How?"

"Sheriff's office. Your dispatcher Joley found it."

Grayson rocked back on his heels. "You should run for sheriff, Dana?"

"Stop feeling sorry for yourself, Walter."

"Yes, ma'am."

"Better call for backup."

"I'll back you, Sheriff," Nancy said, pulling on her leather jacket.

The sheriff radioed Joley before they left the village. Every deputy in the area would be on stand-by, along with a team of paramedics.

"Wouldn't hurt to notify the CHP while you're at it."

"Ten-four, Sheriff. Keep me posted."

Pulling out a county map, he traced a direct route. The road would not be easy to find on a clear night, let alone in fog. "We need flood lights to find the place," he said.

Dana hunched in her seat. "I don't want to rush you, Walter, but time's running out."

He gently patted her hand before shifting into gear. He'd take the highway to the Fuller Road signal, hang a right, and hope for the best. Testing his spotlight, he realized how useless it was.

* * *

Kerrie lost consciousness. When she came to, he was sitting beside her, watching intently.

"Sleeping Beauty's awake and I didn't have to kiss her."

She shuddered. Where were the ants? She then noticed he'd lured them back into their box with sugar.

"Wanna see my bestest spider, Mommy?" He removed his hand from a jar he'd been holding upside down. A huge, hairy creature emerged.

Tarantula.

Flinching, she squeezed her eyes until a voice inside her head reported, "Non-poisonous, but wicked bite. Possible pet if handled carefully."

Opening to a squint, Kerrie swallowed hard, attempting to ignore the tarantula. "Nice spider, Bobby. What's his name?"

"It's a girl. I named her after you."

Kerrie's thought process was hampered by fright as well as fatigue. She knew she had never heard his mother's name."

"Is it Roberta?"

"No." he said. "That's grandma's name?"

"I'm being silly, Bobby. Put the nice spider back in the jar."

"She wants to give you a kiss." Bobby gently lifted the tarantula and placed it on Kerrie's chin.

* * *

They left the highway and followed Fuller Road. Grayson clocked the distance on his odometer. No one spoke as they strained to locate the gravel road on the patrol car's passenger side. When the tires left the pavement, the sheriff nervously jerked the wheel, jolting them in their seats.

"Relax, Walter."

"How relaxed can I get? I've slowed to a crawl." There was an edge to his voice that made Dana cringe.

Nancy leaned in her seat. "You missed the gravel road, Sheriff."

"Where?" Grayson ground to a halt and shifted into reverse.

"Back there," she said, opening the door and getting out.

"Doggone, Murray, you want to get lost in the fog?" He depressed the brake pedal so she wouldn't lose sight of the patrol car. She was back within moments, breathing heavily.

"About twenty feet," she said, rolling down her window. "Hand me the flashlight."

He passed the flashlight over the seat, then carefully soft-pedaled the accelerator.

"Stop, Sheriff. You passed it. Again."

"I can hardly see the hood," he said, easing forward until a vague space was visible between the weeds. The steering wheel jerked as the patrol car lurched forward, the front wheels leaving the gravel lane. When he tried reverse, he found the tires were embedded in mud. He hoped it wasn't an irrigation ditch. Swearing beneath his breath, he tried to rock them free. Spinning wheels only bogged down deeper.

Grayson left the patrol car, slamming the door. He hoped they didn't hear him cussing through the glass.

* * *

Bobby sat rocking on his haunches, humming to himself. When Kerrie's heart eased its pounding, she worried he would suddenly revert to Robert. The tarantula's hairy legs had been plucked from her lips before she suffered a coronary, but what would he whip out next? An alligator?

"I love you, Bobby," she said, mentally crossing her fingers.

"No, you don't."

"Of course I do. If you untie me, I'll give you a queen-sized hug."

"Like Grandma did before she locked me in the basement?"

Kerrie gasped. "Why'd she do that?"

"Because I squeezed her cat."

"Killed it?

"I didn't mean to."

"Of course you didn't, honey."

Bobby stopped rocking to smirk at her. "Let's play with my snakes." Getting to his feet, he started from the room.

"No, Bobby. I hate snakes."

"I know," he said, giggling.

* * *

The sheriff shrugged off his leather jacket and bunched it behind a tire. Nancy did the same on the passenger side. Dana thought they'd lost their minds.

"Get in the car and ease her back," he said.

Dana slipped behind the steering wheel and backed carefully onto the road. Trembling, she slid across the seat. The sheriff and his deputy shook out their jackets and eased back inside.

"The house should be half a mile on the right," he said. "You stay in the car, Dana. Murray and I will—"

"Surround the house—the two of you?"

"Somebody has to monitor incoming calls."

"Is there a shotgun in the trunk, Walter?"

"Yes, but..."

"My husband taught me to shoot pheasant."

"Even so…"

"You're not leaving me behind."

* * *

Bobby cradled two long snakes, which he draped over Kerrie's narrow waist. Catching her breath, she raised her head in an attempt to determine their species. The tan one was at least three feet long, the gray a little shorter. Both tongues hungrily licked the air. "Not rattlers," she breathed.

"Grandma put a rattlesnake in my bed."

"No."

"You never believe me." he shrieked, his wide mouth contorting.

"I believe you, Bobby. Grandma's a very bad person."

"That's why I killed her."

Stunned, Kerrie couldn't speak. What would he do to her when he realized he'd already killed his mother? She watched the snakes writhe over her hips, seemingly entwined.

Gathering her courage, she said, "Let's play hide and seek, Bobby."

He stopped crying and smiled.

"Untie me and we'll go outside. I'll close my eyes and count to a hundred."

"You will?"

"Honest."

Bobby got to his feet. "Be right back," he said, his grin wide.

"Don't forget your snakes."

"Aw, they won't hurt anybody."

When he left, her attention returned to the snakes. She could detect no rattles, but that didn't mean they lacked venom. Kerrie shuddered as they slithered over her jeans.

The door opened shortly and Bobby was back with a knife. Or was it Robert?

* * *

239

Dana watched him punch the mileage button. With an eye on the gauge he was attempting to stay on the road. Dana saw nothing but a misty barrier volleying light from the headlight's low beams.

"Half a mile," she heard him say.

"Now, ladies, we walk." He shut off the engine.

Quietly popping the trunk, he withdrew his riot gun. Handing the shotgun to Dana, he said, "I hope you're telling me the truth. I'll never forgive myself if—"

"Lead the way, Walter." Dana entwined her fingers in Grayson's belt, as Nancy did with hers. They left the gravel road and waded through tall damp weeds. If they missed the house in the fog, they could be lost until the following afternoon. It wasn't that she didn't trust his instincts. He had, she remembered, field-trained police dogs. He must have a good sense of direction.

The darkness and fog made her claustrophobic, a replay of the experience she'd had with Kerrie. Was this another abandoned farmhouse, and had Robert Bailey's grand-mother actually lived there?

The sheriff halted and Dana bumped into him. Reaching to pull them close, he pointed toward a dim light.

"That's it," he whispered.

Dana's heart nearly pounded from her chest. Clutching the heavy shotgun, she feared it would slip from her sweaty grip.

"Watch the front door," he whispered to Dana. They had reached a gnarled tree, whose bare limbs drooped mournfully.

"Hide right here," he said, in a voice that discouraged argument. "Don't shoot unless I tell you. Hear me, Dana?"

"Yes."

"Murray and I will go around back."

"Be careful."

* * *

Holding the knife, he stood over her for an alarming length of time. The grin he'd exhibited earlier now seemed a taunting leer.

"So you wanna play hide and seek?"

Was she mistaken, or was that Robert's voice? Too frightened to speak, she held her breath, waiting for him to stab her.

Laughing, he knelt to cut the tape.

"Scared you, didn't I, Mommy?"

Heart in her throat, she managed a breathless, "Yes, you did, son."

When her hands were free, she quickly rubbed her wrists and reached to untie her feet.

"It's foggy outside," he said, pouting. "How will you ever find me?"

"More exciting this way, Bobby. All you have to do is call my name and run—" Kerrie bit her tongue. What if he asked again about his mother's name?

"You'll never catch me," he said, racing for the door, the knife still clutched in his hand.

"Wait." She had to know the direction he was taking. He might lie in wait, or stalk her in the fog.

Bobby stopped short, his wrist striking the door frame. The knife skittered from his hand. Howling with pain, he watched her rush to retrieve it.

"You tricked me." There was no doubt now that it was Robert's voice.

Stamping his foot on her hand, he pried the knife from her fingers.

"You wanna play?" he said, gritting his teeth.

Pulling her upright, he forced her back against his chest. Pressing the blade to her throat, he said, "Let's take a walk in the fog. You stumble, you lose, and I win."

She walked slowly into the littered yard, the knife blade sharp against her throat. She could see nothing but the darkness of her inner eyelids.

"Move faster," he demanded, pushing her forward with his body, his feet in step with hers. "Run like a stallion. Gallop like the wind."

Kerrie's shriek of terror was muted by clinched teeth. She knew if she lost her balance, she would die.

When they were even with the eucalyptus tree, a branch nicked her face. Before she could make a sound, a cold, breathless voice demanded: "Drop the knife, Robert, before this shotgun relieves you of your head."

Chapter Twenty-Six

"You think they'll put Robert in a padded cell, Mom?"

"I feel sorry for Bobby and total loathing for that old woman who warped him. How could anyone mistreat her grandson that way?"

"She was obviously insane." Kerrie hugged herself. "Speaking of crazy, for an instant in the yard, I thought Bobby's grandmother had returned from the grave. He must have thought so too, or he would never have dropped the knife."

"At that moment I wasn't sure either one of us would survive. I acted on pure instinct."

"You were brave, Mom."

"Not nearly as brave and quick-thinking as you. It took a cool head to deal with a dual personality."

Kerrie smiled. "I have a great role model. You dealt with a temperamental teen. How can I ever make it up to you?"

Dana hesitated. "By getting another staff writing job and a nice place of your own."

"You're pushing me out of the nest?" Kerrie said, smiling.

Dana pulled her daughter into a hug. "There's a better way of putting it."

"I know, Mom. I was thinking similar thoughts."

"By the way, dear, Sarah and I are selling out and buying a motorhome between us. We plan to do some traveling before we need a chauffeur."

"What about Harold and Sheriff Grayson?"

Harold has fortunately discovered Nurse Thompson. And Walter will have a lot of commuting to do if he wants to court me."

#

Read an excerpt from book two of the Logan and Cafferty mystery/suspense series next.

Diary of Murder
by Jean Henry Mead

A Preview:

Chapter One

"Nothing worse than a Rocky Mountain blizzard." Dana's hands tightened on the wheel. "Not even our San Joaquin Valley fog."

Her friend whimpered like a frightened puppy when the motorhome swerved on the ice. A massive storm had assaulted them without warning, spattering the windshield with flakes the size of sand dollars. They had already decided that March was *not* the month to travel Colorado.

"We should have listened to the weather report, Dana."

"That wouldn't have stopped me. I have to know why Georgi died."

"But they said it was suicide." Sarah's grip on the grab handle was turning her fingers blue.

"She would never kill herself and we're going to prove it."

"If we don't get off this highway soon, we're going to kill *ourselves*."

Dana lifted her foot from the accelerator. "If we pull over now, we could wind up in a ditch or hit by a truck that doesn't see us." Activating the emergency lights, she squinted to locate the center line, which had already disappeared under more than a skiff of snow.

Snowfall increased, forcing Dana to adjust the windshield wipers. At their highest speed, they clattered like a band of castanets. The motorhome swayed, prompting something heavy to crash to the floor behind them. My laptop, Dana thought, her attention returning to the windshield. The snow was swamping the wipers so their only hope was to prevent the coach from leaving the highway. She prayed there were no unseen curves ahead in the road.

Wind picked up, striking the windshield in hypnotic swirls. Nauseated, an acrid taste in her mouth, Dana blinked repeatedly, feeling trapped inside a kaleidoscope. Snow fell so heavily that it seemed they were standing still.

"We'll never get out of this," Sarah shouted over the wiper's clattering noise.

"Sure we will," she shouted back, doubting her own words. "Watch for highway signs and delineator posts."

The lonely stretch of interstate between Denver and the Wyoming border had already drifted in with snow, with visibility reduced to several feet. If they managed to survive, Dana vowed she would never leave an RV Park again, without a weather report. A brief glance at the temperature gauge told her it was ten degrees. So why did she feel that she'd just stepped out of a shower?

Hours seemed to pass before visibility increased. Then intermittent lights appeared in the midst of a blinding whiteout.

"Snow plow," Sarah said. "Stay a ways behind him."

"Or her."

"Women don't drive snow plows, Dana. At least not while I lived in Nebraska."

"That was before the snowplow was invented, Sarah."

Their laughter helped to relieve the stress, but her fingers would have to be pried from the wheel when they reached their destination. *If* they reached it.

"Steer into a skid," her friend advised. "At least I remember that."

"Maybe you'd like to drive."

"No, no, you're doing fine." Peering out the side window, Sarah said, "I think an off ramp's coming up. I can't wait to wade through all that white stuff in my tennis shoes."

"And I can't wait to get to Wyoming. My sister loved life too much to have taken her own."

Snow tapered off by the time they reached Cheyenne, where an early truck stop lunch revived them. Sarah replaced her shoes with boots while Dana fueled the motorhome. Impatient to resume their trip, she hurriedly removed ice from the wipers and swiped at the windshield. She then noticed road grime coating the front of her parka. Their recently purchsed RV appeared to have developed Progeria, rapid aging disease. Dana sighed, feeling a similar fate.

The flakes disappeared a few miles north of Wheatland, and she relaxed enough to loosen her grip on the wheel. Checking the map, Sarah told her they had less than two hours remaining. Glancing up, she said, "I wish I'd met your sister before she died."

"I still can't believe she's gone."

Sarah reached across the console to pat her arm. "Sometimes illnesses cause people to act in strange ways."

"Georgi would have told me if she were sick."

"Tell me again what her husband said."

"Rob was nearly incoherent when he called. He said he found her in bed when he arrived home at noon. She was still wearing her nightgown and her hand was on her throat as though she were choking."

"What kind of sickness would cause that?"

"I wish I knew. That's something we need to find out."

"Agreed.

"We also need to talk to her doctor and insist on an autopsy."

"What if her husband objects?"

"I assume he'll agree, but I really don't know him that well."

They rode the rest of the way in silence. Before they reached the outskirts of town, Dana called her sister's number. Her brother-in-law answered and gave her directions to his home in a rural subdivision. When they reached the circular drive, they stopped to stare in awe at the elaborately built house with its towers, wings and gables.

"Dana, this place looks like Queen Elizabeth's castle."

"It's actually a Queen Anne colonial. Breathtaking, isn't it?"

A shiny black sports car, with its engine running, was parked in one of three stalls.

"Nice car," Sarah said. "Looks like somebody's leaving."

Dana remembered Georgi mentioning the sports car, a birthday gift from her husband.

Why was it running now when Rob was expecting them?

Sarah sighed as she removed her seatbelt. "I knew RVing would be an adventure but I never imagined this."

"Good thing you talked me into buying a cell phone. I wouldn't have known Georgi died until we arrived here next month."

Dana climbed from the motorhome and opened the passenger door. "Take a deep breath," she said, "and climb down. We've got some investigating to do."

Chapter Two

A tall, tanned, well-built man opened the carved entry door. For a moment she didn't recognize him. He appeared much older and haggard than Dana remembered. Rob Turnsby gasped when he noticed her standing on the expansive wood porch.

"I thought you were expecting us, Rob."

"I'm sorry, I forgot how much you look like Georgi."

"I'm fifteen months older but some said we looked like twins." We were once as close as twins, she thought as she stepped across the threshold.

She wasn't sure why Rob made her uncomfortable. Maybe it was his standoffishness, as though he didn't want anyone to invade his space. He led them into the living room, motioning them into two matching arm chairs. After introducing Sarah, she glanced about the well-appointed room with its mahogany mantle, landscape paintings, and oriental rug. The oak floor gleamed as though recently polished. Rob had done well for himself since marrying her sister.

"Can I get you something to drink?"

"Thank you. I'll have some herbal tea." She glanced at Sarah, who nodded her agreement.

"I was thinking of something a bit more relaxing, after your long trip," he said.

"Water's fine if you don't have tea."

"Oh, I'm sure there's herbal tea in the cupboard." His eyelids appeared to twitch.

Glancing again at Sarah, she noticed her questioning look.

Her former brother-in-law started from the room but turned back to ask, "You don't mind if I have a drink, do you?"

"Of course not. You look as though you need one."

His face seemed to have lost its previous tan. "What are you implying, Dana."

"Nothing, you just seem on edge."

His sigh was heavy and drawn out. "It's been a nightmare since Georgi's death." His body sagged, creasing his obviously expensive clothing.

"Please sit down. The drinks can wait."

"No, I insist." Rob turned and left the room.

Sarah leaned toward her, whispering, "What's going on?"

"I don't know but we're going to find out." Dana rose from her chair and moved to a large, elaborately draped window. From the corner of her eye she noticed a young woman carrying a packing box to the garage. She turned to watch as the shapely redhead slid into the sports car and backed it from its stall. *Who can that be? And isn't that Georgi's new car?*

Dana walked back and resumed her seat. "Keep your eyes and ears open," she told Sarah, "and do your best to act as though nothing's wrong."

Patting her short blond curls into place, Sarah nodded and glanced about the room. "What did you say Rob does for a living?"

"He owns a construction company."

"He built this gorgeous house?"

"I believe he did."

6

"Very expensive house and furnishings. He must be quite successful."

"I've noticed."

"And young."

"Yes, ten years younger than Georgi."

"Sounds like a mystery novel plot."

Dana shifted uneasily in her chair. "It's strange that you should say that. Are you aware that Georgi was a writer?"

"Yes, you mentioned it."

"Did I tell you she's been writing mystery novels for the past nine years?"

"No, is that why you had so many of them in your library?"

"Partly. Her books piqued my interest in the genre. She was a very gifted novelist." Dana bit her lip and quickly wiped the dampness from her eyes. She then nodded in the direction Rob had taken. Raising a finger to her lips, she settled back in her chair, resting her head against the leather back. Within seconds Rob returned with a tray.

"I hope you don't mind that I microwaved your tea. The kettle takes forever."

Sarah grinned. "As long as you don't microwave our dinner. It destroys the food value—"

"My friend's been reading alternative medicine books," she said, placing a hand on her arm. "We need to discuss Georgi's death certificate as well as the funeral arrangements."

"Already taken care of." He set the china tea service on a marble-topped coffee table. "I wasn't sure you would arrive in time, so I took care of the arrangements, myself."

"But Georgi's only been gone two days—"

Rob excused himself and made his way to the bar in an alcove adjoining the living room. He returned with a cocktail. "I knew you would be exhausted from your long trip and I didn't want to burden you with it."

"What are the arrangements?"

"Cremation tomorrow morning."

"Cremation? But Georgi wouldn't—"

"She said that's what she wanted, Dana. I'm surprised you didn't know."

"She had a living will?"

"No, but there's an estate will. I thought that would interest you."

"Why?"

"She left you some money as well as her books. You're her only blood relative, other than your daughter, Kerrie, so naturally she would leave you something."

"I see."

"By the way, where is Kerrie?"

"Working as an editorial assistant for a news magazine in California. I haven't called her yet."

Rob seated himself in a burgundy leather recliner. "Georgi didn't leave you much because the majority of our assets are tied up in the construction business."

Dana felt her scalp prickle. "I didn't expect any—"

"The housekeeper's packing her books so you can take them with you."

"We'll have to put them in storage for the time being."

"In that case, you're welcome to leave them here until you've finished traveling." He smiled benevolently and raised the recliner's foot rest.

"Thank you, Rob. That's very accommodating. By the way, was that the housekeeper I noticed leaving in Georgi's sports car?" She watched him wipe his shiny upper lip.

"Uh–yes, I'm allowing her use of the car until her pickup is repaired. She's been very helpful about packing Georgi's things."

"What are you going to do with them?"

"Give them to various charities."

"Would you mind if I go through them and keep a few mementos for Kerrie and myself?"

He shrugged. "By all means. I know that sisters have a special bond. I'm sure you even wear the same size and would like some of her clothes."

"You're most generous." Dana rose and offered Sarah her hand.

"You can do that tomorrow after the memorial service," he said, sitting upright.

"Would you mind if we look through them now before the housekeeper finishes packing?"

"Not at all. I'll show you to her room." He glanced at his watch. "I have a business meeting in half an hour. I should be back for dinner." His left arm swung in a generous gesture. "In the meantime, make yourselves comfortable."

Rob guided them up the oak stairs to his wife's room, which was filled with packing boxes. He left before she could ask about the official cause of death. Mentally tabling the question for his return, she opened the closet door.

Shocked, she turned to Sarah. "It's empty. My beautiful, talented sister has only been gone two days and he's already getting rid of her clothes."

"I wouldn't be surprised if the housekeeper's making off with them, Dana."

"From the looks of her, she's taken Georgi's place, including Rob and the sports car."

"We need evidence to go to the police."

"I have to stop the cremation so cause of death can be determined."

"How?"

"I'll think of something. Let's go through these packing boxes to see what we can find."

The first carton contained leisure clothing, the second high-heeled shoes. Five additional boxes were filled with formal wear wrapped haphazardly as though dirty laundry. Dana cringed when she noticed the expensive labels. Her sister had probably

9

worn them while married to her first husband, a San Francisco lawyer.

While sorting through a box of designer jeans, Sarah said, "Look what I found. A black velvet box. "

"It must be some of Georgi's jewelry. I'm surprised it's still here."

"It's heavy, Dana. Do you think we should open it?"

"How? Pry it open? I don't feel right about that."

"The key must be here somewhere." Sarah opened dresser drawers to feel beneath them. Disappointed, she turned to the white Victorian desk, which matched the four-poster bed. Opening the drawer, she extracted a carved wooden pill bottle, which rattled when she shook it. Removing the lid, she discovered a key.

"This has to be the one."

Dana was surprised when the box opened. Carefully lifting the lid, she discovered a matching book, its black velvet cover etched in gold with the name Georgiana Turnsby. Hands trembling, she opened the cover and discovered a diary. The beginning entry was dated June 21st, which she quietly read aloud:

I had serious misgivings about moving to Wyoming, but it's beautiful here. I miss San Francisco Bay, but the air is so clear that you can see the mountains forever. I'm so glad that I allowed Rob to talk me into moving to his home state . . .

"Sounds like she was happy, Dana."

She scanned the next few pages and stopped. "Listen to this:"

I can't tell anyone that I've made a terrible mistake. I should have listened to my friend, Angela. Now, I'm too embarrassed and ashamed to tell anyone. How could I have been so blind that I allowed myself to be fooled and rushed into this. What am I going to do?

"Oh, my." Sarah dropped a black sequined dress back into a packing carton. "What do you think she's referring to?"

"If my instincts are right, she's referring to her marriage, but the entry was made several years ago. Why didn't she confide in me?"

"She said she was embarrassed."

Turning the page, she noticed that the next entry was dated four days later:

I've decided to make the best of it. I've secretly transferred half my divorce settlement to an offshore account. The rest has been loaned to my husband for the business. He promised to build me the most beautiful home in the state, and seems so eager to please me. How can I turn him down?

"Sounds as though she changed her mind."

"Georgie was a generous person. I'm sure she was willing to help Rob establish himself in business."

"Then why would he kill the proverbial goose?"

"The housekeeper, maybe. Georgi may have discovered they were having an affair and threatened to divorce him."

"Wasn't there a prenuptial agreement?"

"I would hope that she was smart enough to have one, but Rob's a former salesman and a very charming guy. He could have talked her into nearly anything. And I think prenups are only legal for five years. They were married nearly six."

Dana had turned another page when she heard a door slam somewhere in the house. Thrusting the diary into its box, she hid them under a pile of clothing.

About the Author

Jean Henry Mead began her writing career as a news reporter/photographer in California, and staff writer and correspondent for the statewide newspaper, the Casper Star-Tribune. She later served as editor of In Wyoming Magazine and Misty Mountain Press. While freelancing for the Denver Post's Empire Magazine, additional articles were also published domestically as well as abroad. She published seven nonfiction books as well as six novels and edited and ghostwrote a number of others. While serving as national publicity director for Western Writers of America, she established the Western Writers Hall of Fame, and wrote Maverick Writers, a book of interviews with famous authors, including Pulitzer Winner A. B. Guthrie, Jr.; Louis L'Amour; and Elmore Leonard.